"Forget it, Rive

Sam watched June, she spoke again. "Leave me with a little pride, and let me pretend I didn't just make a fool of myself."

She pushed the door again, but when he held his position, she threw up her hands and retreated inside. A smart man would let her go.

"June, let me explain."

She angled a hesitant, wounded gaze over her shoulder. "I'm mature enough to take no for an answer, Rivers. But it's time you left."

The cool and clearly false bravado in June's tone only made Sam feel worse. Damn, she was tough. She could have begged, cried, thrown a tantrum or slammed the door on him. He would have expected, and knew how to handle, any of those reactions. Instead, she acted with dignity.

This was one firefight he wouldn't win no matter what he did.

Dear Reader,

Writing this letter is bittersweet. While I get to share the story of one of my favorite heroines, I'm also saying goodbye to Quincey—a town that has become like my second home.

Deputy June waited patiently in the background of my previous two Quincey stories, but it wasn't until an accident forced hardcore marine Sam Rivers to question everything he knew about himself that I discovered why June refused to get out of my head. Despite Sam's repeated efforts to push her away, she's determined to help him become the man he was meant to be—whether or not he wants her assistance. And in June, Sam finds the one woman he considers his equal.

There are times in our lives when we or someone we love needs a June—someone with a positive, persistent, kick-butt attitude and the life experience to help us through a rough patch. I hope you enjoy watching a woman who is everybody's champion take on a man determined to stand alone.

Emilie Rose

USA TODAY Bestselling Author

EMILIE ROSE

———

Starting with June

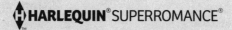

Recycling programs
for this product may
not exist in your area.

ISBN-13: 978-0-373-60887-4

Starting with June

Copyright © 2014 by Emilie Rose Cunningham

Printed in U.S.A.

USA TODAY bestselling author and RITA® Award finalist **Emilie Rose** lives in North Carolina with her own romance hero. Writing is her third career. She's managed a medical office and a home day care—neither offered half as much satisfaction as plotting happy endings. Her hobbies include gardening, fishing and cooking. Visit her website, emilierose.com, or email her at EmilieRoseC@aol.com.

Books by Emilie Rose

HARLEQUIN SUPERROMANCE

A Better Man
The Secrets of Her Past

HARLEQUIN DESIRE

Her Tycoon to Tame
The Price of Honor
The Ties that Bind

SILHOUETTE DESIRE

Pregnant on the Upper East Side
Bargained Into Her Boss's Bed
More Than a Millionaire
Bedding the Secret Heiress
His High-Stakes Holiday Seduction
Executive's Pregnancy Ultimatum
Wedding His Takeover Target

Other titles by this author available in ebook format.

In loving memory of my mother-in-law.
I wish I'd met her sooner.

CHAPTER ONE

SOMETIMES LIFE SUCKED. This was one of those times, Sam Rivers decided as he exited the building on MCB Quantico with the words he'd never expected to hear still ringing in his ears.

Separated from the corps. Medically discharged.

Over. His military career was over.

He caught a trace of movement near his Charger. Instantly alert, he squinted through the glaring sunlight that not even his Wiley X sunglasses could block. Was the subject a friend or foe? A foe on a domestic base was unlikely. But old habits were hard to break.

The man slouched against the car's front fender was none other than Roth Sterling. As close to a brother as Sam would let any man become. Sam should have known the former sniper who'd watched his back for years wouldn't leave him to face the bad news from the Medical Evaluation Board alone. But Sam hadn't called him. How had Roth known today was D-day?

His buddy straightened as Sam approached. Roth had been out a few years, but civilian life and his recent marriage hadn't changed his parade-ready posture.

"Who called you?"

"Does it matter?" Roth answered.

Did it? Not really. The end was the end. Unless he could heal and convince his superiors it wasn't.

"I appreciate you coming up, Roth, but it wasn't necessary." Sam clasped Roth's fist and bumped his shoulder. An invisible hand wrapped a choke hold around his throat. He blocked the rising tide of panic and uncertainty. He and Roth had been through some deep shit together, but he wouldn't drag his buddy into this pig pond. This was his problem and his alone.

"Yeah, it was necessary. Meet me at the Fire Breathin' Dragon, and I'll tell you why." Roth about-faced and made his way to a pickup parked two rows down.

Sam debated arguing, but he needed something better than his own company at the moment. And he could use a drink. Or three. Maybe more. It'd been a long time since he'd needed a ride home. But tonight might be one of those rare evenings.

Thirty-one and washed up.

Done.

He slid into his car, slammed it into gear then headed to the old biker bar with Roth's truck on his tail. Neither he nor Roth rode a motorcycle, but the hole in the wall was close enough to base to be convenient yet far enough away that they weren't likely to run into anyone they knew. The other patrons would leave them alone. And the beer was cheap.

Thank you for your service. The words echoed in his head. He'd heard them hundreds of times from civilians and they'd filled him with pride. Today the words had been a death knell to the life he'd lived and loved for thirteen years—the life he'd planned to continue until they sent him home in a box.

His superiors had sat across the table from him today and told him that surgery had failed to completely correct the detached retina he'd sustained compliments of his last deployment, and the chance of a full recovery was slim. A visually impaired scout sniper wasn't of much use to anyone, they'd said. A blind spot, however small, could put him on the receiving end of a round rather than on the sending end. Plus, the risk of reinjury from another explosion was too great. So they were letting him go. For his own good.

He was expendable.

His knuckles whitened on the steering wheel. What in the hell was he going to do with the next fifty years of his life? He'd go crazy with nothing to occupy him but reliving stories of his glory days. He'd done a lot of good. Saved a lot of lives—taken a few, too. His data book was impressive, but that was history. He'd never planned for life after the corps, because statistically, he shouldn't have made it out alive. Not in his line of work.

He was a hunter. But he'd also been the hunt*ed*.

He hadn't feared death. But he sure as hell feared living...broken. He'd prepared for every eventuality. Except this one.

He parked and followed Roth into the shadowy interior of the bar. The last time they'd been here, they'd been celebrating Sam's return from a nasty but successful deployment. The uneven wooden floorboards creaked beneath his Danner boots. Except for two gray-haired, ponytailed dudes in leather vests bearing multiple motorcycle patches at the end of the bar and a bottle-redheaded bartender who'd spent too much of her time tanning, the place was empty. Not a surprise given it was midafternoon and midweek.

Wednesday. Hump day. Or dump day, as his career went.

As if they'd last been here yesterday instead of years ago, Roth straddled a chair at their usual table. Sam did the same, bracing himself for a blast of pity or platitudes. He couldn't handle either. Not today. Until two hours ago he'd planned to return to duty once he healed. Or at least transition into an instructor role if he had to leave the field. He hadn't come to terms with the end of his military career and didn't want to talk about being cut from the corps. Not even with Roth.

Sam's jaw hurt from hours of clenching his teeth so tightly. "How much do you know?"

"All of it. But that's only part of why I'm here. I need a favor."

Sam narrowed his eyes, suspicious of the timing. Someone had leaked intel—info he had deliberately not shared with anyone. Not even his family. But he doubted his circumstances involved a security clearance. "Yeah?"

"You've been so entangled in red tape I didn't bother you with the details, but four months ago I arrested and fired my senior deputy. He was dirty." He signaled the bartender for two beers, pointing at the neon sign on the wall above their table to indicate the brand. "That's where you come in."

Sam had been surprised when Roth had told him he'd taken a job in his hometown as chief of police since his buddy had always hated the place. Armpit of America, Roth had dubbed Quincey, North Carolina. Roth's plan had been for it to be a short duty station while he settled a few old scores before he returned to his old job with the Charlotte SWAT team, a job he'd loved almost as much as the corps.

Instead, Roth had discovered he had a pubescent kid he'd known nothing about. Shortly after that he'd rekindled an old flame with his son's momma, and now a gold band glinted on his left hand. Sam hadn't seen that one coming, since both of them had sworn off long-term relationships, but Roth had seemed happy and hunkered down for the long haul as a family man when Sam had visited Roth, his new wife and his kid last month.

"How can I help? I don't know any of your men."

"I need to know how deep the corruption runs in

my department. I want someone I trust to infiltrate. Recon is your specialty, Sam. Your ability to smell dirty from a mile away kept us alive too many times to count. You'd see something that didn't add up. I want to hire you to replace the deputy."

Only Sam's training kept him from reacting. There wasn't anyone he trusted more than the man sitting across the scarred wooden table from him. He would—and had—put his life on the line for Roth Sterling. "You fabricated this job to keep me busy. I appreciate your effort. But no."

"Don't flatter yourself. I'm being straight with you, Sam. I have a job opening. And I need help— help I can trust."

Roth looked serious. But the timing was too coincidental, and Sam hated pity parties. "I'm not a cop. No MP training. Not interested. But thanks."

"That's the beauty of Quincey. I can hire and fire whoever I want. I want you. Your military training is sufficient to cover the minimal qualifications. I'll provide the intel you need to cover the rest. You're a damned good detail man, and you have time on your hands while you figure out your next step. You'll be in and out in a couple of months, tops. Work with my team, feel 'em out and give me a report—then you're free to go and do whatever you line up next. I've already found a house for you to rent. Fully furnished. Just bring your Skivvies and a toothbrush."

Still sounded fishy.

"What makes you think I want to do anything but sit back and collect my dis-dis—" crap, that was hard to say "—disability check? I have a severance package coming, and I've squirreled away some money over the years. I'll be okay."

Financially. Mentally was another story. He might never recover from what he considered a betrayal of the corps. But he'd give 'em a chance to make it right once he healed.

"No one hates a handout more than you, and you'll go crazy with nothing to do. You're too smart to sit and watch TV all day. Do you have a plan?"

"To get back in." He tried not to snarl, but Roth more than anybody knew Sam never wanted to be anything but a marine and he damned sure wasn't a quitter. "But right now they won't even let me apply to come back as an instructor or as a private contractor in the Precision Weapons Section."

He'd begged for a job. *Begged.* And damn it, this marine didn't beg for anything.

"I swear to you, Sam, this isn't BS or pity. I need you. A few months in Quincey will buy you time to put a plan together while you heal. I'll help in any way I can. The salary isn't bad either."

Sam searched the strained face across from him, seeing how difficult it was for Roth to ask for a favor. "How many on your force?"

Not that he was considering it.

"Five, including me."

Nope, not even thinking about it. Stagnating in

a backwater swamp wasn't anywhere on his bucket list. He'd lived in North Carolina during one of his dad's stints at Lejeune. He hadn't hated it. But he hadn't seen any reason to return either.

"How many do you suspect?"

"All four until proven otherwise."

Not good. "You don't have anyone you can trust with your six?"

"No. I'm telling you, Sam, this small-town department isn't run like any operation either of us has ever seen. There's no black-and-white. It's all shades of gray, and the corruption went on for a long time. What I have to figure out is where a favor for a friend or looking the other way crosses the line into illegal activity and how many of my officers are doing it."

Sam stalled by wrapping his lips around the bottle and letting the cold beer roll down his throat. He had that itch between his shoulder blades—the one that told him he was in somebody else's crosshairs. Time to seek cover.

But how could he refuse Roth's request? Roth never asked for anything. Not only did Sam owe him, Sam had nothing better—nothing, period—to do. He sure as hell wasn't going home to his family. Not that his dad, a recently retired marine, wouldn't try to be supportive. But his mother and sisters would smother him.

Short of going to ground, did he have a choice? Maybe he could hang in Quincey until he healed enough to approach the corps again. "It'll take 'em a few weeks to process my paperwork."

"I can wait."

He had to be crazy. "Shoot me whatever you have on your deputies."

"No. I want your unbiased first impressions—they're always damned accurate."

Flying in blind. But as Roth had said, the assignment would keep Sam occupied while he healed and plotted his next step. Working with Roth again might be fun.

How bad could it be?

"I'll see you ASAP."

To ALLEVIATE THE scorching heat, June Jones spritzed herself with the water bottle and kicked her feet in the four-foot-diameter plastic wading pool she'd bought for her nieces and nephews. She had three days of vacation with nothing to do but work on her tan and wait for the new tenant to arrive.

Idleness was not her thing, and vacations…well, she rarely took them. Someone else always needed the time off more than she did, and she loved her job. Why leave it? Labor Day weekend was just one of fifty-two in the year for a single woman whose friends had recently paired up with their Mr. Rights. The unofficial end of summer didn't mean family trips to the beach or mountains for her—unless one of her siblings needed an on-site babysitter. Labor Day meant the opportunity to earn some overtime.

But not this year. Even though she'd volunteered to cover the holiday shifts, her new boss, who happened to be the husband of one of her two besties, had ordered her to stay away from the office.

She squinted at her watch. Approaching one o'clock on her first day off and she was already climbing the walls. She might go crazy before the seventy-two hours passed. Shifting in the lawn chair for a comfortable position, she dredged her brain for something more productive to do than sit here and sweat. But she'd already done everything that needed doing.

She'd risen at five and fed her landlord's animals, baked cookies, brownies and cheese puffs for the new tenant's welcome basket and cleaned both houses, hers and the rental next door. Her friend-slash-landlord, Madison, was spending the long weekend with her fiancé and had told June she had no idea what time the new tenant would be arriving. But June took her assignment as deputy lessor very seriously. That meant twiddling her thumbs for as long as it took even if it drove her to adding tequila to her pitcher of virgin margaritas.

Determined to prove to her naysayers that she knew how to relax, she refilled her glass and took a sip of the tart slushy beverage, then tilted her head back, sprayed herself with the water again and tried to pretend she was enjoying the final day of August. Why hadn't she planned ahead and picked up books from the library, rented movies or bought ammo?

The cackle and scatter of the chickens brought her to instant alertness. Remaining still, she eased her eyelids open, scanned the area and the sky from behind her dark lenses and listened for what had set them off. She heard nothing—not even the usual country critter sounds—and she didn't see a hungry hawk. Animals didn't lie. Their silence spoke volumes. She wasn't expecting anyone except the man who'd rented the cottage beside hers. But in Quincey, North Carolina, neighbors tended to drop in unannounced, especially when they wanted to know your business. But neighbors made noise.

Movement drew her eye to the corner of the empty cottage thirty feet away. A blond-headed guy just over six feet tall eased around the back corner with slow, silent footsteps. He wore dark wraparound sunglasses, charcoal cargo pants and an olive T-shirt that conformed nicely to his torso—not too lose or tight.

He wasn't from around here. Was he her new neighbor? She hadn't heard a vehicle drive up.

"Can I help you, sir?" she called out while sitting up. And without seeming to move, he suddenly seemed more alert.

Madison had given June no details beyond the name of the new tenant—which June wouldn't volunteer. Cataloging his erect bearing, muscular build, hyperalertness, and military-style pants and boots, June rose and so did the warning hairs on the back of her neck. This wasn't a hunter or antiquer who'd wandered off course.

Dang it. She'd left her service revolver inside.

Even though he barely moved and she couldn't see his eyes behind his tactical sunglasses, she felt his gaze raking over her and cursed her choice of attire. Of all the days to wear her sister's discarded bikini. But the elastic in her only other swimsuit had dry-rotted from disuse and her sister had handily stored her prepregnancy-sized clothing in June's attic.

"I'm renting this place." He jerked a head toward the white cottage. "The note on the front door said 'Pick up key at yellow house next door.'"

Wow. The women of Quincey were in for a treat. The town's newest citizen was a hunk with a hard jaw, full lips and a voice as deep as a rock quarry. They didn't grow men like him around here. She ought to know. Except for a short stint at the police academy up in Raleigh followed by a few months of blind stupidity, she'd lived here all her life.

She snuffed the memory and stuffed her feet into the idiotic flip-flops that matched the bikini, then crossed the grass snip-snapping with every step. She hated the sandals, but nothing said vacation like the useless rubber thongs. She wished she had a towel or a cover-up or something with her, but inexperience with loafing meant she'd come outside ill prepared.

"I'm June. Your name?"

"Rivers. Sam Rivers."

That matched what Madison had told her. "You have ID, Mr. Rivers?"

He dug into his back pocket and flipped out a worn wallet with precise movements. She checked his name, Samuel Zachariah Rivers; age, thirty-one; eye color, blue. "You're from Virginia?"

"Yes."

Had she imagined that hesitation? "I've been waiting for you. I have your key and the lease. What brings you to Quincey?"

"Work. The key?"

Okay. Not the friendliest guy. Quincey would either fix that or run him off. "I'll get it."

She hustled into her cottage as quickly as possible, then retrieved the key and the goody basket she'd prepared. She debated covering up, but her skin was slick with suntan oil and she didn't want to ruin good clothes. Digging for old ones would take too long. Besides, covering up would imply he made her uncomfortable and give him the upper hand. Nope. Not doing that.

He stood where she'd left him and extended a hand as she approached. She hooked the basket handle over his palm. "I've baked you a few things to tide you over until you can get to the store."

He shoved the basket back in her direction. "Thanks, but I only need the key."

Wasn't he charming? She left the hamper hanging and passed him, heading for his front door. A huge duffel bag sat on the porch. How had she missed his arrival? And how long had he been skulking around before the chickens had alerted her? She scanned the driveway.

"No car?"

"In town. I hiked in."

Strange. Maybe he was a health nut—he was definitely built like one. "I'll show you around the house."

"The building's only twenty by forty. I'm sure I can find my way."

Mr. Personality he was not. "No doubt. You won't even need to leave a trail of breadcrumbs."

No smile. "There's only one exit. Isn't that a fire code violation?"

That hitched her step. Interesting observation. "Not around here. But if you're worried, you can always escape through the bedroom window. It's not painted shut, and with the weather we've been having, you'll probably want to leave it open at night to catch the breeze anyway."

She climbed the stairs, inserted the key, gave it its customary jiggle and opened the door. Shoving her sunglasses on top of her head, she entered the cottage. "Most folks around here don't bother locking their doors. The citizens of Quincey are good people."

She'd locked this door only so he'd have to check in and sign the lease before moving in.

After grabbing his duffel, he followed her, saying nothing. He kept his sunglasses on. Too bad. She'd like to see those blue eyes. It was easier to judge a man's character that way. He carried her basket as if it held fresh manure, but she wouldn't let his poor manners get to her.

"As you can see, the place is fully furnished. Sofa, chairs, TV, but no cable. Madison, our landlord, provides wireless internet. The password is written on a card in the basket, along with a listing for local TV stations, fire and police departments' numbers, a trustworthy auto mechanic, etc. Your copy of the lease agreement's also in that envelope. I'll give you time to read over it before you sign, but I'll need it back this evening.

"Water, electricity and internet are included in your rental fee. If you want satellite, you'll have to pay for it and have it installed yourself. There are plates, utensils, and pots and pans in the kitchen, but there isn't any bakeware. If you need that, I have some you can borrow."

"I won't."

She suspected his good looks had contributed to his lack of personality. At least, that was how it had worked with her siblings. The better-looking their dates, the worse their dispositions. And Sam Rivers was definitely top-notch in the looks department, from his short, spiky hair to his stubble-covered square chin and fitness magazine–cover body.

She walked down the short hall. "Water from the tap is safe to drink. You don't have to waste money buying bottled water." She flipped a wrist. "Washer-dryer here. Spare sheets and towels are on the shelf above them. Bathroom there. Bedroom here. I put clean sheets on the bed today. I have a grill on my back patio. You're welcome to use it. And of course, you saw the pool, but you'll need to bring your own lawn chair and swim at your own risk. There's no lifeguard on duty."

He didn't even crack a smile. What a grouch. He stepped into the bedroom, being careful to keep a few yards between them, and glanced around.

"The chickens are egg layers," she added. "You're welcome to as many as you can eat. The eggs. Not the chickens." Again, nothing. Man, he was a hard case. "Don't worry about the skunk in the barn. He's descented."

"Skunk?"

Of all she'd said, *that* was what got his attention? "Yes, he's the landlord's pet. Don't let him out of the cage—no matter how much he begs. Do you need a ride back to your vehicle? I'll help you unpack it."

He lifted his bag slightly. "This is it."

"Not staying long?"

"Do you always ask so many questions?"

"Do you always avoid answering them?"

"Thanks for the tour, June. I won't keep you from your pool party any longer. Better get back before someone steals your seat."

So he got her jokes. He just didn't have a sense of humor. And he was observant. "I'm next door, if you need anything. My cell number's in the envelope, too. Text or call if you have a question or problem. I've lived in Quincey most of my life. If I don't know the answer, I know where to find it. Also, there are some pretty good hiking trails down near the river. I can show them to you sometime, if you're interested. Welcome to the neighborhood, Sam."

She stuck out her hand. He ignored it and jerked a nod instead. She couldn't help but feel insulted. Good thing her landlord was about to move to a larger, more affluent veterinary practice and didn't need the rent money from this jerk, because June was hoping Sam Rivers wouldn't be around for long.

SAM SET HIS keys on the dresser after a fruitless trip to town. Movement outside the single bedroom window caught his eye. He paused to watch the blonde make her way toward the barn. She'd released her hair from the stubby ponytail and put on clothes.

Too bad.

Negative. He was grateful she'd covered all that golden skin. June might be nice eye candy, but he didn't need the complication. Slip in. Slip out. Leave no trace or ties. That was his MO in the field and out of it. And nothing would change that.

Jeans skimmed her legs and a red polo shirt clung to the breasts that had been about to spill out of her bikini top. The lace-up boots on her feet were a surprise. Her ruffled bathing suit and sequined flip-flops had led him to believe she was a heels kind of girl…even without pedicured toenails, which his sisters considered a necessity of life.

June hadn't been the least bit self-conscious playing tour guide in a bikini, but then, she shouldn't be, with her compact, fit figure. He hadn't seen any fat on her, just curves. Oh yeah, she had those. In all the right places. And slipping her number into the food basket she wouldn't let him refuse… He shook his head. He had to hand it to her. She wasn't shy. But then, women weren't these days—especially around a military base. Sometimes that was convenient. Now wasn't one of those times.

Roth must have put her up to it. His buddy probably thought Sam needed the distraction. Why else park him next to a beauty? Thanks to the surgeries and the end of his career, Sam hadn't been up for any drama of the female variety in months. It had been one hell of a long five months. But his life was a three-ring goat screw at the moment. He had no direction, and he wasn't dragging anyone else into that mess—even temporarily.

June disappeared into the barn. His neighbor was nothing more than another meddling female, albeit an attractive one with her bright green eyes and blond hair that dusted her shoulders, but the last thing he needed was another nosy woman trying to manage his life. He grimaced at the reminder that he hadn't informed his family of his status change or relocation. He should, but if he made that call, his parents, three older sisters, their husbands and their entourage of noisy teenage daughters would convoy down from Crossville to offer love, support and advice he didn't want or need.

Translation: they'd smother him, try to baby him and tell him what to do.

After watching the way his mother and half sisters had worried each time his dad was deployed, Sam had learned to keep his trap shut regarding his location. The less they knew, the less they worried. His family had his and Roth's cell numbers, in the event of an emergency. That was all they needed. And Roth had his momma's.

The whole lot of them resided in Tennessee, eight hours from Quincey, the same distance it had been from Quantico. Yet the long drive hadn't kept his family from ambushing him. After a surgery a few years back, some shavetail Louie had called Sam's mother instead of Roth, Sam's primary contact, and the whole extended clan had descended on him like ants on a picnic. While he'd been laid up in the hospital, his sisters had rearranged his tiny apartment, thrown out food and possessions and replaced them with crap he'd never touched except to put it in the Dumpster. They'd grilled all his apartment neighbors to find out who he was dating and how long he'd been seeing them. He'd learned his lesson, and he wasn't setting himself up for that kind of "help" again.

Sam would show up at his parents' place when he

was ready for company and the females' tag-team analysis torture. That wouldn't be anytime soon.

Separation from the corps still ached like a recent amputation. Until he was past the rawness and had an idea of what he was going to do with his future or how he'd get reassigned to a base, he didn't need a bunch of hens clucking around him and telling him how to live his life. That included his temporary neighbor.

His phone vibrated. The screen indicated a text message from Roth.

Settled in yet?

Affirmative. In my hide, Sam tapped back. Streets rolled up at dusk. Grocery store closed before I could stock up.

Yep. At six on Saturday. Welcome to Quincey. Backwoods, USA. Need anything?

Calling would have been easier than texting, but Roth had insisted no one, not even his wife, know the real reason Sam was here until he reported for duty. Conversations could be overheard, and info was on a need-to-know basis.

Negative. I have rations. Did you send her?

Who?

The blonde.

There was a pause before the next text came through.

June?

Yeah.

No. Why?

She brought food.

Eat whatever she cooks—especially her brownies. She's famous for those.

Except for extracting the lease, Sam had left the basket untouched on the coffee table. For dinner he'd planned to eat one of the MREs in his bag. Brownies sounded better. He couldn't remember the last time he'd had one. He headed for the living room/kitchen combo.

The cottage wasn't luxurious by any means, but it was clean, comfortable and a hell of a lot nicer than most of the places he'd slept since enlisting. He kept a rat rack in Q-Town. It was more like a hotel room than an apartment, but it came furnished and made dealing with his stuff during deployments uncomplicated.

Had kept, that is. Everything he owned was

packed into his Charger. Turning in the key this morning after keeping the place so long had been… an adjustment.

Did she ask about your job? Roth wrote.

Tried. I didn't crack.

Good. Word spreads faster than flu in Q, and it's imperative that no one know you're investigating my squad.

Affirmative.

What do you think of her?

What did he think? Words tripped through his head. Attractive. Annoying. Aggressive. Available. But he settled for typing, Nosy.

Everyone here is. See you Tuesday 6 a.m. Acclimatize till then.

Roger.

Sam deleted the texts, pocketed his phone, then filled a glass with tap water and returned to the basket. Beneath the red-and-white-checked cloth napkin he discovered neatly stacked resealable plastic containers. He located one neatly labeled Brownies with Walnuts, grabbed it and headed for the front porch with his makeshift dinner. The minute he opened his door a mouthwatering aroma assaulted his taste buds. His stomach grumbled. Trying to ID the scent, he parked his tail in a rocking chair.

A rocking chair, for pity's sake. Like a geriatric retiree. He pushed that U-G-L-Y visual aside.

Chicken. Someone was grilling chicken. One from the henhouse? His lips twitched when he recalled June's remark. Blondie had a sense of humor. Blocking out the memory of her sparkling green eyes and the tantalizing smell, he bit into a brownie. The rich chocolaty taste of the moist treat almost made him groan. He shoved the remainder of the square into his mouth and reached for another.

"Do you always eat dessert first?"

He jumped. His neighbor had snuck up on him. Nobody ever got the drop on him. In his line of work—former line of work—that meant death or torture. Preferably the former. He swallowed.

"I didn't mean to startle you." June stood on the ground beside his porch watching him through the pickets.

"You didn't."

Her megawatt smile revealed she knew he'd lied. "If you say so, Rivers. I heard the store closed before you got there."

Had she spoken to Roth? "How?"

"Lesson one about Quincey. People here know what you're doing before you do. And they talk about it. Gossip is our local sport and we have the championship team."

He'd known he was being watched when he'd hiked back to get his car, but he'd hoped to blend in with the weekend antiques hunters wandering the streets. He'd have to work harder at moving under the radar if he was going to do his job well.

She lifted another plastic container the shrubbery had hidden from view. "Here's half a beer-can chicken, a couple of ears of grilled corn—locally grown—and some garlic-cheddar biscuits."

His taste buds snapped to attention, but the rest of him balked. He wasn't stupid. There was only one reason a woman baked and cooked for a man, slipped him her number and offered to show him hiking trails while wearing a bikini that displayed the smorgasbord on offer. The phrase she'd said when they first met echoed in his head. *I've been waiting for you*, she'd said in that throaty voice of hers.

Sam did not need any local honey sticking to his feet and making extraction difficult. The best thing he could do was head her off at the pass. It would save them both a lot of embarrassment later.

"June, I appreciate your generosity, but I'm a no-strings kind of guy. I am not looking for a relationship."

Her spine snapped as straight as a new recruit's. Then crimson flagged her cheekbones. "Zip it, Rivers. I'm not trying to get into your britches. I'm only being neighborly and looking out for you the way Madison asked me to. I brought food to get you through until you can get to the store tomorrow afternoon. They don't open until twelve-thirty on Sundays—after the owner gets out of church. Ditto the diner."

She shoved the container under the porch rail. "It's not like I lit candles, slipped into something sexy and invited you over. Eat this or don't. I could not care less if you starve. But don't leave my dishes outside. The nocturnal critters will destroy them.

"You're on your own for breakfast, though. Like I said, there will be eggs in the coop. Get 'em yourself. If you dare. Brittany has a sharp beak and a mean streak. I'll let you figure out which hen she is."

Then she pivoted and stalked across the grass toward her rear patio. Chagrinned, Sam mentally smacked his forehead and silently cursed as he watched the angry swing of her departing hips. Infiltrating meant making nice with the locals and blending in—something he'd done hundreds, no, thousands, of times. But he'd struck out on both counts with his new neighbor. Her observations also made him realize that if he wanted to keep his privacy, he'd better shop outside of town.

As for donning something sexy…if June could see the way those jeans hugged her butt, she'd realize she was far off target on that comment.

Worse, he'd forgotten to give her the signed lease. He'd have to face her again tonight...unless he could figure out a way to circumnavigate that land mine.

CHAPTER TWO

JUNE HIT THE punching bag hard enough to rattle her teeth and make her wish she'd put in her mouth guard. Then she gave her leather target a one-two combination. The smacks of solid contact didn't give her much satisfaction.

She usually took the Sunday shift so the other deputies could go to church with their families. But not today. Today she was wailing the tarnation out of an inanimate object. Because she couldn't wallop her new neighbor.

Sam had taped the signed lease to her front door last night while she'd been out on her run. He hadn't even had the decency to give it to her face-to-face. And he'd rumbled down the driveway this morning in his black Charger without visiting the henhouse for eggs. She wouldn't mind if he never returned. The last thing Quincey needed was another sexist prick.

"Idiot." Cross. *Pow.* "Jerk." Uppercut. *Thump.* "Coward."

As the only female deputy on the Quincey PD, not only currently but in the history of the department, she'd had her fill of males who considered her weak or inferior. She had to work doubly hard and be twice as good as her male counterparts to be taken seriously. There were those who claimed she had been hired only because she'd spent a chunk of her childhood at the retired chief's house playing with his daughter. That might be half-true, but she'd make darn sure Piper's dad never regretted his decision.

Liver punch. Hook. Elbow stab. Pivot. High kick. Sweat rolled into her eyes. She impatiently swiped it away with her forearm.

"Who rattled your cage?"

June spun around. Piper, the retired chief's daughter, stood just outside the barn. June lowered her arms. "The new tenant. He's a chauvinistic ass."

"He's here?"

"Moved in yesterday. Drove out at seven this morning."

"What'd he do? I've never seen you so worked up."

"I prepared a welcome basket and then took him dinner last night. He thought I was making a pass and let me know it was an unwelcome one." Her skin burned anew with a fresh rush of humiliation.

Piper wrinkled her nose. "He's not from around here, is he? What does he do?"

"He's not a local, and I don't know what he does."

"*Your* interrogation skills failed? Because I know you tried."

Okay, so she asked a lot of questions, but knowing what people were doing was part of her job description. "He wouldn't say and since your husband ordered me to stay out of the station, I can't run the guy's tags *or* do a background check on him." Though she had memorized his driver's license number just in case she got a chance to slip into the office.

"Do you think you should check him out?"

"I'm going to live next to him. None of us lock our doors. And he's…" She tried to find the words to explain her gut feeling. Sam made her uncomfortable. She didn't know why. "I don't know. He has a hard edge and he hides behind wraparound sunglasses all the time—even inside. Something's not right."

Piper frowned. "Your instincts aren't usually wrong. I'll ask Roth to check him out."

"Why don't you just call your dear hubby and tell him to let me go into the office and I'll do it myself?"

"Roth looked at your file and said that you never use your vacation time. He claims you don't know how to take one. Which is true, by the way. He's the one who suggested I invite you to attend church with Josh and me to keep you from trying to sneak into the station."

June prickled as the comment hit its mark. "I do too know how to relax. I sat by the pool yesterday for thirty-six minutes."

"Wow. Thirty-six whole minutes. That's a record. And you timed every wasted second. You have just enough time to shower and change if you want to go with us."

"Thanks for the invitation, but no. Until I get a feel for this guy, I'm not leaving the property unprotected unless it's for work. Madison will be returning late tomorrow night, and I don't want her walking into any surprises."

"Understandable and commendable. I'm going to miss our lunches with her when she marries Adam and moves to Norcross. Don't get me wrong. I'm happy for her and thrilled she found someone after all she's been through, but..." She shrugged.

"Yeah. Me, too." June had known Piper forever. They'd both grown up in Quincey, and when Madison had bought June's grandfather's farm and veterinary practice six years ago, the two of them had taken her under their wing. The trio had formed a single-gal alliance of sorts. Now June was the only single one left. An outsider. A fifth wheel. "I hope she'll call if she needs us for anything."

"Speaking of people calling when they need something...have you heard from any of your siblings lately? Aren't they overdue for wanting or needing something?"

June grimaced and tugged off her gloves. Her twin older sisters and two younger brothers were notorious for contacting June only when they wanted something.

"No, I haven't heard from them, and I don't know what they could possibly need from me. They already have everything." Perfect spouses, children, homes and jobs. She was proud of them. But a little envious, too. She couldn't find Mr. Right with a compass, a map and a bloodhound, and three of her siblings were living the American dream.

"Oh, I don't know, maybe a loan they'll never repay, a free babysitter or storage space, to name a few. You'll be strong this time when they call?" Piper asked.

June rolled her eyes. "I will resist the urge to empty my bank account for them *if* they call, but my nieces and nephews are adorable, and it's hard to say no when they need something." Though she wouldn't spoil her own kids nearly as much—if she ever had any.

"I know you like being needed, but at the rate your siblings spend, they're going to burn through your inheritance. They've already burned through *theirs*. Am I right?"

"Yes, ma'am."

The lecture wasn't a new one. Unfortunately, it was deserved, so she couldn't protest. But she felt guilty that her grandfather had made her his primary beneficiary and left her father and his other grandchildren very little. PawPaw claimed it was because he'd given the others more than they deserved while he was alive and only June had asked for nothing. But her brothers and sisters didn't want to hear that. "You sure you don't want to join us? The tenant's out somewhere and your dad's a decent preacher."

"I've heard Dad's sermons all my life. We all did. Why do you think all my brothers and sisters moved away? And remember, I'm the black sheep. He'd have to make an example of me if I showed up. I've sinned. Big-time."

"June, you made a mistake. We all make them. But I get your point. And it would probably give him a heart attack if he saw you in one of his pews. I'll see what I can get out of Roth. In the meantime, if the new tenant does anything shady, don't hesitate to call it in."

"If he does, I'll handle it. I might not be in uniform, but that doesn't mean I can't take care of business."

Because if she called her fellow deputies for help, it would only reinforce their opinions that little Justice Jones didn't belong on the force.

SAM DRIED THE last of June's dishes Sunday afternoon and stuck it in the picnic basket with the others. He had to return them. And apologize. He'd read her wrong and embarrassed her. For the sake of his assignment he had to make nice.

He'd walked or crawled into hostile territory too many times to count. He was *not* afraid of five and a half feet of angry female, for pity's sake.

So why was he stalling?

He didn't have an answer for that.

He grabbed the basket and exited his quarters, heading next door. Except for paint color, externally, the structures appeared identical, but hers, unlike his, looked lived-in. Pots overflowing with flowers cluttered the outside edges of the steps leading to her porch. More flowers spilled from baskets hanging on the railings or from hooks in the eaves, and another bucket of blooms sat on the coffee table between her twin white rocking chairs—chairs bearing thick ruffled posy-print cushions. A water fountain—made from a series of brightly colored tilted ceramic pots—babbled on the far end.

There was so much color it looked as if someone had bombed a paint factory. With all the girly stuff littering the porch, the utilitarian boot scraper at the bottom of the stairs looked out of place. Then he spotted a toy box with a cartoon train painted on it tucked into the back corner, and every cell in his body screeched a warning.

Kids? She had kids? He'd seen and heard no sign of them. Maybe she was divorced and the rug rats were away for the holiday with their father. He'd seen plenty of that in the corps. But where would she put them in the one-bedroom house? More than likely she wasn't the primary caregiver. But what kind of mom lost custody of her children?

Her front door stood open. A wood-framed screen was the only thing between her and anyone who might enter uninvited into her home. Absolutely no security. Through the mesh he registered that her floor plan was identical to his.

He could see June bustling about the kitchen concocting something with a series of bowls scattered across the countertop. She wore cutoff jeans that showed off her legs and a white T-shirt that molded every curve. Her feet were bare, her hair held behind her ears with a wide black band.

He rapped on the door. June startled, turning. "C'mon i-n."

The last word fractured into two syllables when she saw him, and her smile melted. "What do you want?"

"I'm returning your stuff." He swung the picnic basket into view.

Wiping her hands on a towel, she made her way across the room. "You could have left it with the lease."

He ignored the jab. Not one of his finest moves to drop the paper and take cover. "I would have, but you said not to leave your dishes outside."

She unlatched a hook inside, making her smarter than he'd thought, and pushed the screen open just enough to take the basket. "That's hardly any security, June. Anybody who wanted access could cut through the screen and be inside in seconds."

Her tight smile and the glint in her eyes took him aback. "That would be a mistake."

"What would you do about it?"

"I can take care of myself."

"Overconfidence can get you hurt. If you're not worried about yourself, at least think of your children."

Confusion clouded her eyes. "Children? I don't have children."

He nodded toward the toy box. "Whose are those?"

Her face softened with what could only be love and…was that yearning? "My nieces and nephews. I babysit as often as I can. Don't worry—I'll keep them away from you."

She reached for the basket and pulled the handle. He held on. He didn't know why he was so determined to make her see sense. Probably because he'd worry about his sisters if they were in a remote place like this. "The owner of the farmhouse is away. You're a half mile from your nearest neighbor. Who would hear you if you screamed for help?"

Her eyes narrowed almost imperceptibly. "Who says I'd scream or that I'd need help?"

Not the answer he'd expected. "You weigh what? One twenty-five? No match for a man."

"My weight is none of your business. Was there anything else you wanted—besides to pester me, Mr. Rivers?"

This was not going as planned. "I apologize if I misunderstood earlier."

"If?" She looked angry enough to spit. Red flagged her cheeks and chest, and fury burned in her

eyes. "Don't worry. I won't give you the opportunity to misinterpret my Southern hospitality again."

His teeth clicked together. He was trying to be nice. She wasn't making it easy.

June snatched the basket quickly and with enough force to remove it from his relaxed grip. He hadn't seen that coming. Then she stepped back, letting the screen slap shut, and closed the solid interior door in his face. The lock clicked.

"Guess you got tired of being neighborly," he called out. "Thanks for the food."

No answer. But then, he wasn't expecting one—at least not a polite one. She was probably shooting him the bird through the door. He headed back to his temporary quarters. Antipathy between him and Blondie was a good thing. She wouldn't ask questions about why he was here, and he wouldn't have to lie. His mission was to help Roth, then get the hell out of Quincey. In. Out. Over.

June would have been a complication.

So why was he disappointed?

SAM ZEROED IN on his target—a ten-point buck—exhaled, slow and steady, then squeezed his trigger finger. His camera reeled off three rapid-fire shots. The deer stiffened, his ears pricking forward and the hairs along his back going erect. He searched for the adversary he hadn't yet spotted and pawed the ground. Sam pressed the shutter button again. The buck's head snapped up, his big dark eyes locating

Sam in the tree above him. The deer snorted a warning, lifted his white tail, then bounded off through the woods. Beautiful.

Sam relaxed into his borrowed hide—a hunter's tree stand that he'd come upon during his morning hike. In his line of work—*former* line of work—he'd seen a lot of nature as he'd crept up on his insurgent targets, and he'd learned to appreciate it, but during a mission, he'd never been able to take pictures. He'd been too worried about getting in undetected and out alive.

He checked his watch. He'd been perched in the tree for almost five hours. Time to call it a day. If he didn't leave soon, it would be dark before he made it back. Not that darkness was an issue, but hunger was. He hadn't eaten since breakfast.

He rose. Old injuries protested. They'd stiffened up while he'd sat practically immobile.

He turned and eased down the ladder, and only then did he notice the rain tapping on his jacket—he'd endured and tuned out far worse conditions. The rainy weather had worked to his advantage today. The people who should have been hiking the trails by the river on the Labor Day holiday had stayed inside. That meant he'd been able to explore Quincey's surroundings without interference—and without his neighbor as a tour guide.

Using his compass, he hiked back toward his temporary quarters. Eight klicks. He circled the perimeter of the farm. From the edge of the woods he noted June's diesel crew-cab truck still parked in the driveway. Diesel engines and sparkly sandals didn't go together. He filed away the incongruity.

It didn't look as though she'd moved her vehicle since he'd left just before dawn this morning. There were no tracks in or out of the gravel driveway and the rocks beneath her vehicle were dry. He returned the same way he'd left—on the blind side of his house where his nearest neighbor couldn't see him coming or going unless she was looking out her window at his porch. He climbed the stairs, eyeing no-man's-land—the strip of wet grass between his quarters and his neighbor's.

June's blinds were open and her lights on as dusk approached. He could see her clearly through the window. Her sports bra and low-waisted knit pants clung to her curves, revealing the narrowing of her waist and swell of her hips. Her pose was unmistakably yoga. Power yoga had become popular on base. One of his commanding officers had required the platoon to attend classes because the exercise supposedly improved physical training scores and helped with PTSD. Yoga hadn't been a total waste of time—it had increased his flexibility. But Sam preferred relieving his tension through other means. Emptying a couple of dozen clips on the range. Swimming or pumping iron until his arms felt as if they would fall off. A good run. The latter had a purpose because it could save his life if he was detected and had to haul ass.

A pang of regret hit him. He wouldn't be running for his life anymore unless his eye healed and he could convince brass to let him re-up.

June shifted from a low lunge to a shoulder stand, then rolled smoothly down into a boat pose. She held the V shape steadily, toes pointed up, arms forward with nary a wobble. That explained her flat abs. Tight. Strong. He'd underestimated her muscle tone.

He shook himself. What in the hell was wrong with him, standing here on his porch gawking at a woman working out? His knuckles bumped the gun on his hip as he dug his keys from his pocket. He didn't have a concealed-carry permit for this state, but he wouldn't be here long enough for the paperwork to clear, and there was no way he'd go into foreign territory unarmed. He'd better mention that to Roth. He'd have to open carry when he wasn't wearing his police issued weapon, and he wasn't sure how Quincey's citizens would take that.

He unlocked his door and entered his lodgings. His gaze immediately swung to the window but he kept out of sight and didn't turn on the overhead light. June had her legs spread wide and her breasts pressed to the floor between them. The woman was flexible. That took his brain down a path it definitely did not need to travel. Undeniable hunger burned in his gut. It was unfortunately not an appetite that could be satisfied with a bowl of the stew he'd left simmering on the stove before he'd gone out this morning.

It was not one that would be satisfied—period—during this assignment. But she provided one hell of a view.

JUNE PUSHED OPEN the station door Tuesday morning feeling as if she'd been away for months rather than exiled for three days. Thank heaven her vacation was over. It felt good to be back in uniform and back to her home away from home with her family by choice rather than blood.

Unfortunately, Madison, her friend/landlord, had returned sometime last night after June had gone to bed, and her house had still been dark when June left this morning. Getting answers about the new tenant would have to wait until lunchtime when June could swing by Madison's office to see if her friend had any details.

But on a positive note, June had managed to avoid Sam this morning. His cottage had been dark when she'd left for her prework run, and his Charger had been gone when she'd returned. If she was curious about where he'd gone at such an early hour, well, it was none of her business as long as he stayed out of trouble. If she was lucky, she wouldn't see him all day. Nevertheless, she'd locked her doors last night and this morning—something she'd rarely done since returning to Quincey, and she'd silently locked Madison's while her friend slept.

The other two deputies were already at their desks. That surprised her enough to make her toe catch on the tile with a noisy squeak. Once in a while the chief beat her in, but usually she was the first to arrive. She liked coming in early while the building was quiet and then preparing and sipping her coffee while she reviewed files and bulletins that had come in overnight. She had a lot of ideas about bringing the antiquated filing system up to current-day standards, and her new boss seemed receptive to them.

"Morning, Justice," Alan Aycock, the oldest and most chauvinistic of her fellow deputies, stated.

She'd given up long ago on convincing them to call her June rather than by the name her father and his cronies used. "Good morning, Alan. Mac. What's going on? Did I miss a memo about a morning meeting?"

"Nah. Chief hired a new man. He starts today," Mac replied. "We wanted to check him out."

How had she missed hearing that? "When did he tell you that?"

"Yesterday. You gonna make the coffee?" Aycock asked. "We've been waiting."

"You go ahead. I have to clock in and check the bulletins." She ignored his sputtering and headed for the old-fashioned time clock. It was original to the building, which was only a few years short of historic. That meant it was temperamental.

"What's in the bag?" Aycock pestered.

"You'll find out after you make the coffee."

She heard him grumbling. Then his chair squeaked as he pushed to his feet. "Do I use four scoops or eight?"

"Depends on whether you want to read through it or drink it."

She'd learned early on not to pander to Alan's passive-aggressive personality. If he could get out of doing something by doing it wrong, then he would. But to her way of thinking, a man was never too old to learn new tricks. Like how to make coffee. And other than that and his chauvinism, he wasn't a bad guy. He'd raised his two kids single-handedly after his wife had run off with the propane deliveryman. The kids had turned out all right. Both were on the high school honor roll. You had to give him credit for that *and* for being a fair deputy.

"Hope you enjoyed your time off," he groused.

"Been a long time since you worked a holiday, hasn't it, Aycock? Years? Right?"

He stiffened at the reminder that she always covered for him and his complexion turned ruddy. "Yes. Which was nice... Time with the kids and all that."

"Thought so." She went through her morning routine by rote, clocking in, then depositing the homemade donuts in the break room. The station door opened as she returned to the main room. Roth, the chief, walked in followed by Sam.

Sam in a uniform identical to June's.

Shock glued her feet to the floor, and her stomach

did a loop-the-loop up her throat and down again. It was small consolation that when Sam's eyes—the first time she'd seen them without sunglasses save his DMV photo—fixed on her, the same dismay registered on his face.

"Deputies, I'd like you to meet our newest officer. Sam Rivers."

Sam's unblinking gaze held hers, then skimmed downward, taking in her badge, her equipment-loaded duty belt and her polished shoes, then returned to her face.

"Sam, this is Alan Aycock, my senior deputy, and Mac Morris."

Sam's attention abruptly shifted elsewhere. June used the reprieve to gather her composure while Sam shook hands with each of the men. But her break was short-lived.

"You've already met Justice Jones," Roth added.

Sam paused a fraction of a second before extending his hand to June. "You told me your name was June."

His grip was warm and as firm as his accusatory tone. He held on a second longer than necessary, then released her, but the tingle traveling through her tissues lingered. "My friends call me June, but you can call me Justice or Jones since we'll be working together."

A slight tightening of his lips was the only sign that he'd understood her insult. "Justice because you're a cop?"

"Justice was my mother's maiden name. It's Southern tradition to tag daughters that way."

"Jones is a native of Quincey," Roth continued. "She'll be showing you the ropes."

June's and Sam's heads snapped toward Roth's.

"Me?"

"Her?" they chorused in horrified unison.

"That's right. Sam, you'll ride along with Jones until you get a feel for Quincey. Then you'll get your own cruiser."

"But, Chief—" June protested. Something dark and dangerous in the boss's eyes severed her words. "Yes, sir."

Roth tossed her a key ring. "Jones, would you get Sam's weapon and badge from the safe? The mayor will be here in a few minutes for his swearing in."

She took advantage of the excuse to escape to the solitude of the back room and regroup. Her day— heck, her month, her year, her life—had just taken a nosedive into the manure pile. Her obnoxious neighbor wasn't going anywhere anytime soon. Having him as her shadow was the last thing she wanted, but as the officer with the least seniority, she had no authority to complain.

She was stuck, and she didn't like it one bit. Maybe Piper—

No. She would not put her friend in the middle and cause friction between the newlyweds. She would get through this. One way or another.

Without shooting the new deputy.

CHAPTER THREE

SAM FELT AS IF he'd been ambushed by his best friend and the betrayal stung. He stabbed Roth with a hard stare. "Can I speak to you in your office?"

Roth nodded and strode into his space, closing the door behind Sam.

"You set me up."

"No. I dropped you into position without bias so you could get a feel for June without either of you knowing who the other one was. I didn't even tell Piper you were coming, and trust me, I'm gonna catch hell for that. But those three women—Piper, June and Madison—are as tight as cellmates. What one knows, they all know. It helped that Madison was out of town. You met her when you had dinner with Piper and me."

"Back up. You wanted me to get a feel for June without bias?" Roth's words and matter-of-fact tone rolled around in Sam's head until the answer sifted through. This wasn't about getting Sam laid. "You think she's a dirty cop?"

"What do you think?"

Sam considered her bright eyes and straightforward conversation, the flowers littering every surface of her porch, the toy box, her goody basket, ruffled bikini and ridiculous sandals. Crooked? No. Too sweet and naive for her own good? Definitely. Sexy—

Do not go there.

"No."

"Good." Roth rubbed the back of his neck. "I hope you're right because of her connection to my wife, but I don't trust anyone at this point. Keep your eyes open. Again, I apologize for the deception, but I didn't see any other way."

"How old is Jones?"

"Twenty-seven."

"I would have guessed twenty-one at the most. How long has she been with the department?"

"Four years, almost five. Less time than the corruption has been going on."

"Where was she before that?"

"She trained and worked with Raleigh PD before moving into the rental house on Madison's farm—a farm that June inherited from her grandfather, then sold to Madison. She applied for a job with Quincey PD, and Piper's dad, the former chief, hired her on the spot, cutting through the usual red tape like a hot knife through butter. That caused a little friction in the department, I've heard, and it raised a lot of questions for me as to the presence of corruption in this department."

"Is she qualified?"

"I wouldn't jeopardize your safety by partnering you with an incompetent."

"An incompetent under investigation." Everything in Sam wanted to retreat. Roth must have read it on his face.

"Jones graduated in the top five percent of her class. C'mon, Sam, you've had women in your platoon before. You're no sexist pig like the other two out there."

That raised his hackles again, but only because he didn't like to think of his sisters being treated unfairly. "This isn't about her being a woman, Roth. How am I supposed to investigate her when we live twenty feet apart and she brings me food?"

"You're not a hostage dependent on her. A few brownies won't give you Stockholm syndrome. And don't feel too special. June feeds all of us. How else do you think I knew she could cook? The close quarters puts you in a perfect position to see who comes and goes at her place. I'm not asking you to date her. Just keep your eyes open."

"You're a native, too. Why can't you show me around?"

"I've been away too long, and, of course, I arrested one of their own. Never mind he was caught red-handed moving moonshine. I pissed off a lot of people by calling in the ATF instead of handling the situation discreetly in-house and giving him a gentle tap on the wrist. Locals don't trust me yet.

"Aycock and Morris worked with that deputy for

more than a decade. That makes their conduct the most suspect. The Feds questioned them and don't think they were directly involved, but I need your help deciding whether they looked the other way, if they're good liars or not smart enough to see what was right under their noses."

"Your father-in-law wasn't."

"That's different. Lou and the dirty deputy were buddies. Lou trusted too much and ignored the obvious—something Butch White used to his advantage."

Sam shook his head. "It's strange hearing you defend a man you once cursed, the same man who ran you out of Quincey and threatened to lock you up if you ever returned or contacted his daughter again. But pairing me with June—not a good idea. She's my neighbor…"

"You'll deal with it. As a female, June is less likely to be part of the good-ol'-boy network. But she's lived in Quincey long enough to know how this town operates and to possibly have been contaminated by all the I'll-scratch-your-back-if-you-scratch-mine crap."

Sam still wanted no part of being strapped to his pretty neighbor. "Let me recon solo. It's what I do best."

"You should have realized by now that Quincey's like a fishbowl. Our fine citizens have been watching your every move since you drove into town. You don't fit our typical tourist stereotype. That's one reason we didn't get together before this morning. Here, solo, you'd be suspect. But June is Quincey's sweetheart. With her by your side, folks will let down their guard. Give it a month, Sam. Then you'll have your own car *or* you'll be finished with the assignment. Can't you handle four weeks—less if you provide evidence to who's dirty and who isn't sooner?"

Sam gritted his teeth. What choice did he have? He'd made a promise. "Affirmative."

"Good. Then let's get you sworn in. Our esteemed mayor has arrived."

The sarcastic bite to the word *esteemed* caught Sam's attention. "Not a fan?"

"He's a big fish in a little puddle. Likes to throw his weight around. What do you think?"

They'd both had their share of abuse of power—usually the short officers with big mouths and bigger egos. "Roger. Trust him?"

"He's a butt-kissing politician."

Negative. "'Nuff said."

Roth yanked open his office door. "Jones, bring Rivers's gear. We need a witness. You're it. Let's get this show on the road. We have work to do."

THIRTY MINUTES LATER June closed her cruiser door and turned to face the man riding shotgun. Her goal was to make the loop around town, introduce Mr. Bad Attitude to as many people as possible, then dump him back at the station.

"Why didn't you tell me you were the new deputy?" she demanded.

"I didn't know you were with Quincey PD."

"How long have you known the chief?"

"What makes you think I do?"

Anger and exasperation vied for supremacy. "Can't you just answer the question? Your evasions are really irritating."

"What makes you think I'm dodging?"

She battled an urge to bash her head on the steering wheel. "You answer every question with a question. But the answer you're seeking is—when you're with the chief, your body language isn't that of two men who just met."

"You're a body-language expert?"

Cocky bastard. "Let's just say it's a hobby. Where did you train?"

"Marine Corps."

"Mar—" And then it hit her. "You're Roth's friend. The one who—" Lost his career over an eye injury. Piper and Madison had mentioned him. But Sam had the sunglasses back in place, so June couldn't check for visible damage. "You just got out," she amended when he stiffened.

"Affirmative." His head turned toward her. There was no reflection in his lenses despite the sun rising behind her back. But then, a sniper wouldn't want to give away his position with a glint in the sunshine, and Sam, according to the stories she'd heard from Piper, had been a scout sniper like Roth.

"How much visual impairment do you have?"

Tawny brows slammed down behind his shades and those soft lips compressed into a firm line. "Enough to lose my job, but not enough to keep me from doing this one."

Dear Lord, please keep me from beating this man to death with my baton.

"What made you become a cop?"

"Roth needed help. Do you put everyone through an interrogation or am I special?"

June was the patient one in her family, the peace-maker, the temper soother, the freakin' Rock of Gibraltar. If her siblings could see how close she was to totally losing her control at this moment, they'd be shocked.

"You're carrying a loaded weapon and supposed to be watching my back. That makes you pretty darned special—to me. I don't doubt your skills as a marine or at handling weapons since you and Roth are still alive, but have you had Basic Law Enforcement Training or worked as an MP?"

"Negative. As the chief knows. But I don't engage without intel. Roth sent me BLET textbooks and Quincey's regulations. I'm prepared."

Textbook trained. No practical experience. Sam must be desperate for a job. And Roth...well, he was a really good friend to Sam. Sympathy battled frustration. Sam might be an obnoxious ass, but his career had been taken from him, and he was struggling to find a new place. The way veterans were treated was shameful. As her godfather had been, Sam would be a fish out of water until he found his footing. That went a long way toward explaining his defensive behavior and bitten-off responses.

She could help him adjust. But to do that she had to accept that he wasn't going to be an equal partner for a while. He'd be like a rookie, a liability, and she was responsible for making sure nothing happened to the chief's pal until Sam was ready to work on his own.

The real challenge would be helping him without smacking the inconsiderate, rude jerk upside his handsome head. No small task. But she, the mediator and voice of reason in the Jones clan, was up to it.

She hoped.

OVER THE PAST three hours Sam had been grilled by what seemed like half the population of Quincey. He felt like a carcass—after the buzzards had finished their meal. Capture and interrogation would have been easier because at least then he wouldn't have had to be polite.

June checked her mirrors, then pulled the cruiser back onto the road *again*. Sam spotted yet another citizen a quarter mile away "checking her mail," and June, predictably, lifted her foot from the gas pedal.

"Are we going to stop every fifty yards?" Sam groused.

"The chief ordered me to introduce you to the people you've sworn to protect and serve."

"My sisters are less nosy."

The smirk on her face was unmistakable.

"You're enjoying this," he accused.

"Oh yeah." She flashed a blinding white smile. His heart jolted—but only as a result of her driving through a pothole that should have broken the front axle. The irregular rhythm had nothing to do with the mischievous sparkle in her green eyes.

"How old are your sisters?"

He had a feeling she hadn't missed one thing the citizens of Quincey had tortured out of him. "Forty-four, forty-one and thirty-nine," he bit out through clenched teeth. He'd managed to avoid answering June's questions, but he hadn't been able to bring himself to tell the octogenarian at their last stop to mind her own business.

"And you're what? Thirty-seven? Thirty-six?"

Did he look that old? He tried not to be insulted. But hell, he was. "Thirty-one."

"Big age gap. I would never have guessed you're the baby."

Something in her tone stiffened his spine. "Why?"

"Youngest children are usually charming people pleasers, and you are definitely not, Deputy Rivers. Were you a surprise baby?"

She was just full of joy today, wasn't she? "My mother's second marriage."

"Ah."

"What in the hell is that supposed to mea—" The squawk of their radios cut him off.

"Jones. Report."

Sam ID'd Roth's voice.

"On Deer Trail, Chief," June responded. "Still making the rounds."

"Someone's egging cars over on Oak Hill. Check it out."

"Will do." She flipped on the blue lights, accelerated and waved as they passed a senior citizen waiting by her mailbox. Despite the woman's obvious disappointment, June didn't stop. Sam said a silent thank-you. He'd been grilled enough today.

"Eggers are usually kids, aren't they?" he speculated. "And kids should be in school."

"Speaking from experience?"

He refrained from answering. A few miles later she rounded a bend, slowed and turned off the lights simultaneously. He spotted two heads rising from the ragweed in the ditch, arms reared back. Boys. In their early teens. They dropped their ammo and took off.

"We have runners," she said into her radio. June threw the car into Park, flung open her door and raced after the kids. Sam followed, a beat behind, logging details as he sprinted through the waist-high weeds. Deputy Jones was fast and agile. The boys split up.

"Take right," June called over her shoulder, then veered after the one on the left.

Sam thundered across the unfamiliar terrain. He was used to creeping undetected, not trampling plants, careless of the noise he made. Adrenaline pumping, he went down into a shallow creek bed and back up the other side, gaining on his target and ignoring the briars ripping at his clothes. "The farther you run, the more you'll piss me off," he shouted, but his quarry didn't slow.

Sam could take down and incapacitate an insurgent in seconds, but he had no clue how to deal with a troublemaking kid not wearing explosives. This one showed no signs of surrendering. Sam made a running tackle, banded his arms around the brat and hit the dirt. He rolled to take as much of the impact as he could and skidded across the leafy forest floor holding on to the bucking boy. When they stopped, he pinned the kid to the ground and scrambled for the cuffs on his belt. It took a couple of tries with the unfamiliar equipment before he had the subject hog-tied. Now what?

He rose and yanked the redheaded, freckle-faced youth to his feet. They were both breathing hard.

"I didn't do anything," Freckles shouted.

"Then why'd you run? Running from cops can get you shot."

"It was Joey's idea."

No loyalty. A marine would never give up his man. "Let's go."

Grabbing the narrow biceps, he frog-marched the teen back to the patrol car and met June and her quarry strolling side by side out of the woods. No cuffs. She took one look at Sam and though she said nothing, her disapproval was clear in the hiking of those golden eyebrows and her down-turned lips.

"Suspects apprehended," she said into her shoulder radio. "It's Joey and Tyler."

"Affirmative," Roth responded.

"What were you thinking?" she asked the boys as they approached the patrol car.

"Aw, c'mon, June, it's not like we were hurting anything."

"Eggs damage paint. Get in the back, Joey."

"But, June—"

"Save it."

Sam circled to the opposite side of the cruiser and opened the door. That was when he noticed neither June nor her kid were covered in leaves, twigs and debris the way Sam and his prisoner were.

"Deputy Rivers, please remove the cuffs before putting Tyler in the back."

The kids referred to her by name, and she knew theirs. Frequent fliers? She returned to the ditch, grabbed a basket, which she put in the trunk, then climbed back behind the wheel. She acted as calm as if they'd taken their guests on a picnic. His blood was pumping. This was probably routine for her. Not so for him.

"That's Miss Letty's basket, isn't it? Isn't it?" she repeated when they ducked their heads and didn't answer. "You know she and her son live off what she grows. She's poor, and Jim Bob isn't like the

rest of us. And you took their food. Shame on you."
The boys shrank into their seats.

"You're not gonna call our parents, are you?" the
one Sam had nailed wailed.

"Oh, I'll talk to your parents, but first I have
something else in mind."

Sam glanced through the grate and saw worry
and dread in the faces too young to shave. "Vandalism is a crime. Do you want a criminal record
to ruin your futures?" He used his sternest voice,
trying to scare the piss out of them. Their pale faces
and wide eyes told him it had worked.

"Guys, this is Deputy Rivers. Sorry you had to
meet this way." June put the car in motion, heading
away from the station instead of toward it. Was she
going to torture her passengers with the same pa-
rade through town Sam had endured?

Two klicks down the road she turned up a dirt
driveway flanked by overgrown grass and weeds. A
small, old, formerly white clapboard house smaller
than his rental came into view. She tooted the horn.
A tiny woman as weathered as the peeling building
came out the front door. The teens sunk even deeper
into the seat with a chorus of *Oh man*'s.

June got out and released her passenger. Following her lead, Sam did the same. Then she retrieved
the basket from the trunk. Sam kept an eye on the
boys, expecting them to bolt.

"Miss Letty, this is Deputy Rivers. He helped me
catch these rascals. They've been in your henhouse."

June cut a razor-sharp glance at the boys, who shuffled their feet and tucked their chins, then mumbled, "Sorry, Miss Letty."

"Ya stole my eggs?"

Heads bobbed. "Yes, ma'am."

June passed her the basket. "There are a few left. After school tomorrow Tyler and Joey will each bring you two dollars."

They boys eyed June, then each other in dismay.

"Well, I…" the old lady started to protest.

"It's the least they can do, Miss Letty."

The old woman nodded. "I'd appreciate that."

June snapped her fingers. "Back in the car, boys."

Sam was more than a little surprised when they docilely did as ordered. June crossed to the old woman and gave her a hug. "Have a nice afternoon, Miss Letty. Tell Jim Bob I said hello. I'll be back on Thursday with banana bread. If these boys don't show tomorrow, you let me know."

"What was that about?" Sam asked her over the car's roof after the boys were back in the car and before she opened her door.

"Around here we don't steal, and we take care of our own."

Take Care of Your Own was a motto marines lived by and could be iffy if abused. Was June over-stepping her authority by forcing the boys to pay the woman? Seemed like it.

Again June steered away from the station. Approximately ten klicks down the road she turned the cruiser into a church parking lot, and the boys groaned. "C'mon, June. We're sorry."

"You will be."

The building was old enough to have a historic marker out front. Founded in 1898 by Ezekiel Jones, it proclaimed. Signs along the road and driveway advertised a barbecue fund-raiser being held this Saturday.

"Just call our parents, *please*," Carrottop pleaded.

"I did that last time. It didn't work, did it? 'Cause here you are, hitching a ride with me again," June replied. "This is the second time I've picked you two up for malicious mischief."

She stopped the cruiser in front of the stone house beside the church, exited the car and then released their prisoners. The boys exchanged panicked glances.

"Don't even think about running," June warned, and the boys' shoulders sagged. "I'm faster than both of you and I know where you live."

They obediently followed her up the walk with scuffing feet and bowed heads. No cuffs. No use of force. What in the hell? Each one outweighed her but they made no attempt to escape. Sam took rear guard just in case. June knocked on the arched wooden door and a few moments later it opened, revealing an older man in a suit.

"Hi, Daddy."

The words floored Sam. June was a preacher's daughter? Then he noticed the lack of welcome in the man's eyes—the same green as June's—and the absence of a hug. His father would have crushed him with one if he'd shown up on the doorstep. That thought drove a bayonet of guilt into Sam's ribs. He wanted to talk to his father, to get his advice, and yet he didn't want to admit failure. Being separated from the corps was definitely a failure. Unless he could fix it.

"Justice."

"Joey and Tyler have come to volunteer their services to the church this Saturday. They'd like to wash cars during your barbecue. They won't charge the church, but they'll accept donations for the youth mission fund."

The boys grumbled again until the preacher's hard stare silenced them. "Is that so?"

He continued giving them the beady eye until they nodded and *Yes, sir*'d.

"They'll be here at eleven and they'll stay until the last car leaves. I'd appreciate it if you'd feed them and keep them hydrated."

"Good to know some of our members know how to repent," the preacher said, and June paled. "I'll see that they get lunch."

"See you Saturday, then, Daddy." She turned on her heel and headed back to the cruiser. The teens fell in behind her like baby ducks following momma duck.

Sam took another look at the man's harsh face, then at June. He couldn't help wondering if the clichés about a preacher's daughter being wild were true. From the man's comment about repenting and his chilly attitude, it sounded like it, but that didn't fit June's image as Quincey's sweetheart. As Roth had predicted, everybody they'd encountered this morning adored her.

One thing was certain. His fellow deputy had just become a whole lot more interesting if she'd done something her father couldn't forgive.

SAM STALKED INTO Roth's office at the end of his shift. The day had been worse than enemy capture and torture. "You have to pair me with one of the men tomorrow."

Roth pointed at the chair in front of his desk. Sam sat, relieved to see the end of his first day as a deputy. "Why?"

"After we apprehended the egg throwers, June took them to the lady they stole the eggs from and promised they'd reimburse her. Then your deputy took them to her father's church and volunteered them to wash cars for a church fund-raiser. She never Mirandized them. And that's not by the book."

"No, it isn't, but neither is it out of line. They weren't formally charged."

Matter of opinion. Not Sam's. "After that she took them to school and told their science teacher that the boys would like to do a report and a presentation to their class on how eggs damage auto paint. She touted it as a great learning experience for all."

Roth's face remained inscrutable. "Is that right?"

"Only then did she drive each one of the brats to his daddy's office and tell the fathers what their sons had done and where the boys would be on Saturday and about the school project. Instead of wasting an entire afternoon on these little vandals, she should have hauled them here and tossed them into a cell to cool their heels until their parents posted bail and picked them up. June is more mommy than deputy."

Roth rocked back in his chair. "I told you small-town policing is like nothing you've ever seen. I had issues with June's technique, too, when I first started here, and then my father-in-law set me straight. June's approach may be unconventional. It certainly wouldn't work in Raleigh, where she trained. But it works here. For what it's worth, Miss Letty barely scrapes by since her husband died a few years back, and the boys attend Pastor Jones's church. They're probably even going on the mission trip. Reparation might not be a bad idea. As for the school thing...we could do with a few less juvenile delinquents. They're Quincey's biggest problem."

Dumbfounded, Sam stared at his friend. "What has small-town living done to the rule-following marine I knew? June's dispensing her own brand of justice. Hell, she was judge and jury, too."

"Supposing she'd done as you suggested and brought the boys to the station and charged them with petty vandalism, following textbook procedure. Tyler's daddy's a lawyer, a good one, I hear, and Joey's dad was Quincey's all-star quarterback fifteen years ago. He took the team to the state championship and threw the winning touchdown. That's something folks around here don't forget. I suspect the judge would have thrown out both boys' cases."

"You have to be kidding me. We caught them red-handed."

"I hear what you're saying, Sam, and now you understand some of my frustration. In reality, strings would have been pulled, charges dropped, etc. The boys' punishment would have been over before the ink dried on the paperwork, and they'd have learned that their daddies can get them out of trouble. Or if by some fluke the charges weren't dropped, the boys would have a permanent juvenile record for stealing and throwing a couple dollars' worth of eggs. You and I both did worse as kids.

"Now put yourself in their current situation." Grinning, Roth shook his head. "June's going to torture the ever-livin' hell out of them for a week. Tyler and Joey will also serve as examples to their peers when they're stuck washing cars Saturday afternoon while their buddies are eating barbecue and throwing around the football on the church lawn. And when they're forced to stand up and give that oral report, the message will be driven home again. Screw up in Quincey and you pay. You tell me which punishment is more likely to discourage repeat offenders."

As soon as Roth said it, Sam got it. He didn't like it. He preferred rules and clear-cut consequences for breaking them. He liked going through the proper chain of command. But he understood June's angle. He nodded.

"I hear you, but I'd still like to work with Morris or Aycock tomorrow. That woman likes a captive audience. She nearly talked the boys' ears off. Mine, too."

Roth cracked a smile. "Sam, she's the most even-tempered woman I've ever met or worked with. How did you manage to get on her bad side so quickly?"

The chair suddenly felt harder. "What makes you think I did?"

"She's beat you in here by ten minutes to request that your training be handled by one of the other deputies."

That rankled. Sam had never had anyone refuse to work with him before. On the contrary, he'd had more ask to be assigned to work with him than his superiors could accommodate. He was imperturbable, eternally patient, a damned good shot, and top-notch at calculating trajectories, wind velocities and spindrift.

"*She* doesn't want to work with *me*? What's her problem?"

"You. She claims you're too rigid and used excessive force when you handcuffed Tyler Newsome for throwing eggs."

"I cuffed the little bast—brat for evading arrest. He ran."

"He's barely thirteen."

"So were two of the suicide bombers I was sent to take out."

A sobering silence filled the room. Roth had been there, done that. The first kid Sam had been sent after hadn't even started shaving, but the explosives wrapped around his chest as he'd strolled into a crowded marketplace that had included many marines had been impossible to miss. That had been a hard one. The bastards over there had used women and children on a regular basis. Subsequent assignments hadn't gotten any easier. But Sam had done what was necessary to save lives.

He replaced the bad memories by dredging up an image of angry green eyes and golden hair pulled into a stubby ponytail instead.

"What else is she whining about?" Sam groused.

"She claims you were abrupt with the citizens who tried to welcome you. You even refused Mrs. Ray's turtle soup."

That bit him like belly-crawling over a ground nest of yellow jackets. "I don't like turtle soup, and I met a hundred people today. June never got the car above ten miles per hour. And then she took me to the diner for lunch. A cavity search would've been less invasive. It was like being autopsied while I was still alive." He'd barely been able to eat for people dropping by their table and grilling him.

Roth's grin widened. "Welcome to Quincey. Give it time. It'll grow on you."

"Like fungus?"

Roth laughed. "Ah, you remember my description of coming home. See you in the morning. If you're nice, maybe June will let you drive."

Frustrated, Sam rose. "If I wanted to be tortured by females, I'd go home to my sisters."

"Good idea. I'll give you three days' leave if you want to visit your family. But you're still partnered with Jones."

His sisters made the citizens of Quincey look like amateur sleuths.

"I don't need leave."

At least he and June agreed on one thing. Neither wanted to work together. But he'd change her mind. Then when he repeated his request for a different partner, maybe Roth would listen.

CHAPTER FOUR

JUNE PACED HER tiny den, waiting for Madison to get home. But instead of her landlord's truck, she heard the low growl of Sam's high-performance engine rumbling up the driveway. Tension snapped her nerves as tight as overwound guitar strings. He parked in front of his cottage and headed for his front door.

If it had been anyone else, she'd have invited them to join her for dinner. It was the neighborly thing to do. But not Sam. She'd had enough of his impatience and disapproving glares today. Not that she'd been able to see his condemning eyes through the dark lenses, but the way he'd looked at her, with censure pleating his brow and turning down the corners of his compressed mouth, she'd seen all she needed to see.

Why had he taken this job if he hated small-town life so much? Or maybe he just hated her. That bothered her more than it should have. His opinion did not matter.

A minute later her landlord's truck turned into the driveway. June grabbed the Crock-Pot and picnic basket and, juggling her load, hurried across the yard to meet Madison as she climbed from the cab.

Madison spotted June, and her dark eyebrows lifted in surprise. "Hi. Please tell me that's dinner. I'm starving. Piper and I didn't get a lunch break."

June struggled to contain her questions and forced patience she did not feel. "It is. I made white chicken chili, corn bread and salad. Busy day at the office?"

"There are always pet emergencies after a holiday weekend, but today everyone's 'emergency' was more of a need to stop by and question me about my wedding plans and my replacement, Dr. Drake."

"You got in late last night," June said in an attempt to make polite chitchat before getting down to facts as they crossed the yard together.

"It was hard to say goodbye to Adam." Madison's time with her fiancé and his family had been good for her. She looked more relaxed than June had ever seen her.

Madison, June and Piper had often shared meals, potlucking it at each other's houses until Piper and now Madison had become engaged. Once Madison moved to Georgia after her wedding, June would be solo. Except for her annoying neighbor…unless she could convince her landlord to turf him. But she couldn't blurt out that demand. She'd have to work up to it.

Madison twisted the backdoor knob, then frowned

over her shoulder at June. "You locked my back door again. Why?"

"You don't know your new tenant. I don't trust him."

Madison dug her keys out of her pocket and opened the door. "Oh, c'mon. Sam's a nice guy. And I don't think you can get a better referral than from Quincey's chief of police."

Nice guy? June practically choked on her own saliva as she followed Madison into the kitchen. She set the slow cooker, basket and salad bowl on the table. "Why didn't you tell me Roth's friend was renting the cottage?"

"Because Roth asked me not to mention it. He said Sam needed time and privacy to get his head together about being forced out of the military. And Sam was as pleasant as he could be when I met him at Piper and Roth's, so I didn't think it would be a problem. Of course, that was before he lost his job. That might affect his mood, I guess, if he's acting differently with you."

"He's the new deputy. Roth stuck me with training him."

"Ah…you're working together."

Madison's knowing tone raised her hackles. "What is that supposed to mean?"

"It explains the friction between you. You have not had great luck with the men you've worked with. You especially don't like guys who are condescending or boss you around. Does he?"

Had he? No. Not in that way. "He accused me of coming on to him when I took him the key and a welcome basket."

Madison's eyes narrowed. "I'll bet you gave him your phone number, too."

"In case he had questions. What's that got to do with it?"

"A pretty single neighbor brings food to the new guy. And I know you. That basket was probably loaded with delicious home-cooked stuff. Then that neighbor offers her phone number. How do you think a stranger to Quincey would take that kind of overture?"

When Madison put it that way… "As a pickup attempt?"

Madison nodded. Then June put the pieces together and grimaced. Heat climbed to her hairline. "To make matters worse, I was wearing Kelsie's bikini. He showed up while I was killing time by the pool."

Madison chuckled. "Poor Sam. That explains a lot. Your sister's taste borders on trampy. He'd never know you're as comfortable in a bathing suit as you are jeans and a T-shirt, thanks to your siblings' enthusiastic sports matches at family get-togethers.

"You and Sam got off on the wrong foot. Once you get to know him, you'll see he's a decent guy. He made it very clear when I met him that he wasn't looking for a relationship. Again, that was before he lost his job. I don't know if his status has changed.

But to be on the safe side, treat him like one of your brothers and you should be fine."

Even at their worst her brothers had never been so irritating. They had never questioned every decision she made or looked at her as if she was wasting their valuable time. And they never handcuffed children.

Madison gathered plates and bowls from the cabinets and set the table. "I'm glad you're here. I was going to knock on your door later anyway. Adam and I are having trouble deciding where to get married. I value your levelheaded advice."

June would prefer to talk about Sam and find out everything Madison knew about the former marine. But that would have to wait. She gathered utensils, then sat and dished out the food while Madison poured sweet tea. "What's the problem?"

"I don't want to get married in the Drakes' church. That's where I married Andrew."

"I can see where taking vows to your deceased husband's identical twin in the same spot might be awkward."

"Exactly. Plus, it gives a negative vibe. That marriage didn't work out. On the rare occasions I attend services here I go to your father's church with Piper. But I don't want your dad marrying us either. He may be a gifted orator, but I don't like the way he treats you, and I really want you and Piper with me when I promise forever to Adam."

"This is *your* wedding, Madison. Get married wherever you want. I can handle my dad." June would be there—even if it meant going to her father's church, where he'd humiliated her in front of all of Quincey.

Madison shook her head. "No way. I still remember the excitement in your voice when you called to tell me your guy had planned a special dinner and you thought he was going to propose. Then I remember the pain in your eyes when you showed up on my doorstep three days later dragging a U-Haul trailer and telling me you'd quit the job you loved and left Raleigh and you needed a place to stay. Your parents should have been there for you."

"I didn't need them. I had you and Piper."

"And we were happy to help—even though you wouldn't let us castrate the lying, adulterous bastard. But that's not the point, June. You didn't know the jerk was married. You were the victim and not the offender. Your father shouldn't have condemned you then and he shouldn't continue doing so now, years later. I wish your mother would grow a backbone and tell him to go to hell for treating you so badly."

"My mother only has an opinion if Dad gives her one. She never thinks for herself. Can we talk about something more pleasant? Like your wedding? Are we going to have ugly bridesmaids' dresses?"

Madison laughed. "That's between you and Piper. Y'all get to pick them out. I don't even care what color you choose as long as you're both there—wherever 'there' is."

"Have you and Adam considered a destination wedding? Savannah, Charleston and the Outer Banks are close by. Or you could go to the mountains."

"That's a good idea. One I'll run by Adam and research. But I need a promise from you. Promise me you'll be at the wedding wherever it is. It's scary as hell to be doing this when I swore I'd never tie myself to a man again."

Especially with her dead husband's identical twin, June thought. She didn't know the whole story of Madison's first marriage, but she knew it had gone from heaven to hell at some point. "Do you have doubts?"

"Not a one. I've never been more certain of anything in my life. That's the scariest part. He's either perfect for me, or I'm completely besotted and blind."

"I don't think it's the latter. I'll be there no matter where, no matter when and no matter how ugly my dress is."

That was one promise she'd have no trouble keeping.

For the first time ever, June dreaded going into work. She sat in her truck outside the station trying to rally her enthusiasm for the day ahead.

Yesterday had been tough with Mr. No Personality—correction, Mr. *Unpleasant* Personality—riding shotgun and wearing a perpetual scowl. She'd never met a more rigid, disagreeable, impatient, judgmental man…except maybe her father. But at least her father knew how to turn on the charm for his flock. He just didn't waste it on her.

But after her conversation with Madison, June had decided to give Sam the benefit of the doubt and a second chance at being a decent human being. She climbed from the cab, shifted her duty belt at her waist, then marched from the parking lot into the station. As usual, she was early and the other deputies' desks were empty. The only light came from the chief's domain.

"Jones, my office," Roth called out.

She stopped in front of the chief's desk. "Yes, sir? Have you rethought my request to reassign Sam?"

"Not a chance. I had calls from each of those boys' fathers last night. They both think you went overboard with the punishments."

She hadn't even clocked in and her day had begun to circle the drain. "But, Chief, this was their second offense, and after all the vandalism we had with those other teens a few months back—"

He held up one finger to stop her defense. "I disagreed with them. And I told them as much. You turned what could have been a bad and expensive experience into a learning opportunity—not just for these boys, but also for their peers."

Surprised and relieved, she sighed. She and Roth didn't have enough of a track record for her to know how he thought. "Thanks for the backup, sir."

"I also told them if they'd take the time to parent their sons, Quincey PD officers wouldn't have to."

She winced. "That, uh, might not have been a good idea."

"I'm not going to pander to egos. My predecessor was too nice and too lenient. No one will ever accuse me of that.

"Jones, I want you to take Rivers to the shooting range first thing this morning. Introduce him to Tate Lowry and empty a couple of boxes. Sam needs to get a weapon in his hands again and become familiar with the HK. Lowry's expecting you. The department will cover the cost of the rounds."

Sounded like fun—even with the bad company. "Yes, sir. Is that all?"

"No. Don't shoot my new deputy." He said it with a straight face, but humor sparkled in his eyes.

"I'll do my best to resist the temptation, Chief, but I make no promises, because he is a pain in the butt," she responded equally deadpan. The office had changed since Roth took over. Piper's dad had been a good boss, but more things got done with the new chief always pushing for improvement.

"Let me give you a piece of advice in dealing with Sam. His eye is still healing and his vision isn't what it once was. The doctors said it would take up to a year for it to stabilize. He's on shaky ground now—not sure if he'll end up with a permanent visual impairment. He's a man of actions, not words. Let your accuracy do the talking this morning. And show no mercy. Give him all you've got. Understood?"

She bit her lip. As much as she disliked Sam, she wasn't comfortable with kicking the man while he was down. "That seems a bit…cruel given his in-jury, sir. Are you sure that's the best way to handle this?"

"I'm sure. Sam thrives on adversity. He thinks his clearest when under extreme pressure. That skill saved our asses on more than one occasion. The sniper motto is Death Before Capture. There were a couple of times I was certain there was no way out of our predicament, and I was contemplating eating my own bullet rather than surrendering. But each time, Sam's ingenuity got us out of trouble.

"Trust me, Jones, he'll take this as a challenge, and improving his skills will give him something to focus on besides being cut from the corps."

She wasn't convinced, but an order was an order. "If you say so, sir. I'll do my best to wipe the floor with him."

Roth laughed. "That's exactly what he needs."

The exterior door opened, then closed. Silence followed. No sound of clunky footsteps heralded Morris or Aycock. Instead, June looked up and saw Sam standing in the chief's doorway. Without the sunglasses. The impact of his icy blue eyes on hers winded her like a bad tackle in a family-reunion football game.

"Repeating your request to dump me?" he growled.

Be nice, June. It won't kill you. But it might come close.

She stretched her mouth into a smile so wide it nearly cracked her cheeks. "Good morning, Rivers. On the contrary, I'm getting our assignment. Clock in. I'll be waiting in the cruiser. The chief is sending us on an expedition."

She headed for the door and paused for Sam to step out of the way.

"Hold it, Jones." The chief's voice stopped her inches from her new partner.

So much for a quick escape. She pivoted to face the boss. The subtle aroma of man filled her nostrils. Sam. Not cologne. Her mouth dried. She was too close, but she refused to give away her unsettled reaction by backtracking. "Yes, sir?"

"The idea you submitted for modernizing our records and converting our paper files to digital is a good one. When the equipment I've requisitioned comes in, you and Sam will be in charge of that operation. Copy that?"

She wouldn't be passing Deputy Rivers off to someone else anytime soon. Not good news. "Yes, Chief."

"That's all."

She turned and looked at Sam. His cold gaze drilled hers, but he stubbornly held his ground, blocking half the doorway. Was he trying to intimidate her? If so, he was wasting his time. She'd endured far worse from her brothers and her fellow officers in Raleigh who'd been determined to run off the female country bumpkin—especially once she'd shown them up on the range.

She brushed past him, being extremely careful not to bump him, but at the last second the duty pack on her belt snagged on him, jolting her pulse into a wild rhythm. Ignoring it, she headed for the break room. She needed coffee and distance before closeting herself in the car with him.

Treat him like a brother, Madison had said. But neither Michael nor Rhett had ever had this disconcerting effect on her. On second thought, maybe she didn't need the caffeine after all. Her pulse was pounding like a woodpecker against her eardrums, and she was already jumpy. If she wanted to be able to hit the target, she needed to steady her nerves.

Calm. Cool. Whoop his butt.

Yes, he was an ex-sniper. But that meant he was used to long-range rifles. Thanks to her grandfather, she was an expert with handguns. And as Roth had said, Sam had visual issues, too.

Time for some humble pie, Deputy Sam.

SAM HAD NEVER minded silence. Before now. He was used to solitude and didn't need entertaining. He definitely did *not* need or miss June's chatter or stopping every five yards to meet Quincey's people.

Recon was his thing. The scenery—fields, woods, farms—was self-explanatory. He saw what he needed to see and made a mental map of the region. He didn't need her to identify the plants that provided cover or the hollows where someone could hide, or for her to tell him stories about the odd characters who lived up each dirt driveway the way she had yesterday. Quiet suited him fine.

But he was flying blind with no intel to their destination and he didn't like it. June was edgy. He could feel tension rolling off her like heat off an airstrip. The uneasy feeling of being on the verge of walking into an ambush grew stronger by the minute.

Another mile passed without June taking her foot off the gas except to allow a gaggle of geese to cross the road. On the outskirts of town she hit the turn signal. Sam muffled a groan. He should have known the reprieve wouldn't last. After the kid fiasco yesterday she'd taken him to dozens of backwoods holes-in-the-wall to meet the citizens who operated Quincey's mom-and-pop businesses. Was this yet another one?

Then she turned the car into the gravel lot and a plain hand-painted sign came into view. Hunt and Bait Shop. He liked to hunt and fish. Maybe this wouldn't be unbearable.

June parked, climbed out of the patrol car and headed for the long, low cinder-block building without a word. He tracked after her. The sign in the window said the place wouldn't open for another hour, but after a quick knock, she barged through the unlocked door.

Sam followed a little more cautiously. Dozens of taxidermied dark eyes stared down at him from the walls. Deer, beavers, foxes, raccoon, bobcats, assorted fowl. There were a couple of pictures of a guy in ACUs tucked unobtrusively among them. A red steel door marked Live Fire Beyond This Point caught his attention.

A shooting range? In Quincey? His day suddenly looked more interesting. Sam hadn't fired a weapon in over six months—not by choice. He'd been warned after the surgery to avoid anything jarring like recoil for three months, but an hour before giving him the boot, his doctor had given the okay to resume normal activities.

Normal. *Ha.* His life was anything but normal now.

He itched to unload the semiauto in his holster. He'd come back tonight after work.

"Tate?" June called out.

A fifty-something buzz-cut-wearing man came out of the back office. The guy from the pictures—minus the uniform. A scar now marked the right side of his face and he walked with a mild limp.

"June, I haven't seen you in a coon's age." Then his gaze slid to Sam and he extended his hand across the glass display case containing an assortment of pistols, revolvers and a sweet Benchmade knife. "You must be the new deputy. I'm Tate Lowry, Master Sergeant, US Army, retired, but I won't hold being a jarhead against you." He delivered the rivalry insult with a smile.

The guy knew who he was. Sam shook his hand. "Sam Rivers. Staff Sergeant, USMC. *Former* staff sergeant," he corrected, and the words pierced him like an enemy's bayonet. "And I won't hold being a dogface grunt against you."

Lowry guffawed. "That's the spirit." Then he reached beneath the counter and set two boxes of .40-cal ammo on the surface. "Chief called an' told me you two were coming. I don't open to the public for an hour, so you have the place to yourself."

Shooting? That was the detail Roth had in mind for today? *Thanks, buddy.*

"I've set targets on all four lanes," Lowry continued, "and there are more stacked by the door. Have at it. If you need more ammo, you know where to find me." The old guy winked at June.

She grinned back, and her smile hit Sam like a sucker punch. "Thanks, Tate. I owe you a pecan pie."

"You owe me nothing, sweetheart, but I'll take a pie off your hands anytime." He turned back to Sam. "You need ear or eye protection?"

Sam nodded, and Tate added clear-lens glasses and a set of earplugs to the ammo pile. Sam registered that he didn't offer June either safety precaution.

"Use of the shooting range is on the house for QPD. You're welcome anytime. Rifle shooting is done out back. If you need to get in before or after my official hours, just give me a call and I'll make it happen. I got nothing better to do."

"Thank you, sir. I appreciate it," Sam said, eager to see the range.

"You and I need to swap stories sometime. Not many people around here want to listen to an old fart talk about the good ol' deployment days. Might be dumb, but I miss 'em."

"Copy that."

June grabbed a box of ammo and headed for the red door. Sam did the same. It would be good to know if the woman watching his back could hit anywhere close to her mark or if he'd need to take cover if she ever unholstered her weapon. Roth had said she'd graduated at the top of her class, but seeing was believing. The door closed behind them, and the familiar sulfur smell of gunpowder filled his nose.

June stopped by the first lane. "If you have questions about the HK, let me know. Here's the deal—one magazine per target, loser buys dinner. Highest number of winning sheets eats free. Just so you know, it's going to be me, Rivers. I'll be down there shellacking you." She pointed to the far side of the room, then headed that way.

Her cocky wager—not the sparkle in her eyes or the confident swing of her hips—grabbed his attention by the throat. He'd fired more makes of guns than there were weeks in a year. He took the closest lane. "I think I can figure out this weapon, and

I'll take that bet, Jones. I haven't had a good steak in a while."

"You'll be buying those steaks, Deputy."

Her vaunt made him laugh. "Do you know what I did for a living?"

"I know." She pulled ear and eye protection from her small bag and donned both before disappearing into her booth. The fact that she kept her own equipment in the car made him wonder if she needed that much practice. He couldn't see her over the six-foot protective walls, but he could see her target downrange.

He pulled his spare magazines from his belt and lined them up on the rubber-matted board. Anticipation and adrenaline—not her challenge—made his heart race as he emptied his police ammo, then refilled each clip with cheaper target rounds. He was almost done when the distinct crack-thump of June's weapon pulled his gaze to the paper rectangle. She'd hit an inch left of center. Not bad. Lucky shot? Her second round drilled the target. Bull's-eye. Before the paper stopped fluttering, a third round ruffled the edge of the same hole, then a fourth. He blinked and looked again.

The blonde who wore sequined sandals and a ruffled bikini and cooled herself off with a squirt bottle was a sharpshooter?

"No effin' way," he muttered.

Roth would have warned him. Or would he? His buddy had a twisted sense of humor. Had he been messing with Sam's head and enjoying a private joke? That had to be it. Oh yeah, today would be fun. He'd school June on how it was done. Nice to know she'd be a worthy opponent.

She proved her skills further with eight more rounds. Then she ejected her magazine and backed out of the booth. Frowning down the aisle at him, she removed an earplug. "Need help loading?"

He realized he'd stopped to watch her, and that was wrong, wrong, wrong. He was a professional, not a spectator. "No. Where'd you learn to shoot like that?"

"There's nothing to do in Quincey but fish and hunt. I used to hang out with my grandfather and two younger brothers. I'm a bit…competitive, or so they tell me."

"Not bad, Deputy. But not good enough to get a free meal out of me." He stepped to the line. He'd never fired this weapon, had no idea if the sights were accurate, and it had been months since he'd discharged a pistol. But if there was one thing he knew, it was ballistics.

He took a deep breath, then exhaled, slow and steady. His first shot went wide right, barely tearing the edge of the paper. He mentally adjusted for sights that were off and tried again. Low and outside. Damn. He fired a third and missed again.

He was shooting all around the paper. Was it the gun or him? His mind spun, calculating distance, trajectory, velocity and a hundred other things. He was alive because he was a damned good shot.

Was?

The thought rocked him to the core. Had to be the HK.

He tried to focus, to slow his respiratory and heart rates and still his unsteady hands. Damn it, he was shaking. He didn't shake—not even when his life was on the line. He emptied the clip, replaced the target, then braced his elbows on the deck and emptied another magazine with the same bad results.

His surgeon had warned that he might have some depth perception issues for a while due to the unequal pressure in his eyes. Was that the case here?

"Take your time, Sam," June said from behind him, and rested a hand on his shoulder. He hadn't even noticed her moving to the back of his lane. Her palm burned through his uniform. The concern in her tone ratcheted up his tension. He stood, reeled in the tattered target and replaced it, then ejected the magazine and popped in the next one.

Compensate. Figure out what's going wrong and fix it.

Her scent drifted across the booth, disrupting his focus. Mind games? Blondie was playing with *him*—a man who'd been trained to block out biting insects, snakes and other vermin and even bodily functions to get his shot. Hell, he could lie in wait for hours or days, if necessary.

He'd better concentrate if he didn't want to spend a meal looking into smug green eyes.

Come on, Rivers. You're better than this.

He shook off her hand and fixed his gaze on the intersecting lines, very conscious of the woman watching him. He exhaled, ignoring her as best he could, squeezed the trigger repeatedly until his magazine was empty. His anxiety level rose with each shot.

He looked at the Swiss cheese of his target—pitiful—then at June. For a moment he thought he saw sympathy in her green eyes, and his spine turned to steel.

Then she shrugged. "Sixty-one more rounds to go. I like my steak medium rare with a baked potato drowning in butter on the side."

He had to keep his head in the game. "You think you're gonna beat me."

"Of course. I know this weapon as well as I know my own face. You, on the other hand, are still learning your HK's quirks and you're out of practice."

Her cockiness would have been cute if anxiety hadn't been chewing a hole in his stomach. "My sights are off."

She offered him her weapon, grip first. "Use mine."

In other words, put up or shut up, marine. What choice did he have? He exchanged guns with her. "Are you going to yap all day or shoot?"

Her eyebrows arched above the clear lenses. Then

she about-faced. She took lane three. He moved to lane two, beside her.

He heard the telltale sound of her popping in a magazine and loading one in the chamber. He'd do better with her weapon. The sights were on target. Her accuracy proved that.

But he didn't improve. Four magazines later he admitted it wasn't the weapon. It was him.

He was a sniper, a sharpshooter, without a single bull's-eye. If he couldn't hit his target, where did that leave him?

Unemployable and without marketable skills.

Was the blind spot in his peripheral vision not enough of a curse? Was his visual impairment permanent? It had been five damned months since his final surgery. He was counting on healing and proving the doctors wrong.

Movement downrange caught his attention. June reeled in yet another target with a gaping hole in the center. Each perfect sheet had ratcheted up his tension until he was almost ready to burst out of his skin. His targets looked as if he'd used buckshot. A new recruit who'd never touched a weapon before boot camp would have had better results.

Desperation filled him, forcing out oxygen. He had to improve his scores. Again and again he reached for the box, until there were no rounds left. He'd wasted one hundred rounds and hadn't scored a single winning sheet. He'd improved his score by shooting with his injured eye closed, but he was still nowhere near his previous proficiency.

"Nothing more we can do. Give it time," the doctors had said.

Sometimes life sucked.

And then it got worse.

He removed the glasses and wiped his face, then backed out of the booth, facing one cold, hard fact. He was no longer a marine. He was no longer a sharpshooter.

What was he good for now? Nothing. Nada. Zilch.

Would Roth even want him as a temporary deputy with a shot record like this? Maybe sitting on his ass and collecting disability checks would be the highlight of his future.

No. Aw, hell no. He would get well.

June sashayed toward him, triumph all over her face. "You owe me dinner."

Pressure built inside him. His thoughts spun like an Osprey's rotors. He couldn't handle June's gloating. Not now. Couldn't handle the fear crushing his larynx and pounding in his ears. Couldn't handle this feeling of failure slithering over him like a snake in a swamp.

"I'll let you wait until payday to pay up because I want a thick, juicy steak, not a thin, leathery truck-stop special."

He couldn't take any more. Catching her by the elbows, he yanked her close and smothered her cocky smile with his mouth. Her surprised gasp sucked the air from his lungs. Seconds later her stiff body relaxed and the warmth of her soft lips and softer breasts pressed against him. He kissed her hard and deep, his tongue battling with hers. Slick, wet and hot.

She burrowed closer. Her belt buckle raked across his fly, blasting a flamethrower of heat through him.

At least he hadn't forgotten how to kiss.

His brain screamed a warning. What in the hell? He abruptly released her. He was not an impulsive guy and had never made an unwelcome move toward a woman in his life.

But he'd grabbed June. Why?

To shut her up. And to wipe that smug smile off her face.

Poor excuse. But it was all he had. Despite the cold realization that he'd just screwed up *big-time*, the imprint of her body against his lingered. And that was wrong.

If he was lucky, Roth would fire him. If he wasn't, June would sue him for sexual harassment.

Gold-tipped lashes fluttered open, revealing wide pupils. She inhaled a shaky breath through her wet parted lips. "Wh-what was that?"

Her breathy question slammed him like a pugil stick of desire.

"A mistake."

CHAPTER FIVE

EVERY CELL IN June's body reverberated like an evacuation siren. Shock, denial and a tangle of other emotions wrestled for supremacy. Desire topped the heap until mortification flipped it upside down and pinned it to the ground. She struggled to clear her head and make sense of the past seconds.

Sam had kissed her. And she'd responded like a desperate, needy, hungry woman, squashing herself against him and soaking up his embrace like a thirsty sponge. Why?

She'd emasculated him. Shame burned over her, erasing every last vestige of arousal. She had brothers and knew better than to threaten a male's masculinity. Sam had struck back in the only way he could. By proving he was still a man despite the lost marksmanship skills.

That explained why he'd kissed her. But it did nothing to clarify the part of this equation she didn't want to think about. Why did this man she disliked *intensely* have the power to make every cell in her body ricochet like gunfire in a rock quarry? Kissing him should have been revulsive, not thrilling. Skin crawling, not spine tingling. Annoying, not addictive.

No. Not addictive. She did *not* want to kiss him again. No way. Not ever.

The chief had been wrong. There had to be a better strategy to encourage Sam to move forward than by backing him into a corner and beating him down. But if there was another way, she couldn't think of it at the moment. Sam had smoked her brain cells.

"Jones, report," the radio on her shoulder barked. She jumped guiltily and nearly tripped over her own feet backing away from Sam.

Her already-racing heart bounded faster. *Think.* She and Sam had to work together. She couldn't make an issue of what had just happened, because, one, she'd goaded him into it, two, he was her boss's friend and, three, making this public would only confirm her father's low opinion of her. Number three was a biggie.

"Jones, report," Roth's voice repeated, snapping her out of mental paralysis.

"Finishing up at the range, Chief." She prayed Sam didn't hear the strained squeak in her voice.

"Fess Smith reported a stolen truck. Head there."

"Yes, sir. On the way."

Sam's already-intimidating scowl deepened, tearing her between two choices: running or standing her ground. *She* hadn't done anything wrong. Except taunt him. And kiss him back.

"You didn't get the address," he bit out.

"I don't need one. The Smith homestead's where it's always been." She retreated to her booth and methodically reloaded her magazines with standard-issue rounds, one after the other, hoping the monotonous press-click would calm her enough to help her find a way out of this awkward situation.

She'd made a mistake. So had Sam. Offsetting penalties, in sports terminology. The best thing they could do was wipe the slate clean and start over.

Decision made, she gathered her gear and marched back to his side. "Rivers, I owe you an apology. I thought challenging you might help. But until your eye heals, pushing you beyond your limitations is not the answer."

A muscle bunched in his rock-hard jaw. "What has Roth told you?"

"That it might take months for your sight to normalize. You're going to have to be patient."

"Say that when your only skill has been taken from you."

She gave him credit for not whining. Frustration and maybe a touch of fear tinged his voice. Compassion overtook her. Sam's dreams had been crushed, a circumstance she understood all too well.

"I doubt pulling a trigger is your only skill. Change is hard. The transition period is the worst. But you'll get through it. In the meantime, I'll forget what happened if you will. We have to work together and that…just can't happen again."

He searched her face. "Roger that. I'm sorry, I—"

He cut off whatever he was going to say, hesitated, then shook his head. "Sorry."

"Let's go." She hustled to the cruiser without waiting for him, calling out goodbyes to Tate as she passed through the showroom but not slowing down. Sam's door slammed a second after hers. As he buckled in, his elbow bumped hers on the console, jolting her with another unwelcome flare of awareness as his scent filled her nose. Tension flooded the passenger compartment, making the formerly spacious vehicle feel as suffocating as a car sinking into the river's murky water. Needing fresh air, she rolled down the window and debated hanging her head out like a dog.

Six miles. She had that far to get her head back into the game. Heavy silence descended. Her mind insisted on replaying the firm pressure of his mouth, the strength of his hands, the solid heat of his muscular body against hers, making her tongue and brain unable to convey details about the properties they passed and the people waving from their front porches or yards.

A doe and fawn darted across the road in front of the car. June's distracting thoughts delayed her reaction time. She braked hard and automatically threw her arm across Sam's chest. She barely missed the leggy baby scampering behind its mom. Behind his shades, her passenger's face looked as hard as petrified wood.

She snatched her arm back. His residual heat

burned her triceps. "We get a lot of deer out here and the occasional black bear or escaped farm animal. When you get your own cruiser, be on the lookout for four-legged jaywalkers."

A slight dip of his chin was the only acknowledgment he offered.

When they reached the Smith property, June immediately identified the crime scene by the chest-high broom grass surrounding a bare brown patch. Careful not to cross the tire tracks crushed into the vegetation, she swung wide and parked thirty feet away. As if he couldn't wait to get away from her, Sam vaulted from the car before she pulled the key from the ignition. That stung.

She retrieved the department's camera from the trunk and followed him. Lagging behind put her in position to notice he had one of those triangle-shaped bodies her brothers had tried so hard to build. Sam's wide shoulders tapered to a narrow waist and a nice firm butt that his uniform pants accentuated all too well. Strong legs carried the package that all the single women of Quincey would no doubt soon be chasing.

The slap of a wooden screen door yanked her from her wayward thoughts—a good thing since the last time she'd admired a man in uniform, she'd gotten her heart blasted to bits. She gulped and averted her eyes from forbidden territory.

Fess ambled across the yard as if he had all week

to get there. The only time she'd ever seen the man move faster than a box turtle was when he tried to get to the front of the food line at the church picnic. June made introductions.

Choosing his steps carefully, Sam circled the scene of the crime. "When did you notice the truck missing?"

"'Bout lunchtime, I guess. Came out to get the mail and it wasn't there."

"Was it here yesterday?" June asked.

"Think so."

"But you're not sure? What was the make of the truck?" Sam asked.

"Won't swear it was here on my Bible, if that's what you mean. But it was a '78 GMC."

"Did it run?" Sam continued searching the ground.

"Nope. Hasn't in years."

"That means it left here towed or on a trailer. That could explain the widely spaced tire tracks." Sam's lens-covered gaze landed on June, and her stomach swooped. "Have there been any similar thefts in the area, Officer Jones?"

How did he expect her to remember details when he scowled at her that way? She slogged through the sludge in her brain. "A van disappeared earlier this year. We never found any trace of it. I don't recall anything before that."

"Did you check scrap yards? Trucks and vans

are heavy vehicles. They could have been sold for scrap metal."

Despite her time in the city, that never would have occurred to her. "Butch White, a former deputy, was the officer in charge of that case. I'll check his files when we get back to the station, but I don't recall him mentioning junkyards."

Sam squatted, his muscular thighs straining his pants, and brushed back the grass to study a footprint. For some fool reason, June couldn't take her eyes off his big, scarred, masculine hand.

He glanced up and caught her gawking. She pretended interest in the impression. "That's a small print."

"Good-for-nothing teenagers," Fess snarled. "Lazy. The whole lot of 'em. None of 'em wants to work for a living anymore. Just want their video games."

"Does Quincey have the capability of casting for footprints?" Sam asked.

"No. We haven't had a need to in the past."

She crouched beside Sam and stretched out her measuring tape alongside the dent in the soft soil and then took a picture. Sam's nearness made her jittery. She had to focus extra hard to keep her hands from shaking and get a clear shot.

Needing distance, she rose and scanned the area for more evidence, then concentrated on photographing the deep tire tracks. In the process she found a larger footprint, then measured and photographed it.

"Mr. Smith, what size shoe do you wear?" Sam asked.

She felt Sam's gaze on her as he questioned Fess and she heard tension in his voice that hadn't been there before.

"Ten. Why? What's that got to do with anything?"

Sam pointed. "This print's bigger than a ten. That one's smaller. We're looking for at least two thieves."

"Good observation, Deputy," June said, admiring the way he quickly put facts together.

No matter what they'd promised each other, one thing was certain. Forgetting that kiss wouldn't be as easy as she'd thought. That one moment had changed everything. But she would have to try.

ADMITTING DEFEAT WENT against every fiber of Sam's being. He wasn't a quitter. For a sniper, giving up meant dying. But being a liability to anyone was untenable. He sucked as a cop.

He'd debated his decision until after midnight. He knew Roth would never fire him. It was up to Sam to do the right thing. He marched into the chief's office Thursday morning without waiting for the man to get off the phone. Sam took off his badge and gun and laid both on Roth's desk.

"Let me call you back," Roth said and ended the call. "What's this?"

Sam took yesterday's rolled-up targets from his back pocket and fanned the tattered sheets across the scarred surface. "I'm useless with a weapon and unable to safely execute my duty."

"You can't quit."

A gasp yanked Roth's gaze to the open door behind Sam.

"You're quitting?" June, with shock on her face, stood in the opening.

He should have closed the door. "Yes."

"Just because…" Green eyes searched his face. "Because of yesterday?"

He heard the question she hadn't voiced. She thought he was bailing because of the kiss. He saw it in her hesitant expression and heard it in her less-than-confident tone. But he wouldn't address his stupid move here in front of Roth. He was damned lucky she wasn't jacking him up on charges— charges he couldn't defend.

"I'm supposed to be your backup. Do you want to depend on that?" He jabbed a finger toward the pages. "I'm more likely to shoot you than a perp."

June approached the desk, her steps tentative. She kept two yards between them as she had all yesterday afternoon, clearly illustrating she didn't trust him after what he'd done. Could he blame her? No.

She looked expectantly at Roth and when he said nothing, she focused on Sam. "In my almost five years with Quincey PD and in all the cases I've heard the former chief discuss, Roth is the only officer who's ever had to discharge his weapon in the line of duty. If your poor range score is the real reason you're quitting, I can tell you it's not an issue. But if you don't have the guts to work through a problem, quitting is always easier."

His spine snapped straight at the jab. Was she challenging him to stay? Even after what he'd done? He searched her steady but wary eyes. Her chin lifted. Damn straight she was.

Could she forget his kiss that easily? Each time he'd drifted off to sleep last night, she'd been right back in his arms, soft and warm, pliant against him. Over and over, he'd tasted her lips, felt the slick slide of her tongue and been reminded how she'd responded until he'd given up on sleep and hit the woods for a long hike in the dark.

Losing sleep over a woman—that was a first.

"I hope you can live with your decision, Sam," she said, echoing his earlier thoughts.

She turned and headed for the door but paused on the threshold and slowly pivoted. "For what it's worth, your accuracy definitely needs work, but your deductive skills are excellent. I carried a stack of old records home with me last night, and I found one abandoned motor-vehicle theft every six months for the past three years. Like clockwork. All older heavy cars or trucks, as you said. All taken in the middle of the night. Without a searchable database, examining the files is slow going. I have to read each one. There may be more thefts beyond three years, but I fell asleep."

She swung her gaze to Roth. "Butch White was in charge of each case I've found thus far. A few of his comments implied he considered the disappearance of abandoned vehicles a favor to Quincey because they cleaned up the countryside of 'rusty eyesores.'" Her attention returned to Sam. "A veteran officer never made the connection between them, but you did, during your second day on the job. You also eliminated Mr. Smith as a suspect based on shoe size. Those are pretty good observations for someone with no police experience.

"If you stay, you can help me track the thefts and nail our thieves. But if you go, I'll solve this case on my own and happily take all the credit for doing so." She sashayed out of sight.

Flabbergasted, Sam turned to Roth in time to catch him wiping a smirk off his face. "What she said."

Sam didn't know what to make of June's speech. She should be reporting him, not daring him to stay. "Is she always this much of a PITA?"

"I'm never a pain in the ass, Deputy. I just speak my mind." June stood in the hall outside the door, her arms loaded with manila file folders. "Ask my siblings or anyone else who knows me. I'm the most accommodating person you'll ever meet. You just happen to tap-dance on my last nerve every chance you get. I think you enjoy it." Then she continued down the corridor.

Roth's chuckle carried across his desk, and then his smile faded. "Shut the door," he ordered.

Frustrated, Sam did as bid. Roth rose and paced the office, looking intense. "What June just told us reinforces why I need you here. If White turned his head from this, then what else did he ignore? What if it's one of his cronies who's stealing vehicles, one of my deputies or even White himself? I'd love to nail that sonofabitch for something else."

Valid points. "Roth, my limitations—"

"Sam, I didn't hire you to pick off targets. As June pointed out, you'll have no need for those skills here. I hired you because other than my wife, you are the only person I trust completely."

Every instinct warned Sam to take cover, hole up somewhere until the dust settled and his vision and life returned to normal. But he couldn't in good conscience walk away from Roth.

"I'll stay. But I need some range time—without your ringer marksman out there. I won't be put in a situation where I'll have to defend my partner and end up shooting her instead of the perp."

"Deal. June gave you a hard time?"

"Ground my face in the mud."

"My mistake. I told her to. For the record, she objected to kicking you while you were down, as she put it."

But she'd sure enjoyed it.

"Decent of her. Thanks for letting me know." Her guilt over her part in the disaster was probably the only reason she wasn't reaming him with charges.

He reached for his badge and gun and hoped like hell he didn't regret staying on.

SAM WAS USED to living or working with others in close quarters in barracks or tents, but after five hours of wading through old handwritten files with June he was ready to break and run for the forest.

Where was his ability to focus and block out anything except the mission? Where was his patience? AWOL. Because of that damned kiss.

He needed silence, solitude, space and fresh air that didn't smell like a vanilla-scented, cookie-baking Annie Oakley.

June was getting to him. The way she rolled her pencil between her fingers when she was lost in thought. The way she bit her lip, tilted her head and shifted in her seat. The shuffle of her feet on the tile floor, the creak of her chair when she leaned back. The way the hairs escaping her stubby po-nytail drifted across her cheek and she impatiently swatted them back.

Sam redirected his attention to the safer territory of the county map in front of him, pinpointed the next address and added another dot. Roth wanted this investigation into past vehicle thefts kept quiet in case it involved others in the department. That meant privacy—a closed door and a small room with inadequate ventilation. All he could smell was her.

Sam suppressed the antsy feeling crawling over him. Claustrophobia? Nah. Couldn't be. Hell, he'd lain in a drainage pipe barely wider than his shoulders for three days once to get his shot. He just needed a break.

But he knew it sure as hell could have been worse. Roth could have ordered them to work together in either Sam's or June's house, away from the inquisitive eyes of the other deputies. Instead, Roth had told the others June and Sam were preparing the records for digitizing. Morris and Aycock had run rather than be dragged into the electronic age.

June popped out of her chair, launching his system into high alert again. She circled the table once, twice, lapping the small room and tapping her chin. He'd learned during his morning of confined torture that the indention between her brows meant she was pondering a theory—which he would hear once she put the words together, and not before. Thus far, her theories had been pretty good, if long-winded.

She stopped abruptly and studied the pictures of the footprints laid out side by side on the table along with copies of the scant evidence they'd gleaned from the older files.

"We could be looking at a father-son duo," she announced.

He'd come to the same conclusion. "Or a husband and wife. Just because the boots don't have high heels doesn't exclude women."

"I hadn't thought of that. Women don't usually do this kind of crime, do they?"

"You wouldn't believe what I've seen women do." He instantly wanted the words back. He didn't want to talk about the atrocities he'd witnessed.

She searched his face and waited. When he said nothing more, she nodded. "No, I don't imagine I would. If you ever need to talk about it, I know how to listen."

She circled the room once more, picking up a clear sheet of transparency film and a marker before returning to his end of the table and parking by his shoulder. Planting a palm on the surface, she leaned over the map and laid down the film. She didn't touch him, but he could feel her presence to his core. Using the marker, she dotted each theft location, then connected the dots on the page. It formed a rough circle.

"Each of the thefts takes place within a ten-mile radius. A criminal usually works within his comfort zone. As much as I hate to admit it, odds are our thief is one of my neighbors rather than an outsider."

Smart and pretty. He appreciated her not pursuing the conversation about his past right up until her scent wrapped around him like a Heatsheet. At that point he would have preferred describing the horrors of war to dealing with the way she unsettled him.

"Looks that way."

"Sketchy though White's descriptions are, the MO is the same in each case. Which means someone I very likely know has been stealing right under Quincey PD's nose for years and getting away with it."

"Affirmative."

Her watch beeped right beside his ear and he nearly took cover under the table. That was how on edge she had him.

She straightened and blinked at the digital face. Then her eyes widened. "Oh. I have to go. Can you handle lunch on your own today? I have a previous engagement."

A date? The gnawing in his stomach was hunger. Nothing more. "Go."

She bolted out the door, sucking the air out of the room like a fuel-air bomb does when thrown into a cave. It took him a second to get his bearings.

Lunch. On his own. In Quincey.

He huffed out a breath and folded up the map. He'd invaded hostile territory before. He could handle this. Better yet, he would make it work for him. He had an assignment and it was about time he remembered that.

IDIOT. IDIOT. IDIOT. June mentally kicked her fanny all the way to Madison's clinic. She wanted to be rid of Sam. But she'd thrown down the gauntlet this morning, practically forcing him to stay unless he wanted to be tagged a coward.

Darn her peacemaking, ego-soothing, meltdown-managing heart. Most of the time, her middle-child people skills were an asset. Other times, like now, they came back to bite her in the posterior. Her inability to mind her own business had earned her a morning of close proximity with Sam while they'd combed through old files in the interrogation room.

She'd said as little as possible because the chill radiating from him had nearly given her frostbite. And the memory of his kiss had lurked in the corner of the room like a test proctor, mocking her incessantly and reminding her that the most exciting embrace of her life had come from a man she didn't like. And on the job, no less. Two strikes.

Hadn't she learned anything from the fiasco with Peter? Affairs with coworkers were bad. Not that this was or ever would become an affair, but still, if this situation blew up in her face, where would she run to this time? She was too naive and gullible for the big city. Besides, Quincey was her home.

As soon as she opened the clinic door, June heard Madison's and Piper's voices coming from the back of the building. Eager to escape her own chastising company, she hustled down the hall. Both women looked up when she entered.

"We were about to start eating without you," Piper said. "We thought you might have gotten called out on a case."

"Sorry. I had to swing by the cottage to pick up my contribution to lunch. If I'd taken it to the station, there'd be none left for us." June set her items on the table.

Madison shrugged and eagerly reached for the container. "That's because you've trained them like Pavlov's dogs. They all salivate when you come in with a covered dish. I'll never be able to fit into my wedding dress if you keep testing decadent dessert recipes on us."

"Have you found a dress?" June asked.

"I think so. I have a picture of one that I love and the bridal salon has ordered it in my size for me to try on. When it comes in, I'm dragging both of you with me for your opinions. You can look at bridesmaids' dresses while we're there. I want you to find one you'll wear again."

"June should pick them out. She's the expert on which ones collect dust," Piper said, and June fought a wince at the unintentional nick.

The old "always a bridesmaid" cliché could have been coined to describe her. She had a closet jampacked with dresses and no matter how carefully each bride had chosen or what the saleslady had promised, June had never worn any of them a second time. And between her poor choices in men and the shortage of eligible males in Quincey, she doubted she'd ever get to wear a bridal gown.

Shaking off the depressing thought, she nodded toward Piper. "You have the best fashion sense. I think you should choose."

"Make it a joint effort." Madison eagerly cut into

the dessert despite her earlier protest. "What'd you concoct this time?"

"Brownie-bottom turtle cheesecake. Piper, why didn't you tell me Roth had hired his marine buddy?"

"I didn't know and wasn't even aware Sam was in town until the day he started work. The gossip grapevine spread the word before my husband could. I heard it from a patient." She frowned at Madison. "Still, I can't believe neither you nor Roth told me. Roth must've spoken to you weeks before Sam moved here to make arrangements."

"Your husband told me Sam needed time to get his head together after getting cut from the corps. I respected the man's need for privacy. Been there. Done that. But even I didn't know he was the new hire. I just thought he was coming to hibernate for a while."

"I'm sorry to be so aggravated, Madison. It's just…Roth loves Sam's company. Those two are closer than brothers. You'd think Roth would be so excited about Sam moving here that he'd have to tell me, and yet he said nothing. And Sam hasn't even come over to hang out at the house. Josh is crushed. He loves hearing Sam and Roth talk about old times. The whole situation feels…strange."

The fact that Piper was getting the same weird vibes as June only magnified June's uneasiness.

"What's Roth's excuse?" Madison asked.

"Basically what you just said. Sam wanted to be left alone."

"Maybe they're trying to set boundaries since Sam's now Roth's employee," Madison suggested.

"Could be," Piper speculated. "But I still can't believe my husband kept such a big secret."

"You two have only been married a few months. My guess is you can chalk up the lack of communication to newlyweds learning what and how much to share with a partner," Madison said soothingly.

June's instincts told her there was more to it than that. But she kept her fears to herself rather than worry her friend. And Madison had been married before, so she knew better than June.

But something definitely wasn't right at the station. Keeping the auto theft investigation from the rest of the team was a departure from the former chief's we're-all-family policy. Why would Roth do that unless he suspected one of the deputies was involved? How was she supposed to trust the men and have them trust her if there were secrets between them?

She ached to discuss her confusion with her friends. Madison and Piper were often her voice of reason when she had issues to work out. She told them everything. But she couldn't share this or tell them about that kiss. Especially not Piper.

Leaking info about either to the chief's wife could get June fired, and getting fired was the last thing she needed if she was ever going to get back into her daddy's good graces. She didn't miss him or his dogmatic, judgmental ways, but she missed her mom. And you didn't gain access to Angie Jones without Pastor Kevin's approval.

CHAPTER SIX

SAM NEEDED A strategy to keep him focused on the mission and to get him through this deployment.

Roth had asked Sam to investigate all the deputies. June, by bailing on lunch, had unintentionally provided Sam the perfect recon cover. He needed to grab something to eat and was unfamiliar with the terrain. He could rough it solo, but infiltration required connections. Morris, the deputy with less seniority, seemed the most approachable. Translation: the weakest link.

"Morris, can I ride along with you to lunch?"

"Sure."

Ten minutes later Sam was back in the one place he would have preferred to avoid as he would sutures in the field without anesthetic.

"Is this the only place to eat?"

"Pretty much, unless you run up the road and out of our jurisdiction, which we can't do. Quincey's not big enough to interest fast-food chains. Anyway, everything here's homemade instead of processed in some huge plant and trucked in. Barbecue and ribs are slow-cooked over hickory in the shack out back on Tuesdays and Thursdays."

Forty-eight hours' absence hadn't improved the diner's atmosphere. The tiled-and-chromed '50s-style place held just as many, if not more, curious people who smelled fresh meat—*him*—and would ask too many questions. But this time, Sam realized, one of them could be the car thief, and the questioning could go both ways. He could also watch the crowd to see who seemed uncomfortable having two deputies seated at the corner table.

To do his job Sam needed to gain Mac's confidence. "So, Mac, what do you do for fun around here?"

"Fish. Hunt." And when Sam kept staring, Morris's eyes rounded and his face turned red. He slid down in his seat a little. "You mean…women? Because there aren't any eligible ones in Quincey."

Considering Sam lived next to one, that was news to him. "Not necessarily, but sure, women can be a fun diversion."

"The smart ones move away. The ones that are left…well, you don't want to mess with them."

Did that include June? "Why?"

"Either you've known them since they wore diapers or they're not the kind of gals your momma would approve of."

Which category did June fall into? "How so?"

He leaned forward. "Take Tammy Sue, for instance," he said in a near whisper. "If you haven't met her yet, you will. She's pretty and a good cook. She's lookin' real hard for a daddy for her boy, and she's…test-driven quite a few models, if you know what I mean."

Sam knew. "So how do you meet the right kind of women?"

Morris pushed the ice around in his cup with his straw for a good thirty seconds. "A bunch of us guys load up and head toward Raleigh once or twice a month. We hit a few of the dance clubs."

Now he was getting somewhere. But Morris dancing… That was a sight he didn't want to see. "That can get expensive."

"You aren't kiddin'."

"Any of the guys have trouble coming up with that kind of cash?"

Morris shrugged. "Don't know. I guess. Some do odd jobs for a little extra money."

"What kind of jobs?"

"Whatever needs doing. That's where country boys and city boys differ. Country boys are jacks-of-all-trades. City boys are usually only good at one or two things. Out here we can't just call somebody to come and do our dirty work. We have to figure it out ourselves."

Did that include "cleaning up the countryside," as the fired deputy had put it in his reports?

"Which one are you?" Mac asked.

"I'm used to surviving weeks or months miles away from anyone. Finding my own food and building my own shelter. What do you think?"

"I think if you ever were a city boy, the Marines whipped it out of you."

"I was never a city boy. I was a military brat. I grew up on bases."

Morris got a faraway look in his eyes. "Maybe I should've enlisted and seen something of the world. I'll bet you've been a lot of places."

"Not the good parts. Wars rarely take place in paradise. If you had an interest, why didn't you join?"

"My dad was killed in a farm accident my senior year in high school. Mom needed me to help at home. Still does. But I wasn't interested in farming. Like June, all I ever wanted to be was a cop. At least June got to train in the big city. I took BLET at the local community college. I've been with QPD since day one."

The news flash skipped down Sam's sensors like static electricity. "June always wanted to be a cop?"

"Yep. Not in Quincey, though. She planned to stay in Raleigh after her training. But that didn't pan out."

"Why not?"

Mac shifted in his seat and averted his gaze. "I don't know for sure. All I hear are the rumors. And being she's a coworker and a friend, I'm not gonna gossip. If you want to know, ask her. June's about as open as a large-print book."

"You're a lot older than June."

"And older than her sisters and brothers, but we

grew up on the same road attending her daddy's church. Until her brothers were old enough, I mowed her family's lawn, and I used to go fishing with June and her grandpa or play catch with her little brothers when their dad was too busy—which was most of the time." He ducked his head and blushed—*blushed* at forty-plus years old. "Sorry. I shouldn't have said that. It wasn't nice. I'm sure the church takes up most of the pastor's time."

"You make it sound like he never spent time with his kids."

"He didn't. And the twins, Kelley and Kelsie, June's older sisters, well, they did what they could to get their daddy's attention. Not always good, if you know what I mean. And that's all I'm going to say on that subject."

Sam filed the info away. "So you live with your mom. How did you and she make ends meet if you didn't want to farm?"

"I leased the acreage—still do—to the conglomerate that's been buying up land all over the county. I had some good guidance on that score from the former chief. The people of Quincey look after each other, like one big mostly happy family."

"Enough to turn a blind eye when someone does something they shouldn't?"

Mac stiffened. "If this is about Butch White, I already told Chief Sterling I knew nothing 'bout Butch shipping 'shine. Sure, we all knew Butch was living high on the hog, but we just figured he'd put everything on a credit card. That's the American way."

"Is it?"

"Round here it is. You have a bad crop year and you get behind. That's how the conglomerate gets all its land. They're like vultures. Soon as one of us gets in debt, they swoop in."

"Are you in debt?"

"Nosy fella, ain'tcha?"

He tried his most innocent expression. "I'm just trying to find my way. Life outside a military base is foreign to me."

Mac seemed to weigh his words, then nodded. "I don't run up debt. I'm a pay-as-you-go guy. Strictly cash. I only have one credit card, and it's for emergencies, which, praise the Lord, have been few. I may not want to work the farm, but my momma wants to live there until she dies. I'm doing my best to ensure she can."

Cash was hard to trace. Another red flag.

By the time the waitress set their burgers on the table, Sam had already concluded that Mac Morris was an unlikely theft ring mastermind. He was too nice and seemed a genuinely dedicated cop. But given there had been one small and one large set of prints at the crime scene and the fact that Mac, at forty-four years old, lived with his mother, Sam knew he still had to either confirm or eliminate the Morris duo as suspects. Moms had been successful kingpins before and their children merely minions.

Still, Morris was an unlikely candidate for the thefts—as unlikely as June. But Sam would keep his eyes open until he had more than gut instinct to go on.

"JONES, COME IN and shut the door," the chief ordered.

Uneasy, June did as he said. Another closed-door meeting. Roth looked serious, his brow pleated. Her nerves kinked over seeing Sam kicked back in one of the two chairs in front of the big wooden desk, one long leg crossed over the other at the ankle.

His relaxed fingers rested on the scarred chair arms. The private meetings obviously didn't worry him. But he hadn't been part of QPD's close-knit family before the changing of the chiefs. She doubted he felt like a spy and traitor to the rest of the squad the way June did.

"Sit." Roth pointed at the vacant seat and June perched on the edge of it with a white-knuckled grip on her pen and pad of paper and waited to see why he'd called them in.

"What do you have?" Roth asked, looking at June.

Her phone vibrated in her pocket, a silent signal that she'd received a text message. She ignored it and flipped open her notebook.

"Nine thefts over a four-and-a-half-year span, all within a ten-mile radius, spaced almost exactly six months apart. Senior deputy Butch White was in charge of each investigation. There's no record of him asking for assistance or delegating any of the investigations. None of the vehicles were ever recovered. At our most recent scene there were two sets of prints—one large, one small. The tire tracks were wide, indicating either a trailer or a flatbed tow truck. There's no mention of either in the previous reports and there are no pictures."

"How thorough were White's investigations?" the chief asked with a scowl that could curdle milk.

"It looks like he only questioned a couple of people after each incident. None reported seeing anything, so he closed the cases. But here's something interesting, sir, that may or may not be related and it wasn't in his files—tags and insurance had been dropped on each vehicle. That means no insurance companies followed up on the thefts either."

Sam snapped upright beside her and his probing gaze swung her way. "When did you first suspect that and why didn't you mention it?"

"It was just a hunch. I wanted confirmation before passing on the info. I have a friend who works at Motor Vehicles in Raleigh. I gave her the VIN numbers, and she confirmed my theory five minutes before this meeting."

"I want to know everything you know or suspect you know, when you know it."

Sam's gruff voice scraped across her thin-stretched nerves and his silvery eyes made her want to squirm. "There's no sense going on wild-goose chases with unproven theories."

"He's right, Jones. Share everything. I want to

know where those cars ended up before the next one is stolen," the chief said.

"My guess is the scrap yard," Sam said. "White wrote four separate comments to the effect that it was time someone cleaned up Quincey's countryside. He claimed the rusting heaps were an eyesore. The thief is pocketing hundreds of dollars biannually. That's a steady stream of almost untraceable income since scrap yards rarely ask for titles."

The men exchanged a long look, leaving June feeling left out in the cold. Sam, the newest one on the job, clearly knew something she didn't.

June cleared her throat. "About that…"

The chief turned his hard gaze to her. "What?"

"I found out this afternoon that metal recyclers only recently started logging VIN numbers for their purchases and putting them in a database that they're supposed to cross-check before purchasing. But that's assuming compliance. I've made a list of scrap yards within a fifty-mile radius. Rivers and I will have to check them out."

Roth's lips flattened. Then his hand fisted on the desktop. "I want these cowardly middle-of-the-night thieves caught."

June closed her notebook. "I'll divide the cases between Rivers and I and Morris and Aycock, then—"

"No," Roth interrupted. "This investigation stays between the three of us."

That uneasy prickle turned into a sharp jab of

discomfort. The closed door was one thing, but to refuse to share information… Something was definitely wrong at the station.

"But, Chief, given there've been nine thefts, we need to cover more ground and question more people."

"I don't want Morris and Aycock to even get a whiff of this investigation. And I don't want you questioning past witnesses or even revisiting the scenes. Word will get around and someone will start covering their tracks. They've been doing this successfully for years. Let's hope they've become cocky and sloppy and we can get something to nail them with when they fence this truck. Work with what you have."

"Sir? You don't suspect Mac and Alan are involved, do you?" She hated to ask or even think it possible. Butch White had always been a bit of a superior ass, so him considering himself above the law hadn't been that much of a stretch. But Mac and Alan? She hoped not.

The chief rose and strode to the window. "Too much happened right under the former chief's nose. Lou Hamilton's not a stupid man. For someone to keep this from him and to know which vehicles had tags and insurance removed suggests collusion and cover-up, or at least someone with inside information. It's Hamlet all over again."

At the mention of another small North Carolina town, whose sheriff's department had been accused of illegally seizing cars and profiting by selling them to scrap yards, the sinking feeling in June's belly worsened. Surely he didn't suspect his father-in-law? Chief Hamilton had been too good to her; she couldn't turn him in. No. It wouldn't come to that. He wouldn't be involved in something like this.

She wet her suddenly dry lips. "Sam and I discussed the likelihood that a neighbor who knows the victims well enough to know their personal business might be at fault."

Roth nodded. "Seems likely."

She could feel Sam's eyes on her again and cursed the sense of betrayal she hadn't been able to keep out of her voice. But the people of Quincey were her family. When she'd moved back from Raleigh after the Peter fiasco, they'd welcomed her with the open arms her own father hadn't extended. And even though her father had preached on sins, harlots and fallen women for weeks on end after her return, none of them had judged her.

Her phone vibrated again, this time an incoming call. Once more she ignored it.

"I don't think it's Morris." Sam broke the tense silence. "He doesn't fit the profile. But I don't know his mother well enough to know if she could be a kingpin in this kind of duo."

"No!" June protested automatically. "It can't be them."

"Jones," the chief scolded, "if you can't keep personal feelings out of this, then you don't belong on the investigation."

Her cheeks burned at the chastisement. "I can, sir. But Mrs. Morris was my first-grade teacher. She's a sweetheart and a wonderful person. She still teaches Sunday school and is a strict rule follower who drilled into us daily that you didn't take things that didn't belong to you, and that hard work was its own reward. I don't think she could be a party to something like theft."

"Noted. But assume everyone is guilty until proven innocent. And, Jones, if this leaks, your job's on the line."

Panic fluttered through her. The chief was pairing her and Sam against not only the other deputies but also the rest of the town. "Yes, sir."

It was small comfort to know that since Roth had included her in this inner circle, he probably didn't suspect her.

June's phone vibrated again as she left the chief's office. Not daring to take a personal call on work time given the current hostile environment, she ignored it for the third time.

"Are you going to answer that?" Sam growled as he followed her to the cruiser.

She pulled the phone from her pocket, checked the screen. One text and two missed calls from Rhett. "It's just my baby brother. I'll call him after work."

"Your siblings bother you at work?"

"They call when they can." Or when they needed something. "He's a college student. He's probably between classes. I don't answer personal calls on paid work time, if that's what you're asking."

Sam stepped between her and the car. "Give me the keys and the addresses. I'll drive. You've been squirming since the buzzing started. Deal with it."

She checked the text.

Call me.

Rhett probably needed money. If there'd been a true emergency, she would have heard from her other siblings, as well. There was no need to risk airing personal laundry in front of the chief's best friend and get reprimanded when she couldn't do anything about her brother's "crisis" now anyway.

"I'll call him when I get home. But you can drive if you want." She turned off her phone and tossed him the keys. "The closest place is about five miles east of town."

"Jones, report." The chief's voice came over the radio even before the cruiser's tires had warmed up.

"Still in the parking lot, sir."

"There's been an eighteen-wheeler accident west of town on Little Bear Swamp Road."

"What are we looking at?"

"That's all I have. The connection was garbled. Then I lost it. I wasn't able to reconnect."

"We're on the way."

"Quincey doesn't have a dispatcher?" Sam asked.

"It's not in our budget to have someone sit at a desk all day and wait for the phone to ring. We don't get that many calls. Whoever's in the station responds. When we're out, the call transfers to the on-call person's work cell phone."

She hit the lights and siren. "Take a right out of here, then the first left."

THE SITE RESEMBLED a war zone, Sam decided as he pulled up to the carnage. There were bodies scattered across the grass flanking the road and some in the water—some moving, some still. Pigs' bodies.

Thick and deep tire tracks cut through the mud leading to a busted guardrail and a tractor-trailer lying on its side in the murky water. He and June were the first on scene.

"The truck must've been going too fast for the curve," she said beside him. "We've had accidents here before, but nothing of this magnitude."

Sam left the car and paused to survey the scene. The shrill squeals of the pigs weren't unlike the cries of humans. Pain and panic were universal. They sounded the same. Man or beast.

Spanish moss and vines hung from the trees, but there were no power lines, fuel leaks or other hazards as far as he could see. He suspected the swamp water held its own dangers.

June met him by the front bumper. "The truck's acting like a dam in the creek. The water's rising behind it," she pointed out as Sam was registering the same thing.

The stench scalded his nostrils. "Any gators in this area?"

"No sightings reported thus far, but it's always possible. We are upriver from other known gator habitats, and they're expanding their territory across the state. Whew. That smell is horrible."

"Would've been worse if there'd been a fire and charred flesh to deal with," he said, catching her swift, horrified glance out of the corner of his eye. She paled. "Better call a veterinarian."

"Check." Her shocked gaze returned to the wreckage. "I don't see the driver."

"I'll look for him. We'll need help rounding up the loose pigs and probably three more trucks. One for the survivors, one for the dead and another for injured ones. I don't see a diesel spill, but have Roth notify hazmat anyway."

"Got it," June responded. "I see the pig farm's number on the back of the trailer. I'll have Roth give them a call. They can send out another rig."

"Good idea. I'm going in."

She grabbed his arm, frowning in concern. "Sam, are you…are you sure? There may be snakes and—"

He didn't want her seeing what he might find. "I've searched for survivors before in scenes like this, only involving humans instead of animals. I can handle snakes, and even I can shoot a gator at point-blank range if I must."

The crease in her forehead deepened and her sympathy-darkened eyes shone like jade against her pale skin. "That's not what I meant."

"I've got this, Jones. Can you handle the perimeter?"

She swallowed again but nodded and then snatched her hand away as if she'd only just realized she'd touched him. The heat imprint of her palm burned like a new tattoo.

"Holler if you need me. And, Sam? Be careful."

"I always am." He headed toward the jackknifed cab with the sound of her voice speaking into the radio fading into the background. Images flashed in his brain of military trucks in similar condition after being hit by a roadside bomb. The casualties then had been men. Marines. Friends. But at least here he didn't have to worry about enemy fire.

He blocked out the noise and odor and waded into the swamp. The water was cool, but not cold enough to discourage snakes. The muddy bottom sucked at his shoes, trying to pull them from his feet. Wrong equipment for the job. He needed his lace-up boots.

He endeavored to make enough noise as he slogged through the waist-high water to scare away any water moccasins in the vicinity. Then he reached the overturned tractor and paused to study the undercarriage and mentally plan his climb. He needed a way in that would avoid the still-hot ticking engine parts. He planted and tested one foothold and then another on the bottom. His leather uniform shoes slipped on the metal as he hauled himself up the cab. He wished once more for the nonslip soles of his Danner boots.

He reached the exposed driver's-side door, hefted himself up and looked through the open window. The driver lay crumpled against the bottom door unmoving, the water rising in the compartment. Either he hadn't been wearing a seat belt or he'd removed it after the crash. One of the man's hands clung to the headrest as if he'd grabbed it to keep his head and shoulders above water before losing consciousness.

"Sir?" he called. No answer. But the guy's color was still good and his chest rose and fell in the lapping water. Not dead. Helping the victim meant dropping down into the filling vehicle.

"Sir, I'm Sam. I'm here to help you," he said before prying open the door and swinging his legs into the opening. He glanced up and spotted June turning away from the ditch and wiping her mouth. She looked over and her wide gaze locked on him.

"Driver's alive but unconscious. I'm going in."

She shook her head. "Sam, it's not stable. Wait for help."

"No time. Call for an ambulance," he shouted. Then, bracing his weight on his palms, he lowered himself inside. For the first time since getting cut from the corps he had a job to do—one that mattered. He could save a life. Or possibly lose his own.

PANIC AND WORRY grabbed June by the throat the second Sam disappeared from view. They superseded her nausea. If the rescue went wrong, she'd have two victims on her hands instead of one. Sam was her responsibility. She couldn't let anything happen to him. Not on her watch. She had to do something besides hurl in the ditch.

She'd worked traffic accidents in Raleigh, even two fatalities. But this was different. This time she was personally invested because she knew one of the men in that cab. She didn't even know where to begin.

The screaming, panicked animals with gaping bloody wounds compromised her concentration and made her gag. Some were running around, darting into the road and causing another hazard altogether. Others were on their sides kicking and crying out in distress with broken limbs or loose hunks of flesh dangling. Some were clearly dead. She couldn't help those.

For Sam's sake she had to pull it together and prioritize. She quickly made the necessary calls and relayed the pertinent info while fumbling in the trunk for the traffic flares. She sprinted east down the road and set up the flares at ten-yard intervals— five to the east—then sprinted west and repeated the procedure, hoping to at least prevent more accidents.

All the while she kept glancing at the eighteen-wheeler. Fear was an energy-draining emotion she usually reserved for family and close friends, but she couldn't deny she was worried about Sam. Her heart stalled. The farm's logo had been visible when she'd read the phone number to the chief five—or was it ten?—minutes ago. Now it was half-covered by water. The cab was going under. Fast. With Sam in it. She had to stabilize the vehicle. She returned to her cruiser's trunk, hefted the tow strap and headed for the wreckage.

She raced past pig bodies and into the water but sucking mud slowed her down. It seemed to take forever to reach the upturned tires. She looped the tow strap around the heavy metal axle, then sloughed her way back to dry land, stretching the band as far as it would go. Thirty feet wasn't long enough.

Aware of the rapidly ticking clock, she raced back to the cruiser and retrieved a rope from the trunk, connected it to the strap, then tied it to the brush guard on the front of the cruiser. She climbed into the car and backed it until tension took the slack from her makeshift anchor line. Her tires spun, refusing to go farther. The line held, but her eight-cylinder engine didn't have the power to right the heavier vehicle. She couldn't have done that without warning Sam anyway. But at least the vehicle was stable for now.

She hit her radio. "ETA, boss?"

"On the way," Roth responded without pause.

Small comfort. She couldn't afford to wait for help. Heart racing, she ran back to the water and waded in once more. Current swirled around the big chrome front bumper—current she hadn't noticed before. "Sam?"

No answer. She'd heard nothing from him since he'd entered the cab. His muddy footprints were still visible on the undercarriage. Placing her feet in each of his tracks, she hauled herself up the bottom, then climbed onto the side. She spotted him through the open door and relief rushed through her. He was belt-deep in water but okay. And the driver was pale and pasty but conscious. He looked as if he was about to go into shock. No surprise when you combined the wreck with the cool water.

"I have the first-aid kit."

Sam's head jerked up and his gaze found hers. "You should be on dry land."

"No can do." Then she focused on the victim. "Sir, I'm June. What's your name?"

"Leroy Hand," the driver said through gritted teeth.

"Leroy, hang tight. We're going to get you out of here. Help is on the way. Where are you hurt?"

"My leg."

Sam glanced at her. "Feels broken. Some displacement. But I have nothing to splint it."

There were air splints in the car but June didn't want to leave the men. She searched the cab for anything that would be useful, but all she could see was the rising waterline. Then her gaze fixed on the driver's-side visor pressed against the roof. Flat. The right length. She wiggled forward on her belly until she could reach it, then wrestled it free. The adrenaline rushing through her veins gave her strength. "Use this and some of the tape in the first-aid kit."

Sam went to work. Leroy groaned and his pallor increased. The distant wail of a siren caught her attention. "I hear the ambulance, Leroy. We'll all be on dry land soon. Is there anyone you want me to call for you?"

"My wife." He told June her name and number and she wrote them down on the pad she kept in her pocket.

"I'll call her as soon as the ambulance has you loaded up and we know where they're taking you. But relax, okay? We have this. We'll take good care of you."

"The pigs—"

"The farm has been notified. They're sending a truck. I also have a veterinarian and volunteers on the way to round up and patch up as many as we can. You have kids, Leroy?"

Sam flashed her an irritated look, but she ignored him. She had to keep the patient occupied and awake.

"Three."

"Boys or girls? What are their names?"

Leroy rattled off names and ages. June continued to keep him talking.

And then she felt Sam's eyes on her again. When she dared to look his way, he nodded. Sam's approval filled her like a helium balloon. One she needed to pop. ASAP. Or she'd be in trouble. Big. Trouble. Because developing a crush on the new deputy was a *baaaad* idea.

SAM SLOWED THE cruiser and turned into their shared driveway. June should have been exhausted after working sixteen grueling hours at the wreck site, but instead, a surplus of adrenaline made her such a bundle of nerves and tangled thoughts that she could barely sit still.

Images of Sam running toward the wreckage cluttered her brain. She imagined that was how he looked as a US marine charging into battle. Composed. Ready for anything. Filled with absolute confidence and determination about the job ahead.

Sexy.

No. No. No. Don't go there.

Once the rescue squad had accepted responsibility for the patient, Sam had commanded the scene. He'd issued orders and organized every person involved, from the paramedics to the tow truck driver to the steady stream of gawkers and volunteers who'd shown up to help Madison and Piper with the pigs.

June, the supreme organizer of her family, had been in complete awe of Sam's management skills and the ease with which he'd taken care of business.

The cruiser's engine hummed as he rolled to a stop. Sam kept one hand on the steering wheel. He slowly turned his head and their gazes locked. "You threw up. More than once."

Her face burned with shame. "There's a reason I didn't take over my grandfather's veterinary practice. Severely injured animals make me sick. I learned that the hard way when he asked me to help him care for a dog that had been hit by a car. I was fifteen. Changed my career path."

"And yet you sucked it up today and did your job."

"What else could I do? That truck driver needed us."

Exhaustion pulled at his features, but even tired and filthy, Sam was a handsome man. A strange urge to brush the muck from his stubbled face and pick the bits of twig and mud from his short hair overwhelmed her. She reined it in—with effort—and cleared her throat.

"You did a good job tonight, Sam. You kept calm and rational and—"

"So did you. Despite the barfing attacks," he interrupted as if the compliment made him uncomfortable.

His praise poured over her like warm oil. Approval and respect shone in his eyes. The sudden temptation to kiss him T-boned her. She didn't even see it coming. Need scattered her brain cells like car parts in a collision with a train.

Dumb. Dumb. Dumb.

"Thank you," she said, and the expansion of his

pupils proved he'd registered her breathy, want-filled tone.

"June. Go inside." His low voice was more warning growl than words. It paralyzed her. "Now."

Humiliation doused the heat smoldering in her womb. How long had she been staring at his lips? She blinked and jerked her gaze to his. Banked fires had liquefied the usual ice in his blue irises. Her heart thumped harder. Her mouth dried up. She had to get inside and away from temptation before she did or said something really foolish.

With fumbling fingers she hastily unclipped her seat belt. "G'night…I mean g'morning…I mean… bye, Sam."

Eloquent, she wasn't. She hurled herself from the car and skedaddled into her house. Pressing her back against the closed door, she slid down on noodle-limp legs until her butt hit the floor, then banged her forehead against her knees. "Get a grip, June."

She had to stop acting like a thirteen-year-old with her first crush. It was embarrassing and wrong and would undo the progress she'd made with her father.

She needed a cold shower and sleep. Maybe her idiocy was simply a result of sleep deprivation. That had to be it. She couldn't afford to risk her career on it being anything more. She'd already walked that path. If not for Piper's dad, there was no telling where she would have ended up…

Think about something else.

But all she could think about was how much Sam had impressed her today. Probably more than any man in her life ever had. And that was bad. She had to keep her mental and emotional distance from Sam Rivers. She had to work with him, and work and play did not make good bedfellows.

THE MOUTHWATERING AROMAS of barbecue and frying hush puppies made June's stomach rumble despite the potential encounter with her father, which would be civil at best but more likely downright unpleasant. Seeing Sam… Well, that would be a whole different kind of tumult.

"Roth called the hospital on the way over," Piper said as she and June made their way across the church lawn late Saturday morning. "He asked me to tell you the truck driver only has a nasty concussion and a broken leg. He's going to be okay."

"Thanks to Sam." June tried to keep the admiration out of her voice. "If he hadn't held Leroy's head above water until the rescue squad could extricate him, the guy would have drowned."

"You helped, too, despite the blood and gore. I know that was tough for you."

She grimaced. "Sam took all the risks."

"Putting himself in jeopardy to save others is what he did for a living, and from the stories Roth has told me, belly-crawling through snake-infested waters is routine for snipers. I swear, June, every time I hear those guys discuss deployments, I marvel at the miracle of Roth making it back to us. They're heroes."

A conclusion June had reached herself. Maybe Sam's confidence wasn't conceit after all. Maybe he could back up all that swagger with action.

Maybe she needed to think about something besides her attractive neighbor and the hormones he'd set free to run amok.

"You know, I think Quincey PD stands a chance of defeating the fire department this year with Roth and Sam on the team. The match is usually a joke, and we pray for an emergency call to interrupt us and save us from the ultimate defeat and humiliation, but I suspect the outcome might be different today. Sam and Roth seem the type to hate losing as much as I do."

"I agree. In previous years you were the only fit and competitive one on the team. This year you'll have help."

Piper shielded her eyes and scanned the crowd. June did the same, but she was looking for her father. The longer she could avoid him, the better. When she nailed his location on the opposite end of the tent from the big black pig cookers, she took time to study the crowd. They had a good-sized gathering for the church's annual barbecue fundraiser, and nothing looked suspicious, but brawls between feuding neighbors or relatives had been known to happen. Even though she was out of uniform and officially off duty, she could be called into action. Her gear was stashed in her cruiser nearby just in case.

"Hey, isn't that your brother on the bleachers?"

June whipped her gaze to the spectators gathered opposite the sand court and spotted Rhett. The worry on his face swamped her with a wave of guilt. "Uh-oh. He texted and left me voice mails before the wreck and I forgot to call him back."

Piper rolled her eyes. "June, you had good reasons. That wreck was one of the worst I've ever seen and cleaning up took forever. I'm betting you crashed the moment you got home and slept through yesterday."

"I slept like I was in a coma until late afternoon. Then I got up and did a little work." Slipping out while Sam's cottage was still quiet and putting some mileage between her and her illogical thoughts had seemed a good idea.

"You worked close to a twenty-four-hour shift and then again after only a few hours' sleep?" Piper asked in an appalled tone. "I'm going to have to speak to my husband about that."

She should have kept her mouth shut. Withholding information from her friend made her uncomfortable. "Don't. It was my choice. Morris and Aycock were the deputies on call."

June had visited three of the junkyards on her list. Throughout the afternoon she'd been so busy berating herself for almost kissing Sam that she hadn't once thought of her brother.

"I should've called Rhett. I'm usually a better sister than that." She lifted a hand to wave apologetically to her brother, but he wasn't there anymore.

"Cut yourself some slack. Your family seems to forget all about you until they need something. You have a job and a life and can't drop everything the minute they bellow."

True. But it was nice to be needed. She missed that.

"Here come two of your teammates," Piper said. "Hubba hubba. My husband looks good. Sam does, too. Doesn't he?"

June's stomach churned like a washing machine. She wished she could forget the awkward moment in the car. But it had happened. She'd been tired. Not delirious.

"Don't match-make, Piper," she ordered automatically before she turned to face the men—then wished she hadn't moved.

Roth and Sam, wearing black QPD T-shirts and shorts identical to hers, strode toward them. Side by side, their military bearing couldn't be more obvious. The thin cotton clung to Sam's pectorals and washboard abs, and the shorts revealed muscular quadriceps and calves lightly dusted with golden curls. Warmth stirred low in her belly.

Not enough sleep. That was her problem. That and their investigation coming up empty were the roots of her frustration. She was *not* interested in an affair with her coworker.

But if Sam played volleyball as good as he looked, they were going to wipe the court with the firemen. It would be nice to serve crow instead of eating it for once.

"June, I want you to be as happy as I am," Piper said. "But I promise to back off if you insist. On the other hand, if you're interested in Sam…?"

Piper's fishing reply pulled June from her fixation on man and muscle. "I insist. Sam's in transition right now. He needs to regain his equilibrium, not form ties. And he's a coworker. I've walked through that briar patch before."

"True. I'll leave it alone. So are you going to eat before the game?"

With her father guarding the serving line? "No. I think I'll check on Joey and Tyler. They're washing cars today as penance for a little mischief earlier in the week."

"Roth told me what you were doing with the boys," Piper said. "My car was the first in line this morning as a test of sorts. They did a great job— and I told them so. She's sparkling inside and out."

"All right. Then I guess I'll go look for my brother." She turned to make her escape before Roth and Sam arrived and almost ran into Rhett, who'd snuck up behind her.

"You didn't call me back," he accused without preamble or concern for who might overhear.

"Sorry. I was working."

"I need your help."

Acutely conscious of Sam, Piper and Roth nearby, she put a calming hand on her brother's shoulder and tried to steer him away, but he planted his feet. "I'll talk to you after the game."

"This is more important than a stupid game of over-the-hill klutzes trying to recapture their youth."

Rude but apt. "Rhett—"

Piper came up behind her and cleared her throat. "June was about to join us for lunch before the game. You can talk to her later."

Bless Piper's protective heart. "It's okay, Piper. Y'all go ahead. I'll eat later."

With clear reluctance, Piper let Roth lead her away. Sam, darn him, remained by her side. She met his gaze for the first time since yesterday's awkward moment. Frost filled his eyes and distaste curled his lip. But he wasn't looking at her. He was staring at Rhett, and his hard expression showed no remembrance of her near screwup.

"You can go, too," she said through a constricted throat.

"I'll wait." He folded his arms, making his biceps bulge. Standing sentry, he scowled fiercely at Rhett, but after a quick nervous glance at Sam, her brother didn't appear deterred.

"Jolene's pregnant."

June's stomach flipped, then sank. "Are you sure the baby's yours? I hate to ask, but…"

"I wouldn't be here if I wasn't sure. We've had our problems, but cheating wasn't one of them."

He'd picked up the leeching bleached-blonde dimwit in a bar near campus earlier in the year. June had tried hard to find something to like about Rhett's first serious girlfriend, but she hadn't had any success.

"She's due in three weeks," he added when June said nothing more.

Wow. Not good. She couldn't in all honesty offer congratulations. Thoughts raced through her head. She was going to be an aunt. But her in-college-on-an-academic-scholarship brother couldn't afford a child, and he was ill equipped for parenthood. He and the mom-to-be weren't even married. Thank goodness, she supposed.

"Does Dad know?" Their father would have a fit.

"Not yet. I was hoping…" He dug a toe into the grass.

"Not a chance. You're going to have to tell him. I'm not doing your dirty work this time." And then compassion kicked in. "But I'll go with you. You and Jolene aren't going to rush into marriage are you?"

"No! I don't think… I mean, she's not… I don't see us being forever, ya know?"

She wanted to say that he should have kept his pants zipped or at least have been more careful. But she didn't. Preaching and lecturing were her dad's forte. Not hers. "Then what are you going to do?"

"She's talking about giving it up for adoption."

They were two kids in school without jobs who

didn't want a future together… "Maybe that's for the best? You're only twenty."

"He's mine, June. My flesh and blood."

Rhett had always been overly possessive. Understandably so since as the youngest, he'd received only hand-me-downs. But she wished he wouldn't be possessive about this child.

"What do you expect me to do, Rhett?"

"You could take the kid."

She gaped. She'd expected him to hit her up for a loan that would never be repaid. It wouldn't be the first time. But this… "Take it?"

"As a foster parent. At least until I graduate and get on my feet and can handle the dad thing."

She shook her head. "How do you expect me to do that? I have a full-time job. I work twelve-hour shifts."

"There are single moms everywhere. Talk to your friend." He jerked his head toward Piper. "She was one. She'll tell you how to do it. C'mon, you're good with kids and you can afford day care. I can't. You could probably even get government money to subsidize it, so you'll be better off than you were before."

Money. It always came down to money with her siblings. But this time the stakes were higher. An innocent baby depended on her making the right decision.

But what was the right decision? The child would be her niece or nephew—family. She'd always wanted children. But did she want to be a parent right now? And a temporary one, at that.

It was too much to comprehend on short notice.

A whistle blew, signaling the end of the high-school-teachers-versus-students game. "I need to think about this, Rhett, and do some research. You're asking a lot."

He gave her that ingratiating baby-brother grin—the one that always melted her like a snow cone in August. "I know. But you always come through for me, Junebug. You're the one person I can *always* count on."

She smothered a wince. Even knowing that he was playing her by using her nickname, pouring on the flattery and employing that smile didn't lessen the effectiveness of his manipulations. She wanted to promise to help. But Sam loomed behind her, so she kept her mouth shut. Sam would call her a wimp, a pushover.

If she studied the situation, perhaps she could find a solution and discuss it with Rhett later. But she couldn't make promises now. "I'll get back to you."

Frustration flashed through Rhett's eyes but he masked it quickly, gave her that smile again and then a hug. "Thank you, big sister. I knew you'd be there for me."

"I haven't agreed."

"But you will."

And that was the problem. She always gave her

siblings exactly what they wanted no matter the personal cost to her. She was a sucker and everybody in Quincey knew it. But this time…this time she wasn't sure she was up to the challenge.

CHAPTER SEVEN

"THAT LITTLE WEASEL." Sam couldn't conceal his disgust for June's brother.

"What?" June's defensive green eyes found his.

"He's a manipulative little shit."

Anger flickered across her face. "Tell me what you really think, Rivers. Don't hold back to spare my feelings just because he's my baby brother."

He might have been a little harsh, but he had good reason. "My mom was a single parent before she met my father. She juggled her job, day care and three kids, never having enough time or money. It's not something I'd wish on my worst enemy. If you are even considering taking on what your brother's trying to foist off on you, then you're not as smart as I thought you were."

"It's his baby."

"*His* being the operative word. His baby. His problem. Are your maternal urges so strong you'd take a loaner, Jones? Because that's all he's offering you. You'd do the dirty work of babyhood, then hand the kid over when it's potty trained."

"No. I am *not* desperate to be a mom." She puffed

up at the insult. Indignation painted her cheeks dark pink. Five and a half feet of ready-to-brawl attitude. If her loyalty weren't so misplaced, it would be admirable.

"Does he ever take responsibility for his actions?"

"Hey! That's my brother you're insulting."

"If he's man enough to father a child, he needs to man up and figure out what to do with one." Unlike his sisters' father, who'd been a deadbeat.

June's scowl deepened. "This is none of your business, Rivers. I need to think this through and then talk to him."

"Why don't you let him solve his own problem? Then he might learn something and grow up."

The hurt in her eyes pierced his gut. He tried to ignore it but failed. Damn it.

At thirty-one he was an old guy in the corps. He'd counseled plenty of new and overeager recruits—kids old enough to die for their country but too young to make wise decisions with their wallets and zippers.

He was trying to reason with June the way he would any other coworker, civilian or marine. He had to. Because if he didn't and sympathy for her crept in, what he'd managed to prevent in the car yesterday might happen.

He mentally reeled himself in. He'd been on shaky ground yesterday when her eyes had transformed from exhausted to excited. Then her lashes had fluttered and lowered and her lips had parted.

The hitch of her breath had hit him square in the solar plexus. When arousal had flushed her cheeks, his resistance had started crumbling. Thank God she'd come to her senses and scrammed, because he'd been tempted. Tempted to take what she offered. Tempted to take what wasn't his—what he had no right to.

Hell, he had no more to offer a woman than her idiot brother had. Not now. Maybe never. If he didn't get his vision straightened out, he was useless to anyone.

Treat her like a troop.

"It might be hard to hear, Jones, but you're doing him no favors by 'helping.' You're handicapping him. Turning him into a man who can't think for himself."

"I disagree. Family is supposed to be there for you—especially when the going gets tough."

Something in her tone, something in the way she stressed *supposed to* and glanced toward the food tent, sparked questions. But he didn't want to get involved in June's personal issues. So he simply went on. "I've served with too many of his type, and the selfish little turds either got killed, got other men killed or left me to clean up after them."

She gulped, then took a deep breath that drew his attention to the nice fit of her T-shirt. He yanked his gaze front and center—to the scratch on her nose that she'd acquired during the wreck aftermath.

When he'd climbed out of the truck cab yesterday, he'd found the axle tied off and secured and flares marking the roadway. He'd thanked the first responder, who'd then pointed at June and said, "Thank the one puking in the ditch. You're lucky to have her as a partner—even if she has a weak stomach."

Only then had Sam realized the full value of June's actions at the scene.

While Sam had been concentrating on splinting Leroy's leg blindly under the murky water and preparing him for extraction, June had peppered Leroy with questions about his kids, his grandkids, his favorite vacation spot. At first her chatter had been irritating, making it hard to concentrate. Then Sam had noticed the guy's pulse and respiratory rates declining and realized what she was doing. She'd been distracting the driver. And it had worked. By the time paramedics arrived, Leroy had been more stable.

She'd come across like a babbling bubblehead but in reality she'd been the exact opposite. And so much more.

The referee blew his whistle, bringing him back to the present.

"That's for us," she said.

"I hope you're tougher on the court than you are with your brother. If not, stay out of the way. Roth and I will whip the hosers without you, Morris or Aycock."

"Not happening, jarhead. I'm the family volleyball champion. You stay out of my way, and I'll show you how it's done. On second thought, because volleyball's a *team* sport, and *I'm* not a ball hog, I'll tip you a pass or two. Try not to screw 'em up."

Her cocky response shocked a laugh from him. That was more like it. He preferred June vinegary to sweet. Sweet could get them both in trouble. Vinegar kept him on his toes.

"Talk is cheap, Blondie. Put up or shut up."

JUNE DOVE AND STRETCHED, hitting the ground hard enough to knock the air from her lungs and send sand flying, but she connected with her target. The volleyball bounced off her fist and rose above her, still alive and in play.

Sam's thick calf muscles bunched beside her as he leaped and sent a vicious spike over the net. The firefighter on the opposite side of the court grunted as he lunged after the ball. He made contact but his return sailed out of bounds. The whistle blew, signaling the end of an exhausting and exhilarating hour.

"Game and match to Quincey's police department for the first time in two decades," shouted the high school physical education teacher, who was doubling as referee.

Whoops erupted from the bystanders. Flushed with victory, June rolled to her side and gave a thumbs-up to the crowd. Then a hand appeared in front of her face. Sam's hand. She'd recognize that big square long-fingered mitt anywhere. The rush of victory settled into a hot ball in her stomach.

Touching him wasn't a good idea. But ignoring the friendly gesture would have been rude. And public. She pressed her palm to his and let him assist her to her feet. Sam's grasp was warm, firm, strong and gritty. A charge of electricity raced up her arm.

"Good save, Jones."

The approval in his eyes stilled her frantically beating heart for dizzying seconds. Then the organ rebounded wildly. Seeing that look again was almost more than she could bear. Appreciation from males wasn't exactly common for her. Sure, Piper's dad had often complimented her dedication to detail, but since she was pretty sure the former chief had hired her as a favor to Piper, June had always felt that no matter what she did, it would never have been enough to repay him.

Hyperconscious of the fact that she had sand in her teeth, hair, shoes and sports bra, she gathered her scattered wits and scraped up an answer. "Glad you didn't waste my effort."

Humor crinkled his eyes. "Competitive, aren't you?"

"So my siblings tell me."

"Do you always play that hard?"

"Second place is the first loser."

He searched her face. "You'd have made a good marine."

That grudgingly offered praise was probably the

best a man like Sam could offer, and it made her giddy. "Thank you, Sam."

"Nice play, Jones," the chief said behind her, startling June into hastily releasing Sam's hand.

"Thank you, sir. 'Bout time we won one."

Piper stood beside him. The knowing look in her eyes said she hadn't missed June's breath-stealing exchange with Sam. She stepped forward and dusted June's back.

"Good grief, June. Did you leave any sand on the court for the next match? If you guys think that was impressive, you should see her when she and her siblings play each other. It's bloodthirsty and usually requires a first-aid kit."

June's face warmed. "We get into the game."

Piper tilted her head toward the cookers, where her family was. "Can you get away from here?"

"Yeah, I can go. I'm eating with my parents tomorrow after church."

"Good. Roth is grillin' burgers tonight at six o'clock. You have time to shower before you come over. Sam can give you a ride."

June concealed a wince. She'd walked right into that one. She didn't want to spend an evening with Sam, especially when Piper was clearly in matchmaker mode despite June's warning. "Piper—"

"I insist. I made that new Amaretto cake recipe you gave me. Mom loved yours so much I made it as a surprise for her. I spent hours on the thing, and you know how much I hate baking. Mom and Dad are looking forward to seeing you."

June glared at her friend, who innocently blinked in return. June was stuck, a sucker once more. She couldn't for the life of her think of a viable excuse to get out of this engagement. She had nothing better to do and everyone in Quincey knew it.

JUNE TOOK HER PLATE and headed for the picnic table, leaving the others gathered around the grill. Her plan: eat and run. Cowardly? Absolutely. But wise? For sure.

She took a huge, unladylike bite of burger. Juice dribbled down her chin. Before she could wipe it, Sam settled opposite her. So much for avoiding trouble.

Their knees bumped under the table. She gasped in surprise and almost inhaled the wad in her mouth. *Chew. Chew. Gulp.*

"You didn't wait for a ride," he stated like an accusation.

She hastily blotted. "It's a beautiful day. I wanted to ride my bicycle."

"And then ride it home in the dark?"

"I'll be gone long before then. Hungry, Rivers? It's a wonder your plate didn't fold under the weight of all that food." He had a thick burger and a hot dog, each piled high with every topping available, a side of potato chips and a mound of baked beans and coleslaw.

He shrugged. "I doubled the paper plates. Roth's a good cook. His chorizo baked beans are hard to beat. Where'd you learn to play volleyball like that, Jones? On a school team?"

"Dad sent us to Bible camp for a month each summer. When I got older, I worked there as a counselor and coach." The peace of being away from her father for entire summers had been irresistible.

"From vet wannabe to counselor to cop. How did that happen?"

"Keeping the peace is what I do best. Comes from being the middle child, I guess. When I realized taking over my grandfather's practice was out of the question, I needed a backup plan. One of my teachers suggested police work since I'm a bit of…a stickler for rules. She was right. I love my job."

"Piper is chewing out Roth because you worked yesterday afternoon. Why didn't you come and get me?"

"You needed sleep and I—" She ducked her head and picked a stray grain of sand from beneath her nails. Why couldn't the others fill their plates and haul their butts over here *now*? But no one was headed their way. That meant no rescue. As usual, she could count on only herself. And honesty was the best policy even if it was difficult and awkward. "I needed space."

Sam glanced back at the cluster on the patio. Then his gaze slammed into hers and he said, "You know what Piper's doing, don't you?"

She debated playing dumb. But Sam was too smart for that. "The smell from the pig truck was less obvious."

The corners of his mouth curved downward. "It's not going to happen, June."

Mortification torched her face. "I know."

He crumpled his paper napkin in his fist, looking uncomfortable for the first time since she'd met him. Then his gaze found hers. "You don't need me to tell you that you're attractive."

"I am?" Her heart stalled. She lowered her burger to her plate. "Thanks."

Resolve hardened his jaw. "But I'm not the marrying kind. My relationships are temporary. Always. If a woman can't handle that, then I pass. Regardless of the temptation."

He was tempted? Unable to find her voice, she stared mutely.

"There will never be a happily-ever-after or a walk down the aisle with me. Got it?"

She nodded like a bobblehead on the car's dash. "I hear you."

"Unless temporary's what you want, I have nothing for you."

Her insides swooped like a barn swallow. A sex-only relationship. Like her last one. She vividly remembered how cheap, ashamed and stupid she'd felt when she'd realized forever wasn't part of Peter's agenda. Not with her. She'd been planning a wedding. He'd been planning a way to keep their affair hidden.

June's pride kicked in. She aimed her chilliest look at Sam. "You're assuming I'd be interested in a relationship with you."

"You're interested."

Cocky bastard. He was right. Sam was handsome and too intelligent for his own good. And for some crazy reason she was needy and desperate for a physical connection, and he was the only viable candidate within a hundred miles. She respected him and was even beginning to like him…or had been until now.

Another wave of embarrassment washed over her. "I know better than to get involved with a co-worker."

His eyes narrowed and filled with curiosity, then flicked to Aycock and Morris. "Who was it? One of them?"

She recoiled. "Eww. No."

"Before you came back to Quincey?"

"My past is none of your business unless it affects my job performance. It doesn't." Normally, she copped to her mistakes, learned from them and became a stronger, smarter, better person because of them. And that was the case this time, but she didn't want Sam to know what a gullible country bumpkin she'd been.

She'd been the only one at the academy who hadn't known that Peter had a wife. June had vowed on that humiliating day of discovery that she would never again, ever in a million years, put herself in that horrible situation of everyone knowing her business and laughing at her behind her back.

But that didn't mean she wouldn't think about what it would be like to make love—have sex—with Sam. A lot.

"Thanks for your...*generous* offer, Rivers, but I'll pass."

"It wasn't an offer. It was a warning."

"THANKS FOR OPENING EARLY," Sam said when Tate Lowry unlocked the gun shop's door Sunday morning.

"Good to have the company. Everybody else heads for church."

"I'm not keeping you from going, am I?"

"I'm not much on organized religion. I built my own sanctuary."

Sam scanned the gun shop. "Here?"

Tate jerked his head. "Out back. Want to see?"

"Sure."

After locking up behind Sam, Tate led the way around the counter, through a door and into a room that contained a desk and office electronics on one end and a gunsmithy work area on the other. Sam recognized the tools on the bench from his visits to the Precision Weapons Section on base. A place he no longer had clearance to visit.

He tamped down that thought and followed

Lowry through another unlocked door into what was clearly his home—specifically his living room, built log cabin–style with a stone fireplace taking up most of the far right wall. Like the office/work-room, the space was neat and uncluttered.

"I built onto the shop when I decided I was gonna stay in Quincey. All those rocks came off this property," he said, pointing to the fireplace.

"You're not from here?"

"No. But Quincey suits me."

The long room was rustic but comfortable. No-frills. Basic furniture, wide-board pine floors and shelves—lots of shelves loaded with precisely spaced birds. Wooden this time, not taxidermied. "You collect decoys?"

"Carve 'em. Out here in my 'church.'" He shoved open a wide sliding glass door and stepped onto a screened-in porch extending the length of the build-ing. A hammock stretched across one end. Dense woods and a deep gully ran in each direction as far as Sam could see. A creek babbled over rocks at the bottom, emptying into a pond that was no more than a distant glimmer through the trees in the east.

A small bridge spanned the creek, leading to a stout target on the opposite bank. "The rifle range?" Sam asked.

"Yep. 'Bout the only time it's closed is Sundays and after dark."

"This is great, Lowry. Nice view. One hundred eighty degrees of wilderness."

"Nothing like communing with nature to make you respect creation. Pull up a chair, unless you're eager to hit the range."

"The range can wait." His primary reason for being here was that he needed to keep his mind occupied. Lowry was probably the only other person in Quincey who'd been where Sam was mentally. Cast out of the only life he'd ever envisioned. Birds and squirrels chattered, making soothing background noise. On the job, that would have meant he was undetected and most likely safe.

An acorn or something pinged on the tin roof. "Bet the rain sounds good out here."

"You know it. Makes for good sleeping." He jerked a thumb toward the hammock. "I probably spend more nights out here when the weather's tolerable than I do in my bed."

"Can't blame you." Whenever Sam had been on a mission, rain had been both a blessing and a curse. It could cover the sound of his approach or that of the enemy hunting him.

Tate sat in a wide rocking chair, picked up a chunk of wood and a knife from the table and pointed at the seat opposite him. With one foot he kicked open a door in the floor and made a long, slow stroke along the piece of wood with the blade. A sliver of wood curled. Then the shaving fell. He nudged it through the hole.

"Why Quincey?" Sam asked.

Tate smiled and shook his head. "I was canoeing

the river 'bout a decade ago. Hit a rock and sprung a leak. Got tired of bailing, so I pulled ashore and hiked into town for patching compound. Never left. People here are nosy enough to keep me from getting too wrapped up in my own company but not so meddlesome that they interfere with my need for solitude. How long you been here now?"

"Eight days."

"You decided where you're going next?"

Perceptive man. "What makes you think I'm leaving?"

"Restlessness clings to you. How long's your vision supposed to be messed up?"

"The doctors won't give me a straight answer. Could be up to a year. Until I know my final outcome, I can't make plans." He couldn't keep the frustration out of his voice.

"Closest veterans hospitals are in Greenville and Durham. Long drive to either, but worth it. Good folks there. Might be worth a second opinion."

"Might be."

"Life is different on the civvy side. But different doesn't necessarily mean bad." He took one look at Sam's face and shook his head. "You're not ready to hear that yet. You want to go back."

"Yes, sir, I do."

"Being discharged against your will is like a death." He tapped his leg. "You'll have to work through the grieving process. You're still in denial. Next will come anger. At the world. At the Marine

Corps. At the people around you. Then you'll try to make deals, try to find a way to get back what you had. But you can't."

He'd already done those. "If my eye heals—"

"Even if it does and you could go back to the corps, you know you're not invincible now. Some of that brainwashing they poured into your jarhead has spilled out. You'll be different. Less sure. More cautious. Aware of your mortality."

"You sound pretty sure of that."

"Having a prosthetic means I've not only been there and done that, but I've spent a lot of time at VA hospitals. When you're there, you've got nothing to do but talk to the other guys. Guys who've already walked the path you're on. Your best bet is to try to find a new situation normal. I'm not saying you'll ever forget where you've been and what you've done in the line of duty, but you can forgive yourself for it. War isn't pretty. But you don't have to bring it here. And you need to find something to fill the hole your separation left behind."

The hole would be healed as soon as he was well enough to go back. "I'm working on that."

Lowry shook his head. "Not yet, you're not. You talked to your family yet? Told them what happened?"

"No."

"Suspected as much. You're still acting like the Lone Ranger. You should call 'em. It's a step. A big one. Toward accepting the change."

Sam instantly rejected the idea. "My mother and sisters would show up and smother me, and my dad was a career marine."

"If you're scared of disappointing him, don't be. He knows they wouldn't have cut you loose unless they had to. They had too much invested in your training to throw it away. Talk to your family. Or better yet, go see 'em."

Lowry must have read Sam's answer on his face.

"Son, don't fall off the grid like I did. Too much time with my own company made me mean and angry. Not sure what would've happened if I hadn't hit that rock. During the few weeks I was forced to wait on the repairs, I realized I had to change to fit in. Rewired my thinking. But that's skipping past depression and going straight to acceptance."

Sam shook his head. "I'm not depressed. I'm pissed. Pissed that I'm trained, willing and able to accept a lesser position and they won't let me work. I have no skills or education beyond my job description."

"Then you'll have to learn some. Life ain't over. This is just a detour on the road. I know, I know. Sounds like psychobabble bullshit, and I told the shrinks just that when they spouted it at me, but it turned out to be true. Do you have any hobbies to keep you busy while you work through things?"

This wasn't going the way he'd expected. Maybe he should just go to the range. "I take pictures."

"Good. Similar to using a scope but different. If

your eye is up to it, get busy with that while you figure out your next move."

"You sound pretty sure I won't stay here."

"You won't. Not enough excitement in Quincey PD for two ex-military guys. Just try not to break any hearts before you go."

"I won't."

The older man tapped his tool against his thigh. "Did you see the security cameras I have in the range?"

Lowry had seen the kiss. Weight bore down on Sam's chest. "No."

"Good. I thought I had 'em hid pretty well. Point being, your head ain't screwed on straight right now. Don't go messing with somebody else's, especially that sweet gal's, until you get your situation figured out. June's done had it hard enough already."

"How so?"

"Not my story to tell."

That piqued his curiosity even more. "She and I both know where we stand."

So much for a distraction. They'd ended up talking about the one person Sam didn't want to think about. Not that he wasn't disappointed that June had rejected his offer—warning. Nonengagement was for the best.

But damn, now he knew for sure that once he stepped into that range, he'd be remembering that kiss *and* knowing Tate had witnessed it.

"Go shoot. Cover one eye and fire a few rounds.

Then cover the other and do it again. Keep your targets. You'll see improvement over time. Or you won't. Either way, move on, son. You'll always be a marine in your head, but looks like it's time to put your heart into something else."

As USUAL, the Sunday meal at her parents' house was torture, but except for the times June got stuck working a call, she hadn't missed many since moving back to Quincey. The late-afternoon meal was often the only time she got to see her mother.

Dunch, she and her siblings had tagged it because it was too late for lunch but too early for dinner. June had never known any other family who ate lunch/dinner between three and four, but her father wanted to eat as soon as he finished his pastoral duties. That meant her mom attended services, then raced home to put a meal on the table before he arrived.

"Chicken's good, Mom."

"Fried chicken is Rhett's favorite. I had hoped he'd stay in town for the weekend and dinner tonight, but he barely stopped to say hello at the barbecue. He said he had to get back to campus to study for an exam."

An unlikely but effective justification for avoiding services this morning and a few hours in their father's company this afternoon. June had hoped Rhett would show up for the meal and discuss his situation with their parents. Maybe one of them could advise him. But since they hadn't mentioned Rhett's dilemma, they obviously didn't know about the pregnancy. Otherwise her dad would be ranting about the shame an illegitimate child would bring to the family.

Rhett probably hoped June would break his news even though she'd said she wouldn't. But middle kids learned early on to keep secrets, because no matter how good the intentions, the messenger of bad news always got the bad end of the deal— usually from both sides.

Sam's words replayed in her head. Was she handicapping her brother? No, she was just helping him make his own informed decision—one he could live with.

Her father ate in glowering silence. He hadn't spoken since saying grace. June searched for a safe topic to end the strained atmosphere permeating the formal dining room. Her mother still worked half days at the church preschool—the only job her father had ever allowed his wife to hold. That was as good a topic as any.

"Class started Tuesday, right, Mom? How's this year's crop of preschoolers look?"

"It seems like children get smarter earlier each year. Probably all those electronic gadgets they play with and, of course, television. They can see the whole world on a screen instead of through the pages of a book."

"Is this one married?" her father snapped, and June flinched.

"Kevin!" her mother chastised.

"I saw her looking at that man with lust-filled eyes during the barbecue yesterday, Angie, and so did you. Don't try to deny it. And then they ran off together afterward."

June's appetite vanished. Why couldn't they have a pleasant, nonconfrontational visit for once? "I went home to shower. Alone, Dad. On my bicycle. And then I drove over to Piper's for dinner. Again, alone. Sam's a coworker."

"Like the last one."

There was no point in trying to defend herself when she'd told her father countless times before that she hadn't known Peter had a wife. She'd admitted she'd made a mistake, but that wasn't enough for him. In her father's eyes adultery was adultery. She'd broken a commandment. Whether she'd knowingly done so or not was irrelevant. He probably wouldn't be satisfied until she stood up in church and admitted it.

"I've been assigned to train him. That's it." She prayed he would see her intent rather than her illicit thoughts.

"And you conveniently live side by side."

"The chief arranged those accommodations for Deputy Rivers."

"Do not disgrace me again, Justice." His eyes held no trace of the warmth he showed his flock.

A chill invaded her. "No one knows anything about…Raleigh…except Piper, Madison and you. My friends would never betray my confidence, and the rest of Quincey only knows what you've told them."

"I merely preached about the sin of adultery and coveting thy neighbor's wife."

"For weeks on end we heard about David and Bathsheba." That third sermon had been the last time she'd set foot in his church except for weddings. "It was like pouring gasoline on a fire. What people don't know, they speculate about or make up."

"And you have not corrected them, because you can't. You know you did wrong. Our family must keep higher standards, Justice. We must set examples for my flock."

Nothing new in that speech. She'd heard every chapter and verse before. "I know that, Dad. But we're humans just like the rest of them. We make mistakes, too."

She debated making an excuse and leaving, but she would not give him the satisfaction of knowing his constant condemnation got to her, so she cut a piece of poultry, shoved it into her mouth and chewed out her frustration. She hated that his approval mattered, *hated it*, and yet could do nothing to change it. She turned back to her mother.

"How many students do you have this year, Mom?"

"Only ten in my four-year-old class. Less than

that in the threes and twos. Enrollment has declined as more young people leave Quincey."

"They have to follow the jobs. Like Kelley, Kelsie and Michael did."

Her siblings had shockingly all packed up and left Quincey while June was training in Raleigh. She'd often wondered if they'd really left to pursue employment, as they claimed, or if they'd fled because she wasn't here to run interference with their father.

Either way, they were gone and June was back and now the sole focus of his disappointment.

"Have you invited the new deputy to the church?" her mother asked.

"No, Mom, I haven't."

"You should, dear."

So her father could take potshots at Sam? Or tell him how wicked June was? No, thanks. "I'm trying to keep our work and private lives separate. Some people wouldn't understand if Sam and I were seen together off duty. Anyway, I usually work the Sunday shift so Deputy Aycock can take his kids to church."

She glanced at her father, who stiffened. "Do not bring that man into my house of worship if you're fornicating with him."

She wanted so badly to tell him where to stick his self-righteous attitude, but doing so would mean not seeing her mother, so she swallowed her anger and focused on her mom. "I'd love to treat you to lunch one day this week."

"Your mother works with me after the preschool closes."

"Are you in the middle of a project your church secretary can't handle?"

"I've said your mother is unavailable. End of discussion."

And that, unfortunately, was how it had been since June's return. Once her father spoke, her mother never dared defy him. No wonder her siblings had fled his umbrella of control. June had to admit she was tempted to do the same again. But she couldn't. Quincey was where she fit in, where she knew the rules and where her family resided— her parents *and* the citizens she'd chosen to include in her inner circle.

So she'd stay and endure. That might very well be the only "till death do us part" promise she would ever get to make.

And one day maybe her father would forgive her.

CHAPTER EIGHT

THE REPETITIVE THUMP grew louder as Sam approached the edge of the woods near his cottage after his Sunday-afternoon hike. It was a familiar sound but one that didn't fit in this bucolic setting. He debated continuing on to his quarters without investigating, but Roth had asked him to take note of who came and went on the property.

He followed his ears toward the barn, a building he'd yet to explore. June had said there was a skunk inside and, descented or not, he'd yet to have a good encounter with one.

The grunts following each smack reinforced his guess that someone was punishing a punching bag. Did the veterinarian box as part of her exercise routine? An image of his landlord's slender-almost-to-the-point-of-fragile body came to mind and the idea didn't compute. Madison wasn't that muscular, and the boxer in the barn was landing solid blows. Neither was the vet's truck in the driveway.

That left only one person who belonged here—the one he wanted to avoid. But June had left this morning wearing her uniform, and they worked twelve-hour shifts. She should still be on the clock. From his vantage point he couldn't see if her vehicle was parked by her cottage.

The setting sun at Sam's back made it difficult to approach without his shadow giving away his position, but he chose his path carefully and reached the structure by pressing up against the western wall. He eased up to the big wooden sliding door and peered through the three-inch gap.

The first thing he saw was an animal cage, specifically one holding the skunk June had mentioned. Then he spotted June—whaling the crap out of the leather bag suspended from the ceiling.

He leaned back on his heel and once more debated a safe withdrawal, but if she was abusing her time sheet, then Roth needed to know. Corruption came in many forms. Knocking off early was the same as stealing.

Damn, he hoped she wasn't crooked. He nixed that thought. His job was recon and report. Just the facts. No bias. No emotions. No attachments.

He eased forward again and noted the anger pleating her brow and narrowing her eyes as she landed another series of rapid-fire punches. Her focused fury riveted him. He'd seen her pissed off plenty of times, usually at him, but this was different.

A mouth guard puffed out her lips. Sweat beaded on her skin and trickled down her cheeks, chest, bare back and abdomen, all revealed by the curve-hugging spandex bra-top and midriff-baring bottom she wore. He'd seen her in less clothing but the impact of her fit form still hit him viscerally.

Strands of damp blond hair had escaped her stubby ponytail and clung to her forehead, cheekbones and neck, attesting to the force and rotation behind her blows. Her shoulders were sleekly muscled, smooth and round. She bounced on her toes, then pivoted and landed a high kick followed by another powerful one-two combination, displaying both force and flexibility.

He'd hate to face her in hand-to-hand combat. But he wouldn't mind having her at his back during a fight. There weren't many females he could say that about. He wasn't a sexist, but the corps' motto was never leave a man behind. If he went down in the field, he wanted the marine beside him to be able to carry his two-hundred-pound body to safety. Women would have a hard time with that task. Stress fractures from the sheer weight of their equipment alone, packs often weighing as much as ninety pounds, weren't uncommon during training exercises. But he had a feeling June would find a way to haul his ass out of danger. And he'd bet his Charger she could easily ace the Marine Corps PFT. She was as lean and powerful as those who'd passed the physical fitness tests at the top of their class.

A shrill whistle from one of the cages scared the crap out of him. June checked her swing, her eyes going straight to the door and nailing him in place.

She spit her mouth guard into one glove and lowered her hands. "Spying, Rivers?"

He pushed open the door. "I thought you were working today."

"Partial shift. I covered for Mac so he could take his mom out for a birthday lunch and for Alan so he could go to church."

"You didn't go? Isn't the preacher's daughter expected to make an appearance?"

"I can hardly attend services if I'm working."

From her defensive tone, he suspected she'd heard that question before. "You didn't go last Sunday either, and you were off."

"What are you? My keeper? If you must know, I prefer to visit my parents after services." She turned, peeling off her padded gloves, then reached for a towel, which she used to swipe her face, then body. She missed a few spots.

He yanked his gaze from the glistening areas. "Did you visit them today?"

"Yes."

"How'd that go?"

"Fine." The clipped word said otherwise. "Any improvement on the range this morning?"

"Tracking me, Jones?"

"Don't be an ass. I saw your car at Tate's when I made my rounds."

Something had set her off. What? "Did your father give you a hard time?"

"What do you mean?"

He didn't buy her feigned confusion. She held her eyes open too wide, and her body was too still, too tense. "Your dad treated us like bill collectors when we took those boys over last week, and he gave me the evil eye throughout the game yesterday. Just wondering if it's his face or mine you're visualizing on that bag."

Her quick flush confirmed his statement. "He wasn't glaring at you." Then her shoulders sagged. "It was me."

A grudging confession. "Why?"

"None of your business."

"You say that a lot."

"You ask a lot of questions that are none—"

He held up a hand. "None of my business. Yeah, so you've said."

"Don't you have somewhere else to be, Rivers?"

Annoying her was more fun than it should be. "No."

He stepped deeper into the space and checked out the rest of her exercise equipment. The weight rack and bench tucked into the corner, stretching bands, medicine balls and pull-up bar explained how she kept her body in such great shape.

"Nice gym you have here."

Her eyes narrowed. "Thanks. You can use it if you want. When I'm not here."

"Good ol' Southern hospitality." With a dash of vinegar.

"There's not enough room for two to work out comfortably."

"Roth said you used to own this farm. Why'd you sell it only to move back and rent?" He took one look at the scowl lowering her eyebrows. "I know, none of my business, but if you have nothing to hide, why not answer?"

"I sold it to pay for my BLET program and living expenses in Raleigh." She grabbed her water bottle and headed out the door.

He remembered what Morris had said. "You weren't planning to return to Quincey."

"You've been gossiping."

"Just paying attention when others yap— something Quincey's citizens like to do. Why come back if you prefer the city?"

"I never said I preferred the city. My brothers and sisters moved away while I was in training. Mom needed me." The hesitation before her answer said there was more to the story.

"Is she sick or disabled?"

"No." She quickly strode toward the rainbow explosion she called a front porch.

"Does your father abuse her?"

She stopped and turned on the second tread, putting them at eye level and blocking him from following. "You have my folks confused with the chief's parents. His dad was the batterer. Mine's a mild-mannered pastor. Everybody loves him. Just ask."

"It's clear from the way you reacted to your father's dig about some people knowing how to repent that you and he don't get along. What did you do to get on his blacklist? Try to live up to the cliché of the preacher's daughter?"

"No. My sisters demonstrated that wasn't a good idea. You're assuming my father's the warm-and-fuzzy type. He isn't. Do you and your dad always get along?" she countered.

"Don't change the subject. But yes, we do."

"Then why hasn't he visited?"

Disinclined to lie or reveal that his father didn't even know Sam's whereabouts, he sifted through the facts, trying to decide what he wanted her to know.

"If you have nothing to hide, Deputy Rivers, then why not answer?"

Having his words thrown back at him was no fun.

"Does he work?" she added impatiently.

"He retired recently."

"From…?"

"The Marine Corps." Time to go. She'd gotten more out of him than he'd intended. He pivoted.

"You'd think with your injury that loving parents would want to check on you."

That stopped him in his tracks. His mom and dad had never been anything short of wonderful. "My parents don't live a mile away like yours do. And my mother still works."

"Doing what?"

"She's an ER nurse."

"Not a seven-day-a-week job. I'm surprised she

hasn't checked on her baby boy. I'll bet she's glad you're out of danger."

She would have been if she'd known. Hitting the ball back into June's court and putting her on the defensive was the best way to end this discussion. "What made you take up boxing?"

"If a woman's going to work in a man's field, she has to be able to beat him physically and mentally. My size is a disadvantage. That means I have to work twice as hard to be able to take care of myself and my partner. I refuse to be a liability."

She'd said the one thing to make him like and respect her more. How could he not appreciate the effort she put into keeping her body as well maintained as her firearm? He'd thought Roth had saddled him with a cream puff. Instead, his buddy had paired him with the most dedicated deputy on the Quincey force.

Worse, Sam had compromised his mission by becoming personally invested in one of the suspects. If any of Roth's team were crooked, Sam now wanted to prove June wasn't one of them.

Time for him to make a strategic retreat and get his head back on the mission.

JUNE STEPPED ONTO her front porch Monday morning and glanced over to see Sam looking right at her as he locked his front door. His icy blue gaze nailed her feet to the floorboards and trapped the air in her chest. He looked so darned sexy in his uniform. He nodded a silent greeting.

She returned the gesture with a neck that moved as stiffly as a rusty hinge, then hustled to her truck as fast as possible without being obvious, jumped in and quickly headed out. Her rearview mirror revealed Sam's Charger with its menacing grill right behind her. Apparently, she wasn't the only one who liked to get into work early.

If circumstances had been different, she'd have suggested carpooling, but Sam had a way of looking at her that made her feel naked and sexy and uncomfortable simultaneously. She didn't know what to do with those tangled feelings.

Once they reached QPD, she skedaddled inside with Sam hot on her heels. Trying to beat him to the time clock was childish, but she couldn't help herself.

They were waylaid by the chief. "My office," he said.

Mac's and Alan's desks were empty, but Roth closed his door nonetheless. Conscious of Sam shadowing her, she took her usual seat in front of the desk. Sam settled beside her. His scent wound around her like her grandfather's pipe smoke. She caught herself inhaling a big gulp of him.

Jeez, Jones. Are you so deprived of male companionship that you have to sniff one to get your jollies?

"Don Davis saw headlights on his property at two this morning," Roth said, crushing her sensual hedonism. "He fired his shotgun into the air and his uninvited guests raced off. This morning he found tire tracks around his broken-down '75 Suburban."

Another heavy vehicle. June sat up straighter. "Did he see who it was or get the make of a car?"

"It was too cloudy last night and he has no area lights where his truck's parked."

Sam's chair creaked as he leaned forward. "If it's the same thief, he's breaking his six-month pattern."

The chief nodded. "Exactly. Either we have a copycat, an escalation or something else, but whichever it is, it means nighttime patrols for the three of us. Jones, go home. Get some rest. You have first watch, beginning at midnight tonight. I'll take tomorrow. Sam, you have Wednesday. Same rotation until we catch these bastards."

"Don't you want me to visit the scrap yards on our list first?" June asked.

"Sam will do it. Leave him the names and addresses."

Part of her was relieved to be avoiding a long day cooped up in the patrol car with Sam. But mostly, she was frustrated at not being able to follow up on the leads she'd spent hours researching. But this was the lesser of two evils. "I'll leave him the map."

"Good. And, Jones, don't be a hero. If you see anything suspicious tonight, call me."

"But, sir, I'd hate to get you out of bed for a false alarm, and if it's a neighbor, as we suspect, I know these people. They won't hurt me."

The chief's face turned as dark as a thundercloud. "Call for backup. That's an order. Are we clear?"

Embarrassed by the dressing-down, she glanced at Sam only to find his expression more intimidating than the boss's. "Yes, sir."

AT FIVE MINUTES to midnight June opened the patrol car door. Carefully cradling a thermos of coffee and the new night-vision goggles the chief had dropped off earlier for her to learn to use, she backed into the vehicle and swung her legs around. The big body already occupying the passenger seat scared her half to death.

Juggling the expensive vision equipment with one hand, dropping the thermos and reaching for her gun with the other, she was halfway out of the car before she recognized Sam. She collapsed back into the driver's seat, primarily because her legs didn't want to support her.

"What in the heck are you doing here?"

"Riding shotgun."

"You should've warned me. I could have shot you."

He picked up the thermos and set it in the cup holder. "I would have disarmed you first. And if I'd warned you, you'd have left me."

True. "I don't need you to ride with me, Rivers. I'm a big girl. I can take care of myself."

"Overconfidence will get you killed. I need to know where the abandoned cars are located. You know that better than anyone. You drive. I'll mark them on our map."

Good points. So she was stuck with him in the close confines of the dark car. For a while. She'd make one circuit, then dump him at home. "Okay. Hold these, please."

She handed him the goggles she'd planned to put in his seat and headed toward the outskirts of town. "My plan is to loop Quincey in shrinking circles, then work my way back out again."

He rode along in silence. With only the illumination from the dash and the light-up pen he was using to take notes, her other senses intensified. She could smell him, that distinctive scent of man, soap and laundry detergent, and she heard every shift of his body in the creaky vinyl seat. Even the scratch of his pen on paper seemed exceptionally loud. Sensory overload was making her a nervous wreck. She couldn't have been more relieved when it was time to head back for the cottage.

She turned down the road leading home. "As you've seen, not a lot happens in Quincey during the daytime. Even less happens here at night. We're a predominantly agricultural community. We work when the sun's up and sleep when it sets."

"One more loop so I know my pattern well enough to vary it," he said. "And you'd better switch up your routine, too, or someone could lie in wait for an ambush."

She hated that he was logical. Smothering a sigh, she retraced her route.

Three miles down the road, he whipped his head to one side. "What's that?"

June followed his pointing finger and spotted twin pin dots of light barely visible deep in the woods. Leave it to a former sniper to see something that tiny and distant. She slowed the car. "Someone who wasn't there before."

"Kill the headlights and pull over. Have you used night vision before?"

"No." June parked. She expected him to don the goggles, but he passed them to her.

"Put them on. I'll talk you through it."

She fumbled with the head strap. It was awkward and clunky.

"Let me help." His big hands splayed to spread the straps. Then he eased them down over her head. The sensation of having his palm cupping her skull and his fingers threading through her hair sent a shiver through her. She prayed he didn't notice.

"The binoculars flip up out of your way when you don't need them, but use them now." His huskier-than-normal tone said he hadn't missed her reaction.

She pushed that aside and focused. It took a moment to get used to the change in visual acuity. Adrenaline raced through her veins.

"If the headlights swing this way, close your eyes, then take off the goggles. There's a light illuminator sensor that shuts the unit off, but no need to risk damaging your eyes if it malfunctions."

"Got it. All I can see is the vehicle's front grill, and I can't see that well enough to make out a make or model."

"Be patient." The car or truck inched closer, leaving the woods and bumping into a field. "Admit it, you wouldn't have called for backup if you'd seen something. You'd have talked whoever it was to death. Or tried to."

A guilty flush burned her cheeks. She was thankful for the dark. "I know how to follow orders."

"Sure you do, Jones."

Then she recognized the pickup and the driver and relaxed. "It's okay. It's only Jim Bob. Miss Letty's son."

"He could be our thief."

She rejected the idea immediately. "Not Jim Bob. He's…slow. He has the mentality of a ten-year-old."

"Then why's he driving?"

"He's not on the road. A lot of farm kids drive off-road without licenses."

"In the middle of the night? We need to find out why he's here."

She removed the goggles and hit the lights. The headlights, combined with the red-and-blue light bar, illuminated Jim Bob's panicked gaze as she put the car into gear and rolled toward him.

"Sit tight. Jim Bob's wary of strangers. I've got

this." She threw the cruiser into Park and exited the vehicle, determined to prove Sam wrong.

THE GUY WAS HUGE. Sam could tell from the amount of space he took up in the small cab. Had to be six-six and two hundred fifty pounds of what looked like solid muscle. Big enough to hurt June without trying. Hell, his arms were probably more than half her body length. But this was her shift, her bust, her people. She knew the guy's disabilities. Sam didn't. He'd sit tight until—

Then he saw the suspect's anxious sideways glance, and all bets were off. Sam knew that look. He'd seen it too many times before. He vaulted from the car and, drawing his weapon, raced toward the suspect.

"Take cover," he yelled as he sprinted past June, positioning himself between her and the perp. Sam ripped open the door. The rifle on the front seat confirmed his suspicions.

"Out of the car," he shouted.

The giant cowered, but the Winchester beside him spoke its own language. And then the guy took one hand off the wheel. The wrong hand. The hand nearest the rifle. Slow or not, if he could drive a car, he could pull a trigger.

"Touch that gun and you're dead. Get out of the truck," Sam barked, and grabbed the driver's beefy biceps.

"Sam, it's okay," June said from behind him, her

voice level, quiet and calm. She planted a palm on Sam's back and leaned around him.

Damn it, he'd told her to take cover.

"Jim Bob, it's all right. This is Deputy Rivers. He works with me. Do what he says and come on out of the truck, okay? Turn it off first and let me hold the keys." She spewed it all in a calm, friendly voice. Didn't she see the rifle?

Wide brown eyes went from Sam to June and back again. "I didn't do anything."

"Out, Jim Bob." Sam's low monotone would have warned anybody who knew him well that he meant business.

"But, Miss June—"

"Do it," Sam ordered, and the man complied, slowly, awkwardly unfolding from the seat. He towered over Sam and dwarfed June.

"I didn't do anything," Jim Bob repeated, and gently placed the key ring in June's palm. "I'm a good boy, Momma says."

"Yes, you are, Jim Bob. You're a very good boy."

"Over here." Sam motioned him away from the open truck door with a jerk of his barrel.

The perp looked at June, who nodded and cooed, "It's okay." Then he shuffled two steps to his left.

"Why are you out this late with a rifle?" Sam demanded.

"'Only shoot the coyotes that have been eating my chickens,' Momma said."

"Jim Bob?" June waited until he looked at her. "Is the rifle loaded?"

He hesitated. "Yes, Miss June. It won't work without bullets."

She circled the truck and opened the opposite side, then withdrew the Winchester and competently removed the cartridges and cleared the chamber. She slipped the brass shells into her pocket, then tucked the gun behind the bench seat before returning to Sam's side.

"Jim Bob? Tell us again why you're out here in the middle of the night?"

"I'm looking for coyotes, Momma says."

"You are, huh?"

"Are you looking for old trucks, too?" Sam's question earned him a scowl from June and a wide-eyed, nervous look from the giant.

"Just coyotes, Jim Bob?" June asked.

"Yes, Miss June. Don't want no trouble. No trouble at all. Head home if I see any, Momma says."

"That's a good idea. You shouldn't be out this late anyhow. What would happen if your truck broke down?"

He lifted a hand and Sam's muscles locked and loaded, but the guy only scratched his big head. "I'd walk home, Miss June. I know the way. And I'm not scared of the dark. I'm *not*."

"I know you're not."

"Check the bed of his truck for chains or tie-downs."

Sam's order earned him another green-eyed glare. "You do it, Rivers. And holster that weapon. You don't need it."

He pulled his flashlight from his belt left-handed and backed toward the rear of the truck, but he kept his gaze and his HK on the guy standing close enough to harm a hardheaded, overly trusting blonde. He hoped like hell he didn't need to pull the trigger. But surely at this distance he wouldn't hit June. A quick sweep revealed an empty bed. "Clear."

"Jim Bob, no more late-night rides, okay? We've been having some trouble out here, and like your momma, I don't want you to find it."

The big brown headed nodded. "Yes, Miss June. No trouble."

She handed over the keys, then dropped the cartridges into his T-shirt pocket. "Go straight home, Jim Bob. We'll follow you to make sure you get there safely."

"Yes, Miss June." He climbed back in the truck.

She turned and casually strolled back to the patrol car. Sam wanted to yell at her to be more cautious. No one, especially a special-needs person, should be wandering around alone at this time of night with a loaded rifle. He backed toward the cruiser, slid in and faced June.

With her out of immediate danger, adrenaline ebbed from Sam's veins, leaving nothing behind but anger. "Rule number one—never turn your back on a suspect."

"It's Jim Bob." She put the cruiser in gear.

"I don't care if it's Saint Peter. Don't ever turn your back on anyone with a weapon."

"It's unloaded."

"What if he has others? Even if he doesn't, he isn't unarmed. I've seen what insurgents can do with a car."

"How did you know he had the rifle?"

"He looked at it."

"He wouldn't have shot me," she insisted.

"If he hadn't thought about using it, he would have kept his eyes on you. You were an approaching threat, even though he knows you. I've dodged too many bullets from men doing the same thing to take chances."

The crease in her forehead told him he'd planted doubts. Good. "Better proactive than dead, Jones. Show more sense when you're out patrolling alone. Or we might be searching for a murderer instead of just a truck thief."

"Oh, please, Sam. He's not our guy and you know it."

"Are you willing to bet your life on that? Your buddy had a rifle and he thought about using it. On you. If I hadn't intervened and he'd shot you, you could have lain here until the buzzards gave away your location. Coyote food."

She paled and tightened her grip on the wheel

until her knuckles gleamed white in the dash lights, making him feel a little guilty for being so harsh. But her safety was too important.

"You overreacted." But she sounded less confident.

Had he? "No, damn it, I didn't. Don't be naive, June. The threat was genuine. Wise up."

She ducked her head. Remorse hit him hard. He'd hurt her feelings. But better a bruised ego than hauling her body to the morgue. And if the look in her eyes made him feel as though he'd punted a kitten, then tough. He'd done what he had to do, said what he had to say, for her own safety. He wouldn't always be here to protect her.

The real problem, he realized as he stared out the windshield and willed his heart rate to slow down, was that from the minute he'd considered June in jeopardy fear had gripped his gut like a crushing vise. That wasn't something he could explain—to her or himself. She was a temporary partner, a duty station. Nothing more. And he intended to keep it that way.

CHAPTER NINE

BANGING JARRED JUNE from a sound sleep. She forced open tired, gritty eyes and looked around, getting her bearings. Her alarm clock glowed 1:00. But daylight seeped around the curtains. For a moment that didn't compute and then she remembered. She'd worked a night shift. Part of it with Sam.

The whole night came racing back. She buried her face in her pillow. Was she too trusting, too naive and gullible, even for Quincey? No. It couldn't be that. Quincey was where she fit. Sam was wrong. Jim Bob never would have hurt her. He'd looked at his rifle for another reason. She just didn't know why. If it had been anyone but Jim Bob, she could've asked him why and received a perfectly rational explanation.

But she prided herself on her ability to read body language, yet she'd missed that very important glance at the gun. Or had she? She must've. She didn't doubt Sam for a second.

The knock sounded again. At her front door. If it was Sam, she'd kill or at least maim him for waking her after only five hours of restless sleep.

No, she couldn't do that. He'd tried to protect her.

And that was…sweet. She'd never had anyone put himself between her and danger before, and she didn't know what to make of Sam's actions. She'd always been the caretaker. She looked out for her siblings, her mother, her friends and the guys at the station.

She wasn't ready to face Sam and debated pulling the covers over her head, but the knocking intensified. With a groan she disentangled herself from the sheets, yanked on her robe and padded barefoot through the house. Dread slowed her steps as she neared the wooden panel. The knob twisted but didn't open, because she'd locked it.

"Note to self—install a peephole." Something she'd never needed before her coworker had moved in.

"June, are you in there?" Madison's voice called, and then the pounding resumed, harder this time. June sagged in relief and opened the door.

Piper stood behind Madison. Their surprised gazes ran from June's head to her toes and back again. "Hey, ladies. What's up?"

"Were you in bed? Are you sick?" Madison asked with concern puckering her brow.

She couldn't tell them she'd worked last night. Or why. Not if she wanted to keep her job. Quincey deputies rarely worked overnights. They were on call in case of a crisis like the pig truck, but the department budget wasn't large enough to fund an around-the-clock staff. She wondered how Roth was going to explain his overnights to Piper. But that was his problem. Her truck had been here. Madison wouldn't know June hadn't been home.

"I'm not sick. I was just being lazy."

"You're never lazy," Piper said.

"I…um…stayed up late watching old movies on cable." Lying. To her best friends. She'd reached a new low. And she hated herself for it.

"Which ones?" Piper's interest twisted the guilt screw.

The hole she'd dug got deeper. "I…um… A bunch."

Piper didn't look convinced. "Roth said you were off today, so we've decided to take a field trip."

"Are you up for a ride to Raleigh?" Madison asked. "The bridal salon called. My dress is in. Piper moved all of our afternoon appointments until tomorrow so we could go see it."

Excited at the opportunity to spend the afternoon with her friends, she stepped back and opened the door to let them in. "Sure. Give me five minutes to throw on some clothes."

"Take your time. I'll make coffee and fix you something light to eat while you shower. We'll have dinner after dress shopping."

"Thanks. I'd appreciate that." Madison knew where everything was at June's, just as June knew where everything was at Madison's. They had no secrets.

Until now.

Thirty minutes later, June, her guilty conscience and her faithful taupe somebody-else's-wedding heels were strapped into the back seat of Piper's car, heading out for a day of girl talk and fun.

"Have you set a date?"

"No. We can't do that until we choose a location."

June lapsed into silence while the two in the front debated colors and styles of dresses. Her mind drifted back to last night and the way Sam had waved her behind him as he'd charged toward Jim Bob. That unnecessary action had left her feeling cherished and protected, when she was sure it had been nothing more than Sam looking out for a fellow officer.

Piper caught June's gaze in the rearview mirror. "So how's working with Sam going? Are you still having problems or have you finally admitted you're attracted to each other?"

June's excitement over the hours ahead evaporated. "There's nothing between us."

"But you'd like there to be."

"Piper, how many times do I have to tell you? No! And stop match-making. It's embarrassing. It makes me appear desperate."

"The looks between you and Sam at the volleyball game were so hot I thought you'd melt the sand court into glass, and then at our cookout we could have turned off the gas grill and let you guys flame the burgers."

June suddenly wanted out of the car in the worst

kind of way, but bailing at sixty miles per hour wouldn't be smart.

Madison twisted around in the front passenger seat to face June. "You have the hots for Sam? A few days ago you said he was an ass. How did I miss your change of heart?"

"You didn't and I haven't. He is an ass...*and* he isn't." June stabbed a hand through her still-damp hair. "He's a know-it-all who can't answer a simple question without prevarication. But he might have the intelligence to back up all his confidence. The last thing I need is another dead-end romance, and that's all Sam's good for."

Piper frowned. "What makes you say that?"

"He said it."

"So you've talked about getting together?" Piper asked with interest in her eyes.

June grimaced. This was going to be a very long afternoon, and she'd have to be more careful if she wanted to get through this day without perjuring herself further. "We discussed dating and single life in Quincey—or the lack thereof—when he noticed your blatant matchmaking attempts at the cookout. Like I said, embarrassing."

"Oops. Sorry," Piper said, looking not the least apologetic. "At least admit you think he's sexy."

June wanted to scream. "He might be, but that doesn't change anything. He's not date material. Not for me, anyway."

"Piper's just worried because as soon as Adam

and I get married, I'll be leaving, and my in-laws will be taking over my house and practice. You won't have anyone to go out with…unless you decide to bottom-feed with Tammy Sue's crowd."

She made a gagging sound. "Never going to happen."

Piper's gaze flicked her way. "But how will you meet guys?"

"We could set her up with a dating-site profile."

"No! Madison, I had a front-row seat to your dismal failures with online dating. I am not signing up for Loser Patrol."

"There are some nice guys. You just have to weed through a lot of less-than-wonderful ones to find them."

"And we all know how great my ability to tell the difference between them is, don't we? Can't you two just accept that I'm happy alone?"

"No," Piper and Madison answered in unison.

"Well, Sam is not the answer. One, I work with him. Two, his life is in transition. Three, I can't see him staying here long term, and four—"

"What do you mean you don't see him staying here?" Piper interrupted.

She probably shouldn't have shared that suspicion, since he worked for Piper's husband. "He hates everything about Quincey, from the friendliness of our citizens to the lack of things to do. Mac said Sam grilled him about nightlife, and we have none.

And he's made no effort to put down roots. He's in a rental house."

"So are you," Madison pointed out.

"That's different. My cottage was my grandparents' first home. They lived there until after my great-grandparents passed away and they moved into the house you live in. I have emotional ties to it. Sam hasn't even opened a bank account."

"I thought Roth would leave, too, but he likes Quincey," Piper said.

"Your husband has you, his son and his mother to sweeten the pot. Plus, he's in charge. I can't see Sam as the second-fiddle-forever type. He's too smart."

"What will you do about sex? Do you plan to remain celibate for the rest of your life?" Madison asked.

"Good question. One I'll have to figure out at some point, but I've managed fine for the past few years without growing a wart on my nose or developing a twitch. But number four, my most important reason for not getting involved with Sam, is my father. If he found out I'd had another 'licentious' affair, I'd never get to see my mother again. And how could my dad not find out in Quincey? Even if Sam was the sexiest man on the planet, I couldn't risk it."

"No one can see the cottages except me," Madison pointed out.

"And Sam had a pretty high security clearance as a marine. He's trained to keep secrets," Piper added.

"Will y'all stop! I don't want a relationship that I have to hide."

Piper grimaced. "Okay, okay. I'll stop match-making. But I think we need to revisit the online-dating idea. You can do that out of town."

"No. No. *No*."

"But—"

June decided being mature about this whole conversation wasn't possible. She covered her ears and started humming.

JUNE COULDN'T UNLOCK her front door and escape fast enough Tuesday evening. She hastily waved good-night to Madison, then locked herself inside and sagged against the door. Two good things had come out of the day. Madison's wedding gown had been even more gorgeous than the picture, and the bridesmaid dresses they'd ordered weren't hideous. But the rest of the day had been absolute torture.

The girls had never quit chasing the rabbit of June's single status. They'd spent hours cowriting her online-dating profile, completely ignoring her repeated protests. More than once during the outing she'd wished she hadn't opened her door to them. She usually loved spending time with her friends. But not today.

She crumpled the nauseating sales pitch Madison and Piper had painstakingly crafted and hurled it toward the garbage can. It bounced off the rim and hit the floor, but she didn't have time to pick it up now. She'd get it later. And probably burn it. At the moment she had another mission.

The overwhelming desire to eradicate the evidence of how many times she'd been runner-up—a bridesmaid rather than the bride—had tied her stomach in knots. Even the bridal salon manager had recognized her and greeted her by name. "June, welcome back. It's nice to have such a loyal customer who refers so many of her friends. One day we'll be searching for your special dress, won't we?" she'd said with a patronizing smile and pat on the back of her hand.

June opened the spare closet and a colorful bouquet of compacted fabrics blossomed into the hall without the constraining doors to contain them. A decade's worth of dresses, dating from her sisters' and brother's weddings to her high school friends', took up most of the space. She would never wear them again, and there was no way to shoehorn Madison's bridesmaid dress into the overstuffed closet. It was time she donated this lot so someone else could use them, maybe for prom or something. And clearing them out couldn't wait until tomorrow.

She counted the hangers. Eighteen dresses. Eighteen times someone she'd known had found their soul mate and cared enough about June to ask her to be part of their special moment. Eighteen times she'd stood in the circle of single gals—who each time were increasingly younger—to catch the bouquet.

In all those years, June had never caught the bride's flowers and she'd only found one man she'd thought she wanted to spend her life with. But when she'd discovered he was a cheater, she hadn't been able to stand the sight of him—or herself—anymore. How could she have been such a blind fool? She certainly hadn't been willing to continue their affair in secret as he'd suggested. She wasn't as judgmental and unforgiving as her father, but there were some covenants you just didn't break on purpose.

Banding her arms around the gowns, she wrestled them off the rod, then waddled outside with her bundle. In the driveway she stopped, realizing she should have opened the truck door before hauling out the dresses. Letting go of one side meant spillage.

"Need help?" Sam's deep voice came from behind her in the dark.

She jumped, squealed, juggled and nearly dropped her load. Sam dove forward, enfolding the mound of fabric to prevent disaster. His fingertips brushed the sensitive skin of her torso, and her latissimus dorsi muscles danced as if he'd hit them with a Taser. His arms were warm against hers and his face was so close she could see individual beard stubbles in the area light.

"Thanks," she offered grudgingly, breathlessly. And then she wanted to crawl under her grandfather's old truck. Sam was the last person she wanted to see this collection.

"What's all this?"

"Clothes I'm going to donate. Um…could you open the back door for me?"

He did as she asked, but the minute he released her she missed his body heat. Irritated with herself, she stuffed the garments inside, careless of wrinkles. The pile of satins, chiffons and taffetas looked out of place on the old diesel crew cab's utilitarian vinyl back seat.

Sam fingered a shiny crinoline-stiffened hem. The fabric glimmered like iridescent fish scales in the truck's overhead light. "You wore these?"

His appalled tone raised her hackles. "I didn't choose them."

"But they're yours? You brought them out of your house."

Frustration built. So much for a graceful exit. "They're bridesmaids' dresses."

Eyebrows hiked. "You have a lot of them."

She slammed the door before he could count them. "I had a lot of friends."

"Had?"

"Back in the day. They moved away."

"You did, too. But you came back."

And then she noticed the sweat-soaked T-shirt molding his chest and the brief running shorts baring his muscular legs. Both items were faded olive green and worn enough to be slightly clingy. Probably marine issue. Her pulse rat-a-tatted in her ears, making her burn for a reason other than humiliation.

"Been for a run? You're late getting back."

"Yeah. You like weddings."

So much for changing the subject. "I like seeing my family and friends happy. Their wedding days are probably the happiest days of their lives until they have children. I'm blessed to have been included."

"How many of them are still married?"

"That's a bitter view."

"But realistic. I've seen too many military marriages fail."

"But your parents are still married, aren't they? And your dad's military."

"That's because my mom's a rock. She went through hell before she met him. But I saw what stress and worry did to her every time he was deployed. I'd never do that to anyone."

She didn't take the cheap shot of reminding him he was no longer military. "What if you meet someone who's worth risking it?"

"I won't."

Ouch. Not that she wanted a commitment from him. She didn't. But to know he'd already discarded her as a candidate stung. Even though it shouldn't have.

He stood there looking at her and his silent assessment made her uncomfortable. She scrambled for safer turf. "Did you make it to the scrap yards today?"

One corner of his mouth tilted upward. "Checking up on me, Jones?"

She wanted to smack the cocky smile off his face. "Your car was gone when I got up."

"I hit the closest ones. Got nothing. Most of the trucks disappeared before the VIN search software became a requirement. The recent vehicles didn't come through the locations I checked."

"I'll hit the rest tomorrow."

"*We'll* hit the rest."

"You're working tomorrow night. You should be off the clock."

"All I need is a few hours' sleep. I'll ride with you in the morning."

She opened her mouth to argue the importance of a good night's sleep, then snapped her lips shut. As he'd pointed out, she was not his mother, sister, girlfriend or wife and never would be. His poor sleep habits were none of her business. "Okay, then. Good night."

"Do you have a list of the remaining yards here? I'd like to get a feel for distance and location from the thefts. The vehicles are disappearing too easily. It feels like we're missing something."

"I'll get it for you." She headed inside. He followed. She didn't want him in her house—especially after today. What should have been a happy celebration with her friends had turned into a very unsettling experience. She knew Madison and Piper meant well. They didn't want her to be alone, but all their chatter had left her feeling vulnerable and like someone's ugly cousin with a "good personality" who had zero chance of finding the happiness Piper and Madison had found.

She glanced toward the main house. If she left Sam waiting on her porch at this time of night and Madison saw him, there would be an inquisition. So she didn't stop him when he shadowed her into the dark cottage. She flicked on lights to alleviate the intimacy and retrieved the map she'd hidden behind the sofa. She carried it to the kitchen table and unrolled it. "Which ones did you hit today?"

When he didn't reply, she turned. He stood in her tiny kitchen with a crumpled paper in his hand. The profile. Horror crushed her chest, coming out in an agonized squeak. "Give me that."

His eyebrows shot up. Then a teasing light entered his eyes. "What is it? A love letter?"

She snatched at the page. He held it out of reach. Then he slowly straightened out the wrinkles.

"Rivers, I'm not kidding. Give that to me."

He ignored her. She lunged for it again, and once more he easily dodged her attempt. He was a youngest child, an only brother, one who'd probably learned from the cradle that the greater her panic, the more interesting the item in his possession. With three older sisters, he probably found taunting her as autonomic as breathing. She cursed her friends for concocting the stupid, humiliating, over-the-top sales pitch.

He glanced at it. Did a double take. Then bowed his head and read Madison's neat script. Mortification lit June like a gasoline-fueled bonfire as she watched him skim the words. His blue gaze stabbed hers. "You're going to place a personal ad?"

Could the day get any worse?

"No! Madison and Piper wrote it. I told them I'm not going to pay to play loser lotto. But they refused to listen."

"Are you that desperate for your own wedding day?"

"No! I don't mind being alone. What's wrong with being alone?" Then she realized she'd practically screeched the words.

He frowned, looked down at the page, then up again. "You don't have to try so hard."

That answered her question. Yes, the day could get worse. Dig-a-hole-and-drop-a-house-on-me worse.

He read some more and she wanted to die. "You left out the good parts."

"I told you. I. Didn't. Write. That piece of— What good parts?"

"Those, for example." He nodded toward the still-open closet. Without the mounds of material, her rod and gun racks were clearly visible on the wall, and her tackle boxes sat below them on the floor.

"I inherited most of those from my grandfather."

"But they're well maintained and look like you've been using them."

"Yeah? So?"

"Men like women who hunt and fish."

"I'll keep that in mind if I ever get desperate enough to publish that anywhere. And I *won't*!" She snatched again and this time he surrendered the page. She tore it into shreds and dumped the pieces in the trash.

"You'd have better luck finding a husband in Raleigh."

"I prefer Quincey."

"Do you? Or are you hiding from whatever sent you scurrying back home?"

His question floored her. She had never broadcast her reasons for returning. Thanks to Peter, she was scared to live anywhere else. Not physically afraid. She could take care of herself if it came to an attack—with or without a weapon. But she no longer trusted her judgment or her ability to weed out the liars and snakes.

She was all the things Sam had accused her of being on the stakeout last night. Too naive. Too trusting. It had never occurred to her that Jim Bob— whom she'd known most of her life—would hurt her. But he'd looked at that rifle. Would he have used it if Sam hadn't stormed the truck? Probably not. But she wasn't sure. Not anymore. Although she'd never admit that to Sam.

"I don't know who's been bending your ears with

gossip, but I told you I came home to be near my mother. Now, if you don't mind, I'd like to get some sleep before my shift tomorrow."

He didn't budge. "You're a good catch, Jones. Don't forget that. If I were looking for a woman, you'd be at the top of my list."

Surprised by his kind words and the gentleness of his voice, she stared at him. The lack of the usual ice in his eyes sent a flood of moisture to her mouth. She gulped. Awareness swelled to fill the narrow space between them, seeping into her muscles and making them stiffen. Her heart pounded harder, faster, infusing her veins with heat.

Her mind swirled in confusion. She was a good catch, he'd said. She'd be at the top of his list. But Sam wasn't fishing. And she shouldn't be either. Not with him. Definitely not with him. For all the reasons she'd told Madison and Piper, she shouldn't be tempted by Sam Rivers. But she was. Not even Peter had made her feel this fluttery, flushed and out of control. And she'd be lying if she didn't admit she was very curious to see where Sam could take her.

June missed sex—not just the physical release but being held and caressed, and the mental intimacy of being part of a couple. She missed sharing morning coffee and conversation, and fighting over the TV remote control. Witnessing Madison and Piper's happiness only underlined what was lacking in June's life.

Why not Sam? a voice in her head asked. He was attractive. Single. Honest. And as Piper had pointed out, accustomed to keeping secrets and being stealthy. His life had depended on him coming and going undetected. Only twenty feet separated their houses, and as Madison had said, only Madison had a view of that space.

Really bad idea, June.

Or was it?

Maybe Sam needed someone—someone who believed in him. Someone who'd help him recognize his good qualities while he came to terms with his disability. Someone who could help him make the transition between marine and civilian... Someone who already had a serious case of hero worship.

She dampened her lips and dredged deep for the courage to make the suggestion. "Sam—"

Sam snapped to attention and wariness replaced the warmth in his eyes. "You'll find someone who can give you the wedding, the house, the kids, the picket fence, Jones." He jerked a thumb toward the truck parked outside filled with bridesmaid dresses.

"But—"

"I'm not him."

Then he about-faced and left her, sucking all the energy out of her cottage with him. Drooping against the counter with sudden fatigue—definitely not disappointment—she admitted she should be relieved. After all, he'd saved her from making a

big mistake and a fool of herself. Instead, she felt…
empty, rejected and…lonelier than she'd felt in a
very long time.

CHAPTER TEN

THE FAINTEST RUMBLE of June's diesel engine coming down the road carried through the open den window, snagging Sam's attention. He looked up from the file he'd been reading on Quincey's deputies. Shadows filled his living room and kitchen. Dusk—1930 hours. 'Bout damned time. She was late, and worrying about her had made shrapnel of his concentration.

The urge to go out and meet her was as strong as the one he'd experienced as a boy when his father had returned home. He tried to convince himself it was merely the need to ask if she'd uncovered any leads or to make sure her trusting nature hadn't gotten her hurt this afternoon. In truth, it was both of those and more, and the "more" could get him in trouble.

Last night he'd come close—too close—to acting on the desire he'd seen reflected in June's bright eyes. He wanted her in a way he'd never wanted another woman—physically and as a…friend. And he couldn't have her.

She deserved better than a short affair with a guy

who had no job prospects and an undecided future. He'd be unemployed if not for Roth's request, and even if Roth offered to keep Sam on, he couldn't stay. He'd go nuts with nothing more exciting to do than watching Quincey's grass grow for months on end.

This morning's ride to four scrap yards with June had been uncomfortable. Not knowing what to say, he'd kept his mouth shut, but she'd filled the ride with nonstop nervous chatter. He hadn't seen her nervous before. It wasn't an enjoyable sight.

Escaping to the solitude at Tate's should have been a relief, but Sam had destroyed a pile of targets and not in a good way. The doc had said to give it time, but with each day that passed, Sam's chances of reenlisting or getting a job on any base as a civilian contractor decreased. Hell, not even the reserves would take him in his current condition. He'd checked.

He'd never failed to attain any goal he'd set his sights on, but this time he had to face facts. He might need a backup plan. As Tate had said, Sam couldn't tread water indefinitely. He had to seriously consider what in the hell he would do with his life if he couldn't return to the corps or land a contractor job on base.

Being thirty-one years old and trying to decide what he wanted to be when he grew up sucked. And it scared the hell out of him. He'd been a military brat, then a member of the military. He didn't know any other way of life.

With dread, he glanced at the cell phone in front of him on the kitchen table. His mother had called while he'd slept this afternoon and left a message asking him to check in when he could. He didn't want to respond until he had something concrete to tell her. Admitting he was out seemed like acceptance of his civilian status. There would be questions—questions for which he had no answers. But June was right. His family deserved to know he wasn't in danger.

He tossed his pen onto the file folder, grabbed his phone, then typed out, Stateside. All's good. Will call when can. Luv 2 U & Dad. He hit Send at the same time that June's engine went silent.

Love you. Miss you. Stay safe, his mother replied almost instantly, meaning she wasn't working today. He could call her. But he wouldn't. Not yet.

Frustration clawed at his insides. Instead of heading outside to June, he rose and headed into the kitchen to refill his glass, all the while cataloging the sounds of June's truck door closing, her feet crunching gravel, then jogging up her stairs, the opening and closing of her front door. He carried his water over to the sofa and sat in the dark. He had both windows open and a cross draft cooled his skin, but the fresh air did nothing to settle his restlessness.

His investigations were going nowhere. He was

no closer to knowing if any of the deputies were corrupt, because as Roth had said, Quincey had more gray area than black or white. And he and June had almost nothing on the stolen vehicles. He needed to complete these two assignments and get the hell out of town before he did something stupid like take advantage of a naive blonde who he suspected was developing a crush on him. Her growing fondness was there in her eyes, in her smiles and in her stolen glances at him.

It didn't matter that seeing her each day was like feeling the sun on his skin and breathing the fresh air after a week in a stagnant swamp hide. Breaking cover might feel good, but being in the open carried its own hazards. As a sniper/spotter, he'd crept in, then out, leaving havoc in his wake too many times. He didn't want to do that to June.

Music drifted his way. Instrumental. Flutes. A piano. The kind of boring white-noise stuff that would soothe you if you weren't as agitated as a new boot hitting foreign soil for the first time. He looked through his window. June must have opened hers while he was rattling ice cubes in the kitchen. He hadn't heard the usual squeak of the old sash.

She was probably preparing dinner—no doubt a meal more exciting than the ham-and-cheese sandwich he'd consumed. He inhaled, but none of the tantalizing aromas that had tortured him previous nights drifted from her house to his. More than once he'd kicked himself for biting the hand that fed him.

Then a light came on in her living room, and June strolled by the window wearing her exercise gear of a sports bra top and a pair of skintight knit shorts. Aw, hell.

She shook out her mat onto the floor, then stretched her right arm above her head and arched left, sliding her left palm down her quadriceps and baring the ivory skin between her hip bones and rib cage. She repeated the motion to the right and a lump formed in his throat. He stabbed a hand through his hair, then checked his watch. Three hours to kill before he went on duty. And he couldn't spend it here watching her. Not if he wanted to stay sane. But where else could he go? He was supposed to wait until Quincey rolled up its sidewalks before venturing out for night surveillance.

She bent forward, revealing the curve of her back. If circumstances had been different, he'd have relished the opportunity to trace the bumpy line of her spine with his fingertips, then his lips. But no collateral damage meant he had to leave the deputy untouched.

She rolled effortlessly into a handstand and balanced there, pointing her toes to the ceiling. It took strength and control to do that. Her legs parted slowly, lowering until they were parallel to the floor. Like a snake charmer's *pungi* did to a cobra, her smooth movements mesmerized Sam. Watching June work out was more arousing than the erotic dancers that his buddies had dragged him to see for his thirtieth birthday. Those overtly sexual women had done nothing for him, whereas June's unconscious sensuality lit all kinds of fires that needed to be extinguished.

He closed his eyes and emptied his lungs, fighting to slow his heart and respiratory rates the way he did before taking a tricky long-range shot. The tried-and-true tactic failed to decrease the hunger clawing inside him. When he opened his eyes again, June was gone. Relief and disappointment warred within him.

Determined to remove himself before temptation returned, he drained his glass and stood...discovering she hadn't left after all. She'd shifted to a plank position on the floor, toes and elbows on the mat, spine and legs straight, without even a tremor. An image of him stretched out beneath her hit him like a flash bomb and his pulse reverberated wildly again. Need grabbed him by the balls.

Why her? Why did he have to be attracted to Miss Congeniality? Probably because besides her sunshiny personality, she shared the traits he admired most: honor, courage and commitment. She treated everyone they met with respect, whether deserved or not. And she never lost her temper—except with him. She'd yet to hesitate to wade into any situation they'd encountered, and she committed herself one hundred percent to every task.

He'd bet everything he owned that she wasn't a

crooked cop, and he would tell Roth that. One clear. Two to go.

June went through another series of slow, graceful moves, and he couldn't look away. Man, she was killing him. If she'd work out in her barn gym instead of in his face, he wouldn't be fighting this battle between his conscience and his desire. He was trying to do the right thing, trying to stay focused on the job. And he was failing. Miserably. Because she was undermining him at every turn. She had to know what she was doing to him. Had to.

Anger built inside Sam like in a pressure cooker. Some of it was aimed at the instigator, but the majority was self-directed. He'd been trained to control his response to stimuli, but with June he couldn't. And that made him feel as if he'd lost yet another skill that had defined him as a scout sniper.

Then she lifted her chin, looked straight at him and snapped a salute before turning her back and resuming her exercise.

How long had she known he was watching? Was she trying to provoke him? It was about time she learned that this marine didn't back down from a fight. He stalked out his front door and crossed no-man's-land to her porch, where he pounded out his frustration on the wooden door. Seconds later it opened.

June, wide-eyed, stared back. "What's wrong?"

"Close your damned curtains."

She flinched, making him realize he'd barked out

the command like a drill instructor. Then her expression turned rebellious. "Well, excuse me, but it's cooler outside than it is in the house and the breeze feels good. So, no, I'm not closing my curtains. Stop staring if you don't like what you see."

She knew damned well he liked what he saw. "Then put on some clothes, and quit flaunting your perfect body in my face."

He was being an ass. He knew it the minute the words left his mouth.

Her surprised gasp rent the air. "My body's far from perfect, Sam. But thank you."

The pink on her cheeks and sincerity in her eyes told him she wasn't fishing for compliments. She started to shut the door in his face. He blocked it with one hand. "Didn't the idiot from your past ever tell you how beautiful you are? Who was he?"

Her lashes fluttered. She swallowed, hesitated. "Someone from BLET, and he said what he needed to say to get what he wanted from me. I was gullible enough to take his bait and let him reel me in."

Trained with? She must have been twenty-one or two. A kid. The pain in her eyes shredded him. He fisted his hands against the need to reach for her. He'd made that mistake once already.

"Somebody needs to shoot the bastard."

Her lips twisted in a wry smile and humor sparked in her eyes. "Madison and Piper have already volunteered, but trust me, he's not worth the legal hassle." Then she ducked her head and plucked at a piece of lint on her spandex shorts, drawing his attention back to her incredible body. "These are my regular workout clothes. You've seen them before, and I know you've worked out with women who wear similar gear."

He had, but they hadn't affected him the way she did. "June, I'm trying to be smart about this attraction between us. But I need you to do your part. Close your curtains, put on more clothes or exercise when I'm not here. I don't care. Just quit tempting me with something I can't have."

Her surprised gaze found his. Then a bead of sweat trickling between her breasts snared his attention and dragged it downward. The fabric of her bra sucked up the moisture and his tongue curled in disappointment over missing it.

"Sam...what if I decided to take you up on your offer?"

Hoping he'd misheard her hoarse whisper, he zeroed in on her face. "What offer?"

She pushed back her hair with a shaky hand, then crossed her arms and shifted on her feet. "No strings. Just sex. Like you said. At the picnic."

His heart slammed his rib cage. His knees locked. But the fuse in his pants had been lit. He couldn't tell her how badly he wanted to accept.

"I've told you. That wasn't an offer. It was a warning. I'm not marriage material, and judging by the number of weddings you've danced at and the toy box on your porch, you are definitely somebody's bride-to-be."

"I do want to get married one day and have children, but I'm not ready for either of those now. I have things to do first."

Not what he wanted to hear. Temptation gripped him. "You're better off with a dating site."

"I'm not going to pay to play dating roulette, and I'm not the type to pick up strangers in a bar. You and I…we're both in the same boat. Single, available and alone. There are no decent prospects for… companionship in Quincey."

She made it sound feasible, but for her sake, he had to find a reason to say no. "We work together."

"That was my first thought, too. But correct me if I'm wrong. You won't be here long."

Alarm stiffened his muscles. "Why do you say that?"

"Because you haven't unpacked your car or opened a bank account."

Damn, she was observant. "I've been here less than two weeks."

She leveled the kind of look on him that his mother had employed to get Sam to confess all as a boy. "You need more excitement and responsibility than Quincey can offer. Once your eye heals, you'll be gone. If not before. It was nice of Roth to help you make the transition, but we both know you won't stay."

"I never said that."

"You didn't have to. I've studied your body language and behavior. You're trying very hard not to assimilate into Quincey or bond with our people."

She was too smart for her own good. Something else to admire. "June—"

"If we did…this, we would have to be really, *really* discreet. My dad could never find out. And that means *no one* can find out, because he has a way of getting people to confess all kinds of things they shouldn't."

Do the Right Thing wasn't just a Marines motto. It was Sam's personal code. That meant refusing her proposal no matter how much he wanted to carry June down the hall to her bedroom and kiss her until she couldn't talk, then explore every fit, taut, smooth inch of her.

But he shouldn't. Couldn't. Wouldn't.

"I'm not the man for you."

Mortification filled her face before she averted her gaze. "Okay. Fine. Forget I said anything. Good night. I'm sorry if I made you…uncomfortable."

Aw, hell. He'd hurt her. Remorse parked on his chest like a tank. She pushed on the door. He blocked it open with his foot. "I don't know what my future holds. Not even a clue."

Her flush deepened. "I said forget it, Rivers. Now go. Please. Leave me with a little pride, and let me pretend I didn't just make a fool of myself." She pushed the panel again, but when he held his position, she threw up her hands and retreated inside. A smart man would let her go.

Apparently, Sam wasn't as smart as his CO had claimed. A litany of swear words ricocheted through his brain as he followed June inside and closed the door. Determined to make her understand he was refusing for her own good, he grabbed her by the arm. She froze, her backbone going Parris Island straight.

The warmth of her skin and the firmness of her bunched biceps penetrated his palm, then traveled up and doglegged south to settle heavily in his groin. "June, let me explain."

She angled a hesitant, wounded gaze over her shoulder. "I'm mature enough to take no for an answer, Rivers. But it's time you left."

The cool and clearly false bravado in her tone only made him feel worse. Damn, she was tough. She could have begged, cried, thrown a tantrum or stomped to her bedroom and slammed the door. He would have expected and known how to handle any of those reactions. Instead, she acted with dignity.

If he walked out he would hurt her, and that could put a strain on their working relationship, possibly impeding their investigation. Ditto if he stayed.

This was one firefight he wouldn't win no matter what he did.

A GIRL COULD take only so much humiliation in one day. June opened her mouth to repeat her request that Sam go, but something in his alert eyes and stance stole the words.

"We both know I should leave. But if I do, this'll be the only thing either of us can think about whenever we're together." He paused, a nerve twitching above his lip. "Are you one hundred percent certain you can handle a short-term, no-commitment relationship?"

Her heart jumped to her throat. Confusion tumbled through her. "What are you saying, Sam?"

His grip tightened on her arm, then relaxed. He stroked the tender inside of her biceps with a callused thumb and goose bumps chased across her skin.

"I miss the corps, the camaraderie, the sense of purpose in every day and every mission. My goal is to heal, prove the doctors wrong and re-up. Fallback plan is to get a civilian contractor job on base—any base. Either way, I'm outta here. Alone. No wife. No fiancée. No girlfriend sitting by the phone waiting for news. Can you handle that?"

A bolus of adrenaline, excitement and arousal raced through her veins, making her skin tingle. "I can handle a temporary arrangement."

He searched her face and feathered his fingertips ever so slowly down to her wrist. "Do you have protection?"

They were really going to do this.

She strove for composure, but the slow circles he drew on her skin made it difficult to think. Could he feel the frantic, dizzying flutter of her pulse? If he realized how inexperienced she was and how big a step this was for her, would he back out? Probably. Best to keep that to herself.

"I'm on the pill for a woman thing. Other than that, I'm healthy. I've been tested periodically since my last relationship."

"I'm clean, too."

Sam's calm, logical approach was the complete opposite of Peter's calculated seduction of wine and insincere flattery. Even though she was older and wiser now, her reactions were exponentially stronger. Sam had an effect on her that she couldn't explain and didn't understand.

He stepped closer. She met him halfway. The tips of her breasts grazed his chest and the impact zapped her like static electricity. She jumped. Her nipples immediately tightened and ached for his touch.

"Easy." He skimmed his fingertips up the outsides of her arms with knee-weakening effect, outlining the curve of her elbows, her shoulders, her collarbone, the underside of her jaw, then the shells of her ears before delving through her hair and removing the band holding her ponytail.

A shiver rippled through her and heat coalesced in her belly. She tilted back her head, inviting his kiss. She needed him to end this crazy anticipation, but instead he skimmed his thumbs across her cheekbones and massaged her nape slowly, deliberately, all the while watching and gauging her responses.

If not for the pulse beating every bit as fast as hers at the base of his neck, she'd think him unaffected. What was he waiting for? Did he think she'd change her mind?

Determined to rattle his composure as much as he had hers, she wedged her hands into the narrow gap between their torsos and walked her fingertips upward from his waist. His abdominal muscles rippled beneath her touch and when she reached the indention below his pectorals, he sucked a quick sharp breath.

Emboldened by his reaction, she outlined the crease from inside to out, then back again, enjoying the bunch and release of his jaw muscles. Tiny beads appeared beneath his thin cotton shirt. He pressed his palms against her nape and tipped up her jaw with his thumbs. How had she ever thought his eyes cold? They burned with need now—need for her.

"You're playing with fire. But you know that. Don't you?"

"Am I?" She brushed her thumbs across the hard points. His chest expanded, his lips parted and his exhalation fanned her face. But still, no kiss. Hunger amplified her impatience. What was it going to take to break his control?

She smoothed her palms across his pectorals, then over his collarbone. Next she traced the rigid tendons up the sides of his neck, relishing the suppleness of his skin and the velvetiness of his freshly shaved jaw. Then she moved on to the bristly sides of his close-cropped hair until her stance mirrored his. She cupped his face and lifted her lips toward his. Still nothing…nothing except the stamp of desire on his face that made her blood simmer.

He skimmed his hands down her back. The brand of his palms on her bare waist passed so quickly she barely had time to register it before he cupped her bottom. She felt every long, hot finger pressing into her flesh through the thin spandex. Then he pulled her forward until she was molded against him from her knees to her breasts. And yet no kiss.

His restraint would have been admirable any other time, but right now she wanted—desperately *needed*—what he withheld. Then she identified that spark in his eyes as one of challenge. *He* wasn't going to kiss *her*. If she wanted his mouth, she was going to have to take it.

She'd never been the aggressor in a sexual relationship. Was she bold enough to demand what she wanted? Staring into his passion-darkened eyes, she decided for him she could be. Before her courage could waiver, she pulled down on his head and rose up on her toes simultaneously. Their mouths collided.

Sam instantly swept her into his arms, crushing her against his solid flesh and devouring her mouth in a fusion of soft lips and a tangle of slick tongues.

Her stomach swooped as if she'd stepped out of an airplane for a parachute jump.

With his hands firmly planted at her waist, Sam backed her down the hall. Ten heart-pounding steps. He'd let her take the lead earlier in this encounter, but there was no mistaking who was in charge now. The kiss she'd waited so long for went on and on until she broke away to gasp for breath. Her bedroom was dark. The den lights didn't reach this far, and she couldn't see his face. She had to depend on the quick rasps of his breath, the burning heat of his palms to gauge his level of arousal.

Two more steps and they reached the side of her bed. He tunneled his thumbs beneath the elastic of her sports bra and swept the garment over her head in one swift maneuver, then peeled off her exercise shorts with the same efficiency. She had no reason to be self-conscious in the dark room. Then he flicked on the bedside lamp.

She winced at the unexpected brightness and tried not to feel exposed. But she was naked and he wasn't. He stared into her eyes. Then his gaze slowly roved down. Big hands spanned her waist, and the heat of his touch spread through her. Using his thumbs, he stroked lines parallel to her navel. Up to her rib cage. Down to her bikini line. Her stomach muscles spasmed. Then he grazed upward to cup her breasts and tease the taut tips. The sensation was so intense her knees nearly buckled. Her eyes drifted closed and her lips parted to draw in much-needed air. Then he stopped. She whimpered in disappointment.

With effort, she lifted her heavy eyelids. Sam studied her as if he were planning an invasion and she were his topographical map. Then he reached for the hem of his T-shirt, bunched it in his fists and ripped it over his head.

His chest was a work of art with a few small scars scattered across the golden-brown surface. And then he waited, arms by his sides, hands opening and closing. She got it. Finally. Her turn. He'd lobbed control back into her court. Okay, she could play that game.

She was eager to touch him and couldn't resist repeating the torture he'd inflicted on her. Beginning at his wrists, she circled over the paler skin, then drifted upward, savoring the tickle of springy hair on his forearms, the firm curve of his bulging biceps and the strength of his broad shoulders.

She dragged a fingertip across his lips, testing his warmth and suppleness. He caught her hand and sucked her finger into his mouth. His tongue swirled over the sensitive pad and she felt both the pull and the caress deep in her womb.

Then he released her. She floated her fingertips down his chest, over each bump and slope, and slipped them into the waistband of his low-riding jeans. The hiss of his breath and the impressive ridge behind his fly did wonders for her ego. He wanted her as much as she wanted him. Ignoring the obvious next step of lowering his zipper, she lightly scraped her nails outward to his hip bones, then in again, delving a little deeper on the return trip, deep enough to feel his wiry curls. Only when he shuddered did she find the courage to stroke the distended fabric.

Sam's head fell back. A groan rumbled from deep in his chest. He covered her hand with his, stilling the caress and pressing her against his erection. The depth of her hunger shocked her. She'd never wanted to tear a man's clothes off before. But she did now. Urgently. She fumbled with the brass button and zipper until they gave way, then shoved at Sam's pants. He helped her get them over his thick arousal. The tip glistened. She gulped. Peter hadn't been half as endowed.

Sam sat on the bed and pulled her between his splayed legs, capturing a nipple with his mouth. Her reservations vaporized at the first sip from his lips. He suckled one sensitive tip, then the other, alternating his mouth and his hands until she trembled and dug her toes into the carpet. Then he sat back and bent to unlace his boots. Her damp skin chilled. She couldn't wait. Dropping to her knees, she tackled his other boot and seconds later his feet were bare. He rose and shucked his jeans.

She should have helped, but she could only stare. Sam had the kind of body she'd seen only on magazine and book covers. Hard. Muscled. Carved. Long legs. Tight butt. And he was hers to touch and taste. Hers for now.

Then he yanked her forward. His hot skin melded to hers and all she wanted was to satisfy the gnawing ache in her belly. He lifted her as if she weighed no more than her pillow and laid her in the middle of the bed. Then he stretched out beside her. He radiated heat like nothing she'd experienced before. She couldn't get close enough to him.

He lifted one hand and cupped her knee, then stroked the crease in the back and desire raced through her. He drew a line up the inside of her thighs and she quivered in anticipation, but he only outlined the triangle of her curls, then the circle of her navel, the curves of one rib and breast, then the other. First with his fingertips, then with his palms, he mapped her body, never lingering in one place any longer than it took to rake up a crop of goose bumps.

Tension built in her womb. She scissored her legs, trying to ease the need. When that failed, she rolled on her side to face him. He kissed her, long and slow, while his hands played over her back, her waist, her bottom.

Too keyed up to just lie there, she mimicked his caresses until his breathing was as choppy as hers. Then he pushed her onto her back and rose above her. She hooked her legs around his and lifted her hips, but instead of filling her, he kissed and laved a trail from her jaw down her sternum to her belly.

He cupped her bottom as his tongue swirled in her navel, then descended. Surprised and unsure, she clenched her muscles. She'd read about this, heard about this, but had never had it done to her.

Warm breath fanned her skin a split second before the hot wash of Sam's tongue found her center. His rapid flicks hit her most sensitive spot with just the right pressure, and desire blossomed inside her like a morning glory unfurling for the sun. Her release hit hard and fast, before she was ready and with more force than she could handle. She jackknifed again and again as her muscles contracted with each wave of sensation. When her orgasm ended, she fell back on the mattress, stunned, breathless, limp. Sam planted a damp kiss on her pelvis, then rose above her.

Her conscience kicked in. He'd pleasured her, but she'd done nothing for him. She bowed up to kiss his puckered nipple and wrapped her fingers around his shaft. She stroked him, once, twice, savoring his breadth and length. He whistled through his teeth, then covered her hand with his, stopping her.

"Next time. Right now I need to be inside you."

He positioned his thick, glistening head at her core, then slid home, stretching her, filling her. It had been years since she'd taken a man into her body and Sam felt so good, so right, so perfect. When he withdrew, she dug her nails into his buttocks and pulled him back in. He picked up his tempo. Each thrust hit her sensitized flesh and increasingly aroused her until she felt the pressure of another climax building inside her. Surprised, she looked up into his face and found him watching her—watching her pleasure mount. He kept his eyes locked on hers until she teetered on the edge.

"That's it, June. Let go."

The rough low rumble of his voice lifted her even higher. She teetered there, then tumbled over, whispering his name in release.

Before the last quake rocked her, Sam grasped her hips, thrust deeper, harder, then groaned, and it was her turn to watch his face contorting as he found satisfaction. For several moments he stayed stiff-armed above her, panting as rapidly as she. Then he eased down beside her.

June snuggled into his arms, finding a place for herself against his shoulder. Wow. Wow. *Wow* was all she could think. And then it hit her. This was exactly where she wanted to be and who she wanted to be with.

She didn't just have a case of hero worship for Sam Rivers. She was falling in love with him. And he was determined to leave. Quincey. And her.

Unless she could change his mind.

CHAPTER ELEVEN

THE BACK OF Sam's neck prickled a warning. He'd learned two very important things in the past ten minutes. June didn't have a lot of sexual experience, and he had to get out of here before he succumbed to the overwhelming urge to fall asleep beside her. Even if he hadn't had to work, he wasn't a spend-the-night kind of guy. Nights and weekends with a woman only gave her false expectations.

He eased his arm out from under June's warm body, swung his legs over the side of the bed and levered into an upright position. Deep muscle lethargy fought him every inch of the way. He could barely keep his eyes open as he reached for his pants. Not even the chill of the room on his sweat-dampened skin revived him. Man, what had she done to him?

The mattress shifted behind him as he stuffed his legs into his pants, rose and zipped. He glanced over his shoulder to judge June's emotional state. With wary green eyes fixed on him, she sat up and pulled the sheet over her perfect breasts. "You're leaving?"

"Night shift."

"Oh…yeah."

He could almost hear that damnable voice from his GPS saying, "Recalculating."

Had he made a mistake? Had he been wrong to think he could keep this strictly physical? Or that she could? Would sex compromise his investigation of her and the rest of Quincey's deputies?

But she's innocent.

You think, his brain countered. *You have no proof either way.*

"Want me to come with you?"

"No. Get some sleep." He needed space to figure out if this was a disaster. He'd betrayed Roth's trust. That much was guaranteed. Would there be any other fallout? He reached for his boot.

"Will *you* call for backup if you see anything unusual?"

She was really good at throwing his words back at him. "I'm used to working solo."

"Want to be buzzard bait?"

Damn, she was good. He cut her a derisive look. Mistake. She'd tossed back her cover and stood on her side of the bed. Every naked, mouthwatering, overprotective, defiant inch of her called him back to the mattress. *She deserves more than ten minutes.* He checked his watch. He had an hour to repeat the whole process in slow motion and linger over the hills and valleys he'd missed.

But he couldn't, not until he analyzed the situation.

She shrugged on a robe, covering up the buffet he

craved and allowing him to return his focus to the mission—where it belonged. But he couldn't help wondering what kind of selfish bastards her previous lovers had been that oral sex had shocked her into stiffening up. He shoved that question aside. He'd ask later. When he had time for follow-up. And a hands-on demonstration.

And just like that he knew that even though tonight hadn't been his smartest maneuver, he'd be back. The attraction was too strong and his release had been too powerful to ignore.

She looked at him expectantly. He retrieved her question from the mud she'd made of his brain. "I'll call for backup if I foresee a problem."

"Thank you."

He opened his mouth to tell her not to make more of this than it was, but she held up a silencing hand.

"Don't take it personally, Rivers. When we're a deputy short, we all have to put in extra hours. It's been an exhausting few months since one of our own was arrested. I want you around long enough to shoulder your share of the load—at least until Roth can hire and train your replacement."

The woman knew how to deflate an ego. He could have used her in dealing with a few of the shavetails—kids a decade younger with no deployments under their belts who thought they knew everything. "Right."

He stuffed his foot into his second boot, laced

and tied it, then reached for his shirt. "What did you do between high school and the police academy?"

She blinked at his out-of-the-blue question; as well she should have. What did it matter? But the thought had been nagging him. There wasn't a surplus of jobs in Quincey, and she was too smart to sit on her butt. And she was a giver, not a taker—he couldn't imagine her sponging off her asshole of a father.

"I earned my associate's degree in criminal justice at the community college."

Something else to admire about her. She was dedicated to her career. Same as him. "So you could work anywhere."

"Yes, but I want to work in Quincey. Have you ever thought about going to college, Sam? The GI Bill would cover tuition and living expenses, wouldn't it? If you needed to start over, I mean?"

He didn't want to think about starting over, but Tate had opened that nasty can of worms. Suppose he was allowed to re-up and finish out his years of service without another sniper taking him out. What would he do when he retired? He still wouldn't be qualified for anything else.

"I haven't thought about it."

"You should. The world's wide-open for you right now."

Open? Hell, no. A rockslide had blocked his only path. He had to move those rocks. But that wasn't a discussion for tonight. "I need to shower and get into uniform."

She nodded, hugged her arms around her waist and marched down the hall to her front door. She opened it a crack, scanned the yard, then looked back at him. "Be careful. And remember, this stays between you and me. I don't need Madison, Roth or anyone else knowing we made… Knowing what happened."

The comment slid under his skin like a long splinter. Why did it bother him when she was only restating their agreement? "Copy that."

The urge to hook his hand behind her neck and kiss her till her knees shook hit him like recoil from a .50-cal. He resisted. "Get some sleep, Jones. See you in the morning."

He made his escape before he changed his mind. But damn, leaving was hard.

SAM HIT THE BRAKES, then reversed the cruiser. Even with the GPS coordinates Roth had texted, he'd driven past the barely discernible pine needle–covered path Roth had designated for a rendezvous point. Sam eased through the gap between trees and rolled down the bumpy trail.

A hint of sunrise pinked the sky with the promise of another temperate day. Good day for a hike. Maybe after he logged some shut-eye. A half mile in, Roth's personal vehicle sat off to the side, concealed by a bend until Sam was almost on top of it.

Roth, out of uniform, sat on his open tailgate. The bed of the truck was loaded down with fishing gear.

Sam parked behind him, climbed out and joined him. "G'morning."

Roth nodded, then pulled a bottle of water and a wax paper–wrapped item from a cooler.

"What's this?"

"Breakfast. Best pork tenderloin biscuit you'll ever eat. But I didn't bring coffee, since you need sleep."

"Thanks." Sam accepted his loot and took a big bite. The flaky bread and tender, juicy meat were delicious—and not just because he hadn't eaten in six hours. Quincey didn't have any twenty-four-hour stores where you could drop in and grab a bite, and he'd consumed the sandwiches he'd made midshift. He hadn't dared swing by his house, because he hadn't been sure he'd be able to resist dropping in on June.

"See anything last night?" Roth asked.

June naked, flushed and panting from her orgasms. The image Sam's brain had replayed too many times last night returned like a flash bomb and heat ignited in his gut. Remorse quickly followed. He'd broken protocol. Neither he nor Roth had ever compromised a mission by getting blown off course by libido.

He shook his head. "Quincey was locked up tight."

"Damn it. I want these thieves caught."

"You know as well as I do that the best campaigns can take weeks or months of stalking before execution."

"We can't continue overnight details that long without Morris and Aycock noticing. Once they do, they'll ask questions. The more people who know we're looking, the more likely we'll lose the element of surprise. And if my deputies are involved, we might never catch our perps in the act."

"Copy that."

"Find anything on my deputies not related to this case?"

Adrenaline spiked in Sam's bloodstream. He'd discovered a lot about June, but nothing that belonged in his report. "I haven't seen anything suspicious. Morris is a momma's boy but seems okay. Aycock's a struggling single father. Sure, he could use the money, but I don't see where he's getting any extra or spending it."

"And June?"

His heart stalled. "No unusual trips out of town or off-hour visitors." Other than him.

Roth nodded. "Keep looking. But first go home and get some sleep. I'll see you tonight."

"Tonight?"

"At June's birthday party."

She hadn't mentioned it. "It's her birthday?"

"I think the actual day is Sunday, but the party's a surprise, so they're holding it early. Piper was supposed to tell you."

"I haven't seen or heard from your wife since the cookout."

"She and her mother have been cooking up a storm. Every flat surface of my house is covered with food I'm not allowed to sample. Party's going to be in the church fellowship hall. Eighteen hundred hours. Whole town will probably show up. Like I said, it's a surprise. Don't let on."

"Good opportunity to see who's uncomfortable around law enforcement or who doesn't show that should have."

"Good point. Park around back, or hike in and I'll see you get a ride home before I take the night shift."

"Roger."

"And just for future reference, down that path is the best fishing spot on this side of the river. That's where I'm headed."

"Good to know."

"June showed it to Josh. My son was smart enough to bring his ol' man." The grin on Roth's face revealed how happy he was with his ready-made family. Sam would never have predicted that. Hell, he'd have bet a month's salary against it.

"You want to hang around and fish for an hour or two to wind down? I brought an extra rod. Catfish are big down there."

"Nah. But thanks. I'm ready to call it a night." Not that he was tired. He headed for his vehicle and checked his watch. If he hustled, he might catch June before she left for work.

EXCITEMENT BUILT AS June turned into the church driveway. She couldn't keep the smile off her face. Her mother had called. Sure, it was to ask for help setting up tables for a church ladies' luncheon tomorrow, but her mother hadn't initiated anything between them since June's return from Raleigh.

One of the double vestibule-entrance doors opened. Her mother stuck her head out and waved. Surprised, June turned the wheel and parked in the front of the church rather than around back by the door they usually used. Eager to see her mom, she jumped from the cab and jogged up the sidewalk.

Then June noticed her mother was wearing makeup…and nice clothes, and her feet slowed. June had dressed for manual labor in old jeans, a T-shirt that had seen better days and sneakers.

"Hi, Mom. You look nice. We're not going out for dinner, are we? I mean, I'd love to. We haven't had a girls' night out in years. But I didn't dress for it. I can run home and change."

"Oh. No. Come in."

June wrapped her arms around her mother and hugged her tight, and when her mom hugged back, June held on for a few extra seconds. "Thank you for calling. I've missed you."

"I've missed you, too, honey. But—" her mom averted her face and fussed with her hair "—I've been really busy getting ready for school. The first few weeks of September are always hectic."

"Are you okay? You seem uneasy."

"Oh, no. I'm fine. Come on to the back."

The vestibule was cool and mostly dark. The only light came through the stained glass arch above the door. "You sure you don't want to skip out and grab a bite before we get started?"

"No. I have others coming to help. I can't make them wait."

So much for one-on-one time. She tried to mask her disappointment and followed her mother down the center aisle. "Okay."

June had grown up in this church, but she had never run down the wide burgundy carpet or played in the pews. No matter how badly she'd wanted to jump from one colorful puddle created by the windows to another as a child, that would have been grounds for punishment. June had been the rule follower of the Jones clan right up until she left Quincey.

They reached the rear doors and her shoes squeaked down the linoleum hall. Out of habit she automatically tried to silence her rubber soles. The door to the fellowship hall was closed. That was odd. It was never closed unless someone was holding a meeting or a Bible-study class.

"I'd like for us to go out sometime—without Dad."

"I don't know, June. I don't like to upset him."

"Having lunch with your daughter shouldn't upset him. It's not like we'd go to a bar. Just enjoy a meal you didn't have to prepare. We could even bring him back something."

"I'll think about it and get back to you."

Her mother seemed agitated. "I didn't mean to worry you."

She paused with her hand on the doorknob. "You haven't, dear. I love you and I appreciate your invitation. Maybe when he goes on his next mission trip in a few months…"

Then she pushed open the door.

"Surprise!" screamed a chorus of voices, startling June. Then the group launched into "Happy Birthday." Her gaze scanned over the packed room of smiling faces and landed on Sam. He stood at the back of the room off to the side. Her stomach swooped. She hadn't seen him since last night. Their gazes locked and held. At the distance of fifty feet, she couldn't make out the expression in his eyes. He lifted his plastic cup and dipped his head. Instantly, the feel, smell and taste of him came rushing back and arousal flushed through her.

She averted her gaze and looked straight into her father's disapproving face. His condemnation came through loud and clear. Despite that, or maybe to spite it, she forced a smile and waved to the gathering.

She was a tangle of emotions. First, she was disappointed that her mother hadn't actually wanted her company. Second, she was touched that the community cared so much for her to have gone to all this trouble. The room was decorated to the nth degree. And last, she was both excited and apprehensive about facing Sam in front of the people who knew her best. This would be a true test of their ability to hide their relationship.

"Forgive my subterfuge," her mother said when the song wound down. "But I wanted you to have this moment to know how special you are to so many people."

June pulled it together and did her best to cover her nerves. "No problem, Mom. It's a nice surprise." Then she turned to the crowd of friends, neighbors and even her siblings. "I had no idea what y'all were up to. Thank you for coming and for thinking of me."

She let herself be swallowed up by well-wishers, but there was only one person here tonight she wanted to talk to. And he was the very one she couldn't speak to with her father and the eyes of Quincey on her.

JUNE DIDN'T GET a minute to catch her breath until almost two hours later when the party began to wind down. She glanced around the room and spotted Sam cornered by four teenage boys. They seemed to be hanging on his every word, and he looked relaxed and comfortable talking to them.

"The new deputy is a hunk," Kelley, her sister, said. "And he's good with kids."

"Appears to be."

"Is he single?"

"Yes."

"You two have been circling each other all night. He's probably the only one in the room who hasn't wished you a happy birthday."

True. June hadn't realized that in trying not to show preference to him, she'd made her avoidance of him obvious, but if her usually obtuse-to-subtleties sister had noticed, then who else had? She hoped the burn in her face wasn't a blush. "You're barking up the wrong tree."

"Seriously? What a waste. I can't believe you work with *that* and haven't even considered—"

She needed a diversion. Fast. "Where did Uncle John go?"

Kelley groaned. "He probably cornered someone and is forcing them to listen to his war stories. Why?"

"I need to talk to him."

"About what?"

"You don't have to be apprised of every detail of my life, you know." She said it in a joking tone but with a core of truth.

"Yes, I do. I'm the oldest. The oldest must know all." Kelley said it tongue in cheek, but unfortunately, June knew from experience that Kelley took nosiness to an art form.

"Uncle John is ex-military and so is Sam."

"Sam. That's Handsome's name?"

"You're married. You don't get to look."

"Honey, I'm breathing. I can still look! Don't worry—there's no 'lust in my heart,' as our dear daddy says. You don't have to get territorial."

"I'm not territorial, and please don't joke like that around Dad."

"Still hasn't forgiven you, huh?"

"No."

"You should've stayed in Raleigh. Why come back to his criticism?"

"He just holds us to a higher standard. That's all."

"He's overbearing and hypercritical. I practically needed wings and a halo when I lived here."

True. "And you did everything you could to prove you didn't have them. But Mom needs someone nearby since you all bailed."

"Only after you showed us that God wouldn't strike us dead for leaving Quincey and Dad's domain. I have to hand it to you, you were a brave little pioneer to be the first to strike out for new territory and risk his wrath."

"I wanted to be a cop and I couldn't do that here back then. Excuse me, Kelley. I really want to find Uncle John and introduce him to Sam."

"I'll tag along and you can introduce me to the new deputy, too."

Great. "Don't match-make. I already have one friend doing that and it's embarrassing. And don't tell stories about when we were kids."

Her sister just laughed. "You don't want him to know that you were our supreme manager?"

"No."

"There's a lot of Dad in you."

"Please don't say that."

"Not the bad parts, but you're very good with people. You know, motivating them and getting them to do things. Your way, of course."

"Are you done?" June hit her with a hard stare. Then, after Kelley nodded, June located her godfather talking to someone with a glassy-eyed I've-heard-too-much expression. Uncle John was interesting, but his passion for his job sometimes made him a bit…long-winded.

"Uncle John, can I steal you away to meet another veteran?"

She hoped he missed the grateful look she received from his captive.

"Anything for the birthday girl." He made his excuses, then followed June across the room.

"Sam's just left the Marines on medical discharge. He hasn't come to terms with the career change yet, and if anyone can understand that, you can. I thought you could try to convince him there's life after service and maybe tell him about your JROTC program."

"Yes, missy, I'd be happy to do that."

Her two favorite men in the world were going to meet, and maybe Uncle John could offer Sam some guidance and help him find his way…even if that took him away from Quincey. And June.

ONCE THE BOYS SCATTERED, Sam took a quick survey. There had been close to a hundred people here tonight. They were down to a couple dozen now. June was definitely Quincey's sweetheart, and if he hurt her, he'd be a hunted man. Not the first time. But it would be the first in a noncombat situation.

For most of the night, he'd hung back, talking to Roth and studying the crowd. And June. He'd been on the receiving end of too many drop-dead stares from her father to count. He didn't give a rat's ass if the man didn't like him, but June probably did. So Sam had played nice instead of confronting the preacher and asking who had shoved the stick up his ass. When he wasn't glaring at Sam or beaming insincerely at one of the other guests, the man scowled at his own daughter. Not for the first time Sam wondered what June could have done to get on her daddy's dark side. His other children avoided him, too. That said a lot about the man's winning personality.

Sam did a perimeter check and spotted June talking to an older guy. Sam pegged the sixty-something as ex-military by his parade-rest posture, high-and-tight cut and the knife-edge crease in his trousers. Then the guy turned his head and his direct stare landed square on Sam, confirming his guess. Probably a retired officer. The only question was, which branch? June led the man in Sam's direction. Sam had tagged the woman trailing them as one of June's older twin sisters. Her carbon copy had left ten minutes ago.

The trio stopped in front of him. Sam snapped to attention. "Sir."

"Sam, this is my sister Kelley and my godfather, John Page. Y'all, this is Sam Rivers, Quincey's newest deputy."

The old man smiled. "At ease, marine."

"Kelley has to say hello and goodbye quickly before she rounds up her kids and heads home. It's a long drive and Bradley and Hannah have school tomorrow."

The sister didn't look pleased by the brush-off. She offered Sam a limp handshake—nothing like her sister's firm grip. "Welcome to Quincey, Sam. It's a little stifling, but it does have some charms." She cut a look at June, who returned it deadpan. "Well, as June said, I must run." Then she left.

"First Civ Div is not a fun assignment," June's godfather said, clueing Sam in that June must have told him Sam was fresh out of the corps.

"No, sir."

"It's an adjustment. I hope you'll be happy with Quincey PD. Law enforcement wasn't for me. Similar to the service in rules and regs, but not an option for me since my ticker earned me a ticket out of the army and DQ'd me for police work. I teach the Junior Reserve Officers' Training Corps at Central High down in Charleston. Now, that's a job I'm going to miss—even more than the military. Those kids are a little smarter than most new recruits and a lot more eager to learn. Watching them acquire discipline is very rewarding."

"I'll bet it is. But you said you're going to miss it?"

"We've seen the world, compliments of Uncle Sam, but the missus tells me it's time to pack our bags and see some of the old US of A before we're too old."

"Sounds like a good plan, sir."

"I'll be at it until this June, but come the end of the year I'll be checking out."

A commotion at the door diverted Sam's attention. June's younger brother came bustling in. He looked flushed and agitated as he scoped the room. Then he spotted June and beelined in their direction. He jerked to a halt beside them.

"You gotta do something. She's going to sign the papers," he said, without regard to who or what he was interrupting. Speaking of discipline, this kid could use some. "She had it last night. And she's determined to give it up."

June's distress was evident. "It?"

"A boy. She had a boy."

Sam was determined not to let June make an emotional decision she might regret. "June, some of your guests are headed for the door. Why don't you say goodbye to them? And keep your father occupied. I got this."

"But—"

"I need to talk to my sister," Rhett argued.

The little pissant had nerve. Sam calmed his temper and turned back to June's godfather. "Sir, I would love to talk to you another time. But please excuse us."

John looked from Sam to Rhett. "Son—"

"I have this, John," Sam insisted. "I'm up on all the details."

With concern in his eyes, John took one look at June's worried face, then nodded. He dug his wallet out of his pocket and handed Sam a business card. "I look forward to hearing from you. Call or stop by anytime. Here's where you can find me." He shook Sam's hand, then took June's.

"Let's go say your goodbyes, June." And he dragged her off. Sam doubted there was another person in this room who could get away with that, and June didn't look happy.

"Hey—" the brat called.

Sam stepped in front of Rhett, blocking him from following. "Buddy, your timing sucks. This is your sister's birthday party. You have no business dumping your crap on her here."

"What business is it of yours?"

Defiant little brat. "I'm making it my business because your sister is my coworker and my friend. Her job is very important to her, and you're asking her to compromise that dedication to clean up *your* mess. Be a man and stop making others bail you out."

"You don't know what you're talking about."

"Yes, I do. I'm the youngest of four. And everybody wants to 'help' the baby. But I learned about the time I started shaving that a real man doesn't dump his problems on a woman. My sisters and mother would smother and mother me to death if I let them. But I handle my own shit. And for the record, my mother was a single parent raising my three sisters. You don't know squat about the hell she went through if you're trying to put your sister in that position."

"But—"

"You have a decision to make. You. Not June. Either you become the father that little boy needs or you step aside and let someone else do it who can."

"But school—"

"Will always be there. Think of someone besides yourself for a change. Are you ready to be this boy's father 24/7/365, through snotty noses, dirty diapers, teething and puberty, or are you just being possessive because he's yours and you don't know how to share? And quit calling your son *it*, damn it. He's a person, not property."

The kid's argumentative expression faded. His Adam's apple bobbed on a gulp. "What would you do?"

"Doesn't matter what I'd do. This is about you.

I learned a long time ago not to let someone make my decisions when they don't have to live with the consequences of their advice."

Rhett glanced nervously toward the door. "Our dad would never accept a child born out of wedlock. He's a preacher, for God's sakes. But he's the most unforgiving, judgmental person I've ever met. 'Love the sinner but hate the sin,' he preaches. But he sure doesn't live that way. At least not for his kids."

That explained June's relationship with her father.

"Rhett, one day your dad will be gone. And his opinion won't matter. You'll have to live with this decision for the rest of your life. And so will your baby. Think about that."

He could almost hear the wheels turning in Rhett's head. Rusty, from lack of use, most likely. But he could also tell his words were sinking in.

"Go wish your sister happy birthday and get the hell out of here before you cause her more grief."

"Or what?" A touch of defiance returned, but Sam knew how to crush it like a bug.

"I'll have a word with your dad."

The kid paled. Rhett about-faced and did exactly as Sam had instructed. June shot him a confused, questioning glance when her brother left without incident.

"Later," he mouthed.

Ten minutes later the party had dwindled down to a handful and Sam had strategized a way to get some one-on-one time with June. No one would think twice about him hitching a ride home with her. They lived side by side. It made sense, and he knew Roth's car would be full because Madison had ridden to the party with the Sterling family. The beauty of it was, he would ask Madison for a ride, and she'd take care of the rest for him.

He couldn't stay too long at June's place tonight. He'd had insufficient sleep in the past forty-eight hours and needed to catch up. But June deserved more than ten or fifteen minutes. She deserved to have enough orgasms to make her legs too weak to support her. He'd make damned sure she got them before he went home for shut-eye.

His heart rate rose in anticipation of getting her alone. He couldn't wait any longer.

CHAPTER TWELVE

CURIOSITY WAS KILLING June by the time the last trash bag had been carried out. Her parents had left a few minutes ago, and Madison, Piper, Roth, Josh and Sam had gathered by the door.

"Do you mind giving Sam a ride home, June?" Madison asked. "I left my car at Piper and Roth's. I'm catching a ride to their house, and it'll take us a while to separate and wash all the containers."

Normally, June would offer to help. They'd gone to a lot of trouble for her. But tonight she hoped she had other plans. Anticipation hummed through her, quickening her breath, something she struggled to hide from her friends. "Sure. I'll lock up."

"Great. See y'all tomorrow." Then her friends were gone.

Madison wouldn't be there to see which cottage Sam went into tonight. June tried to hide her excitement when she lifted her gaze to Sam's.

"What did you say to Rhett? And how did you get rid of him without a scene? My baby brother loves drama."

"I'll tell you in the truck." He gestured for her to precede him.

They exited the back door and walked through the empty parking lot. The brightness of the cloudless, star-studded, almost-full-moon night sky kept her from reaching for his hand. If her parents' house hadn't been just across the lawn, would their strictly physical relationship have included public hand holding? Probably not. It certainly hadn't with Peter—a clue she'd missed.

Not something she wanted to think about right now.

She unlocked her truck and climbed in. Sam filled the passenger seat. "So?" she asked.

"Impatient, Jones?" The twinkle in his eyes tripped up her heart.

She started the engine and put the truck on the road. "Rhett came in whining and left...without asking for anything."

"I'll trade you that intel for a piece from you."

"What could you possibly want to know that I haven't already told you?"

"No prescreening my questions. That's the deal on the table. Yes or no?"

She sighed in frustration. "Okay."

"I told him either he wanted to be a full-time father or he didn't. This was his decision, not yours. He was the one who had to live with the consequences."

"That's it? That's all you had to say? I can't believe it. Rhett's usually more stubborn and selfish."

His grin tugged at her heartstrings like a fish on a line. "I might have mentioned that if he spoiled your birthday party, I'd have a word with your father about his situation."

"Might have?" She shook her head. "Good thinking. Gosh, I didn't even congratulate him on fatherhood."

"He may not choose to be a parent."

She let that sink in. Hadn't she already decided adoption was best for the baby? There were thousands of couples out there longing to have a child but unable to conceive. Yet if she ever faced an accidental pregnancy, would she have the strength and generosity to put the baby's welfare first? She wanted a baby one day, but with the hours she worked, could she be the parent a child deserved if she had to go it alone?

"Thanks for talking to him and averting disaster. If Dad had caught wind of the situation, the night would have turned out very differently. I don't know what to say. I'm not used to someone else handling my family dramas. You were a little high-handed."

"But effective. A good offense is the best defense."

She couldn't argue with that.

They rode in silence for a minute. She kept waiting for him to ask his question, but when he didn't, she started wondering if he was thinking about what she was thinking about—him coming into her house when they got home.

"Some high school boys asked me to speak on Career Day."

She sensed his reservations. "You said yes, didn't you?"

"They want me to talk about being a sniper. Do you think I should? My MO was assassination."

"Did you enjoy it?"

"Being a marine or eliminating the target?"

"The fact that you're smart enough to make the distinction tells me you should go. They need to know that the violence they see on TV, in movies and in video games isn't fun and games. It comes with a price." She glanced his way and caught him looking at her. "What?"

"You're pretty smart, too."

As compliments went, it wasn't the best or most effusive one she'd ever had. But it affected her more deeply than any had previously. "Thanks. You looked comfortable talking to those boys."

"Watching me tonight, Jones?"

She hoped he couldn't see her blush in the shadowed interior. "You're new to town. I was going to make introductions if needed. And…I was watching my dad, too. I would've interceded if he'd become a problem for you."

"If he does, I can handle him. And why wouldn't I be comfortable with the boys? They're only a few years younger than some of the privates I work with."

His sincerity only affirmed something she'd considered earlier tonight. "You definitely need to talk to Uncle John again. Maybe a JROTC instructor position is an option for you. I know they are few and far between, but you'd have the best of both worlds—structure and discipline of the corps but the freedom of a civilian."

His face went rigid with rejection. "I want to talk to your godfather, but only because he seems like an interesting guy and I had to cut him off tonight. Being employed on base is still priority number one. Don't start picturing me in suburbia."

A reminder that losing her heart wasn't part of their arrangement. "You've made your goal very clear and I respect that. But sometimes it pays to have a plan B."

He said nothing else for the remainder of their ride. They reached their driveway. She parked the truck beside her cottage and removed the keys. Her pulse quickened. Had she angered him by suggesting he consider he might not make it back into the military?

He turned in the bench seat to face her. "What did you do to piss off your father?"

Surprise snatched her breath. He'd found the one topic she didn't want to discuss. "That's your question?"

"He watched you like a hawk all night except for when he watched me."

Folding her hands in her lap, she sifted through what she wanted him to know, while trying to hide how badly he'd rattled her. She wasn't proud of the fact that she'd been an overly trusting simpleton. If Sam had any respect for her as a person or an officer, the full truth could kill it.

"I made a mistake. One he can't forgive," she hedged.

"You'll have to give me more than that, Jones. With the way everyone except him adores you, I can't believe you were the clichéd hell-raising preacher's daughter. Is this connected to the bad relationship you had during BLET?"

The truck's spacious cab suddenly felt airless, claustrophobic. She shoved open her door and headed for her porch and her favorite rocking chair. She'd rocked away a lot of worries in this seat. Sam took the one beside her and waited. A chorus of insects and frogs down by the creek filled the nighttime air.

She gripped the armrests and put the chair in motion. On this very porch her grandmother had said, "Any relationship not based on truth isn't one worth having." Her connection with Sam wasn't going to last, but he'd been honest with her about that from the beginning. The least she could do was show him the same courtesy.

"I fell in love with one of my instructors. I thought our relationship was leading to marriage. I would never have let it become intimate if I hadn't. But it turns out I was stupid and gullible. A few months after graduation he took me out to a very expensive dinner. I expected a proposal. Instead, he informed me his wife was coming home."

"Had they been separated?"

"Not in the way you mean. She was a university professor who'd been on sabbatical in Europe. Apparently, I was the only one at the academy who hadn't known about her. I resigned my position when I found out that my coworkers and fellow students had assumed I slept with him to guarantee I'd pass BLET and get a job with the department. I graduated near the top of my class and everyone thought I'd earned my high scores on my back.

"As for my father, he can't forgive the fact that I committed adultery, knowingly or not." There—she'd said it. She couldn't bear to look at Sam and see disgust on his face.

"Was the cheating bastard fired for fraternizing with a student?"

Surprised, she gaped at him. "I didn't report him. I ran home like a coward rather than face my humiliation. My second mistake was being honest with my father and expecting his forgiveness." She rocketed to her feet. "So if you want nothing more to do with me, I understand."

Sam rose slowly and stepped to her side. He cupped her cheek and tipped up her chin. "I've seen your skills with a punching bag and a pistol. You didn't need help to pass your exam. And you are one of the smartest women I know.

"You were young and trusting, June. That's

hardly a crime. Stop beating yourself up. Your instructor's the one who ought to be hung in the desert by his balls for taking advantage of a student and betraying his wife. And if your father is holding your inexperience against you, then he needs to hang right beside that asshole."

She hadn't expected his support and it touched her so deeply tears stung her eyes. She never cried. Rather than let Sam see the wetness in her eyes, she wound her arms around his middle, rose on her tiptoes and kissed him.

He returned the kiss for maybe fifteen seconds, then peeled her arms from around him and stepped back. Shadows covered his face. Had she screwed up? "I'm sorry, Sam. Did I—?"

"Unlock your door. Let's take this inside."

Sam knew her dirtiest secret and he hadn't rejected her. She fell a little deeper in love. Yes, she acknowledged. Love. This was more than a crush. More than hero worship. She was in deep.

And then an old cliché came to her. *It's not the falling that hurts. It's the sudden stop.*

A doozy of a heartbreak waited just around the bend. And there was nothing she could do to stop this speeding train.

SAM'S RIGHT ARM was numb. Instantly alert, he opened his eyes to pitch blackness. Where was he? A whisper of warm breath dusted his neck.

June's bed. His heart pounded in acknowledgment. He'd fallen asleep after accomplishing his mission to leave her satiated and limp. Problem was, he'd been just as satisfied and enervated. He'd planned to give her five minutes to fall asleep before making his escape. That idea had obviously fallen through, because he felt as if he'd slept a week.

His eyes adjusted and he realized his arm was numb because June had it pinned to the mattress with her head tucked against his shoulder. The heat of her naked body was tattooed to his side and she had one leg hooked over his.

In three minutes he could have her moaning the way she had hours ago. Arousal returned full force, eradicating any lingering drowsiness. Wasn't gonna happen. He had to get out of here before she got any ideas about this becoming permanent. Earlier tonight she'd hit him with that JROTC/suburbia job suggestion. Was she having second thoughts about their arrangement? If she was, he had to set her straight.

But damn, she felt good and smelled good, and the soft tickle of her hair on his nipple was—

Forget it, Rivers.

What time was it? He craned his head until he spotted her digital alarm clock—0300. Double shit. He'd been out four hours. How was he going to get out of here without waking her? Very carefully.

He eased up. Hard to do with a numb arm. Then he tilted her so that her head landed gently on his pillow. She mumbled something. He froze, waiting for her to quiet.

Where were his clothes? They'd tossed them off fast, starting in the den. Despite wanting to take it slow and easy with her tonight, the first time had been lightning fast and just as electric as the previous night. The second time, he'd gotten it right. Now his erection begged for round three. He ignored its call.

Her bedroom was full of shadows. He crept around until he located his boots, socks, which he usually tucked into his boots but hadn't last night, and his pants. He recalled her removing his shirt in the den somewhere.

Bundling everything in his arms, he set off in search of his shirt. He found it by the front door and got dressed. Sneaking out in the middle of the night wasn't his usual MO. He was frank about his comings and goings. But tonight he needed space to figure out how and why she got to him and why he had let himself relax enough to fall asleep in her bed.

Lack of sleep. That was all.

Sounded good, but the excuse fit like skivvies two sizes too small. He liked June. Respected her. Enjoyed her company. If circumstances had been different, then maybe he'd have considered a longer relationship. But he had nothing to offer her.

Fraternization within the department was forbidden. Even if he tried to make it work with her, one of them would have to find another job. QPD was her family. That left him out in the cold with no skills. He would not be a deadbeat who depended on a woman to pay his bills like his mother's first husband.

No, the situation with June, while enjoyable, was definitely short-term. He wanted back on base. And that meant leaving Quincey and her ASAP.

He paused by her door, watching her sleep, and debated climbing back beneath the rumpled sheets for a few minutes. No. It was better for both of them if he left.

JUNE LOWERED HER toothbrush and listened, trying to identify the humming sound that had snagged her attention, but the house was quiet. The buzz must have been a low-flying plane or helicopter. She finished brushing her teeth, shut off the water and heard it again. Nope. Definitely not an aircraft *or* her imagination.

She walked into her bedroom. Silence. Then she cruised through the kitchen and den. The front door was locked. Sam must have done that when he'd slipped out. She wasn't sure how long he'd stayed after making love to her. Surely, a man wouldn't spend that much time on a woman's pleasure if he didn't care about her. He'd fallen asleep thirty seconds afterward—she'd known from his deepening breaths and the weight of his muscles against her.

A happy bounce lightened her steps and a smile covered her face as she headed back to her bedroom for her uniform. Sam's sleep habits reminded her of her nephews'. The boys were wide-awake one minute, then practically comatose the next. He hadn't woken when she'd snuggled into his shoulder in lieu of her pillow. In fact, she didn't think he'd moved until he'd jerked awake before leaving.

Oh, yes, she'd awoken when he had, but she'd gathered from his stealthiness that he didn't want conversation. She'd listened to his every move, including him coming back to her bedroom door to stand and stare at her one last time. Her heart swelled. That had to mean something, didn't it? But she'd let him slip out without asking.

She pulled on her pants and heard the sound again. It hummed like a cell phone vibrating, but hers was on the nightstand, silent and still. Then she pinpointed the location—the other side of her bed. The side Sam had slept on. She padded around and picked up her discarded pillow. Sam's phone lay beneath it. The rectangular face glowed with an incoming call. She picked it up and it vibrated in her hand. She debated letting the call go to voice mail, but the icon on the screen indicated three missed calls. In her family, calling multiple times meant an emergency.

She slid the indicator. "Hello?"

June heard nothing for two heartbeats. "I'm looking for Sam Rivers. Did I dial the wrong number?"

A woman's voice. One who knew him well enough to call at 6:00 a.m. Her heart dropped to the pit of her stomach. She looked out the window. His car was gone. "No. He's not here right now. May I give him a message?"

"Who's this?"

She hesitated. But what if this was urgent? "June. I work with Sam in the Quincey Police Department. Can I relay a message?" she repeated.

"Quincey? Where's that?"

A frisson of unease skittered over her. "Who is this?"

"Erin. Sam's sister. What happened to the Marine Corps?"

Uh-oh. "Sam hasn't told you?"

"Told me what? He's okay, isn't he?"

She heard the alarm in the woman's voice and wished she could start the morning over and ignore the phone. "Yes. Sam's absolutely fine. I'll have him return your call, Erin."

"But—"

June disconnected and sank onto the mattress before she said anything else she shouldn't. The fizzy excited anticipation she'd awoken with over the prospect of seeing Sam at the office morphed into flat-out dread. Sam hadn't told his family about leaving the corps… She had a bad feeling that she'd just revealed information he didn't want shared. He would not be happy with her.

JUNE HEAVED A sigh of relief when she spotted Sam's Charger alone in the QPD parking lot. She would have preferred to return his phone at home, where she could have explained why she'd answered it and how she might have inadvertently let information slip. But at least no one else was at the station yet.

A flash of sunlight on chrome jerked her attention to the rearview mirror. The chief's cruiser was on her tail. So much for plan B. She'd have to concoct a plan C to return Sam's phone.

She joined her boss on the sidewalk and forced a cheerfulness she didn't feel. She hoped he couldn't tell how less than thrilled she was to see him. He hadn't shaved—he must have taken last night's shift. Maybe he wouldn't stay long.

"Good morning, sir."

Roth nodded his greeting and opened the door for her. She entered the building with him on her heels and a spare phone pressing against her hip. Sam looked up from his desk. His gaze collided with hers. Her breath caught and her nerves snarled under the deluge of emotions swamping her. Excitement over seeing him. Desire brought on by memories of last night. Trepidation over what she had to tell him. Disappointment that they wouldn't have a moment alone. And a…fondness for him that he wouldn't welcome.

He started to rise and opened his mouth to say something, then spotted Roth, sat back down and nodded. "Morning."

"You two are both in earlier than usual," Roth said.

"Better to compare notes on the thefts before the others arrive," Sam said. "See anything last night?"

"Nothing." Roth looked at June and hitched a hip on Mac's desk. "Did either of you notice any strange behavior at the party last night?"

"No," June and Sam answered simultaneously, and their eyes met.

"Jones, was anyone missing that you would've expected to show?"

She mentally ran through the guest list and shook her head. "No, sir. There were the true friends and family and the ones who always turn out for a free meal or some socialization. Same old crowd."

Roth's mouth curved down. "What did you learn yesterday?"

She didn't need to pull out her notebook to report. "I visited the remainder of the scrap yards. None has any record of the vehicles reported stolen."

The chief scowled. "How can trucks disappear? Could the perp have carried them over state lines?"

Sam tapped his pen on the desk. "Unlikely. The closest states that don't report to the National Motor

Vehicle Title Information System are Mississippi and Michigan. The costs to transport that far would almost negate the profit."

"If not that, then what?"

"A chop shop?" June offered. "The thief could be parting out pieces. Though taking a car apart seems like a lot of work and would require equipment, time and a building. There are professionals, and I use the term loosely, who can do that in minutes in metropolitan areas, but Quincey hardly qualifies, and our perp must be local considering their knowledge of the area and the vehicles. But we don't have any locals who've ever lived in a big city where they could acquire those…skills."

"Could one of the scrap yard owners be lying?" Sam speculated.

She looked into those silvery-blue eyes and instantly remembered how passionately he'd made love to her last night. She dampened her dry lips and his eyes tracked the movement of her tongue, nearly making her forget what she was going to say.

Blinking, she schooled her expression and looked at her boss. "The…um…owners I've questioned seem pretty straight up, and they're aware of the consequences if they get busted for noncompliance."

"Are you confident in your assessment?" Roth asked.

"Their body language leads me to believe they have nothing to hide. But I suppose there could be other employees who are less—" One of the phones in her pocket vibrated, reminding her she had something very important to hide from Roth. Was it her phone or Sam's? It didn't matter. She wasn't going to answer either now. "Less scrupulous."

Finally, Roth nodded. "That's probably our best bet. But if that's the case, we may have given our thief a heads-up by grilling the owners and managers. Be careful tonight. If we don't find something soon, as much as I'd prefer not to, we'll have to open the investigation up to the rest of the squad. We can't continue night shifts indefinitely without someone catching on. Jones, you have tonight's watch."

"Tomorrow's her birthday," Sam protested. Surprised, she looked at him, then caught Roth's narrowed gaze on him.

"When have you ever had your birthday off?" Roth questioned.

"I'll take tonight's shift," Sam insisted.

"No, Sam," June hastened to interject. "It's my turn. And I celebrated last night." She'd meant with the party, but with the way Sam's gaze sharpened on hers she realized he thought she meant their private fireworks after returning home. Adrenaline pulsed through her in warming waves.

Roth rose. "Rivers, you're riding shotgun with Aycock today. Jones, the night vision is in my car. I'll walk you out."

She struggled to conceal her dismay. How could she return Sam's phone without jeopardizing both of their jobs? And surely he'd missed his phone by now. Had he guessed where he'd dropped it?

Roth opened the door and held it for her. She had no choice but to leave—with contraband in her pocket. And with the chief behind her she couldn't even signal Sam to call her later.

"DID YOU GET my text?" Roth asked when Sam entered the squad room at the end of his shift.

"No."

"I sent it an hour ago." Roth pulled out his phone as if checking to see if his message had gone through. "It says Delivered."

Sam stalled, trying to figure out what he could say without lying to his best friend. He'd lost his phone sometime between last night and this morning. Never before had he been so distracted by a woman that he'd misplaced personal items. He was careful, methodical. Losing stuff just didn't happen. Not to him.

A search outside June's house this morning in the dark had proved fruitless. He suspected his phone was in either her truck or her cottage. Both had been locked when he'd headed out this morning. Because he'd locked them; she wasn't careful enough. He hadn't wanted to knock and wake her and possibly Madison at 0430. And being paired with Aycock all day meant he hadn't been able to track it down.

"I forgot my phone this morning."

Aycock paused on the way to the time clock.

"Why didn't you say something? We could've swung by your house and picked it up."

"I can live without it for a day. What's up?" he asked Roth.

Roth motioned Sam into his office and closed the door. "Erin called."

"My sister Erin?"

Roth nodded and alarm trickled through Sam. His family had Roth's number for emergencies only. "What's wrong? Did she say?"

"No. She called the station's nonemergency number and said it's urgent that you call her back. I tried to get more, but that's all she'd give me."

Shock hit him. The station? How had she known where to find him? The only contact number she had was his cell phone. "Are you sure she said *urgent*, not *emergency*?"

"Yeah. And she said if she didn't hear from you by tonight, she'd have your mother call in the morning."

Damnation. "I haven't told my family I left the corps yet, and the brat is threatening to blow my cover."

"Since I witnessed the last Rivers invasion and the fallout from it, I don't have to ask why you haven't shared your news. But from personal experience, I can tell you that secrets like that come back to bite you in the ass. How'd she find you?"

Sam racked his brain and came up empty. "I don't know."

And then it hit him. June must have found his phone and used it. Anger stirred. She had insisted he needed to notify his family. Had she gone through his contacts and taken matters into her own hands?

There'd been a look in her eyes this morning that he hadn't been able to decipher. He'd chalked it up to last night's off-the-charts activities. But maybe she'd been feeling guilty because she'd meddled in his business. Roth had escorted her out of the building before Sam could ask and there'd been no time to speak to her privately.

June must have given Erin the station number. Time for a green-eyed blonde to get her head chewed off. She'd overstepped her boundaries. "I gotta go."

"Let me know if there's anything I can do or if there's something going on in Tennessee and you need time off."

"Roger." Sam hustled to his car and drove to his quarters as quickly as possible. June's truck was the only one in the driveway. Good. His landlord had stayed in the city this weekend. He could hammer on June's door without witnesses if she wasn't already awake, but the panel opened as he climbed her stairs.

Even in sweatpants and an old T-shirt she looked good. He tamped down the unwelcome desire and focused on his anger. She held his phone in her outstretched hand.

"I found this on the floor under my pillow this

morning. You'd already left. I'm sorry, but I couldn't figure out how to return it with Roth watching."

"Why did you call my sister?" He managed to get the question out levelly despite his anger.

Her eyes rounded in surprise. Innocent or faking it? Then the corners of her mouth turned down. "I didn't call her. *She* called *you*."

"And you answered? What in the hell for?"

She bristled and her face reddened. "I wish I hadn't."

"Then how did she get the station's number?"

"While I was getting ready this morning, I kept hearing a buzzing sound. I finally pinpointed it and found your phone. The icon indicated three missed calls and voice mails. In my family multiple calls in quick succession, especially that early in the morning, means an emergency. I answered, thinking you had a problem on your hands."

"I do now."

She shot a look at him and he could tell she was irritated. "It was a woman. She said she was your sister and asked who I was. I wanted her to feel safe giving me a message to pass on if it was important. I told her I worked with you at the Quincey PD. Then she asked, 'What happened to the Marine Corps?' Then I cut her off as quickly as I could because I realized you hadn't told them, and I promised to have you call her back. But then I got tangled up with Roth, and I was stuck with your phone all day. If you've heard from her, I guess she took it from there."

She wasn't lying. Or if she was, she belonged in Hollywood.

"You must've told her more. How else could she have found me?"

"There was a feature article on you in our local paper last week. It included your name and bio. All she'd have to do is search the internet."

FUBAR. He didn't read the local paper and no one had mentioned the article. Stupid mistake. One he should have anticipated.

"I didn't want my family to know where I am."

She gaped. "They don't know where you are? *That's* why they haven't visited?"

She made it sound as if he'd committed a crime. "Affirmative."

"That is wrong, Sam. So wrong. Did you at least tell your parents you're out of the corps and no longer in danger?"

"Negative to the former. Positive to the latter."

Shaking her head in obvious disapproval, she opened the door wider. "Come in. Dinner's ready. We can hash this out while we eat."

"June, I don't want you cooking for me." It was too domesticated, too permanent. Especially given he was counting the days until he got out of Quincey. Besides, there was nothing to "hash out."

"Don't get excited. It's only meat loaf. I have to

eat and if we share, then I won't have to choke down leftovers for a week."

A plausible explanation. He debated refusing. Then she stepped aside and gestured to the already-set table. Plates and utensils. No candles or flowers. Maybe it wasn't intended to be romantic. He let the mouthwatering aroma floating past her lasso his taste buds and reel him in.

He was a sucker for this woman *and* her cooking.

She cut a thick slice of meat loaf and laid it on a plate, then added creamy macaroni and cheese—not the boxed junk he sometimes made—and green beans.

"Take a seat." She waited until he did before sitting opposite him and serving herself. Then she bowed her head for about ten seconds. Saying grace? Well, she was a preacher's daughter. She and her father might not get along, but apparently some of his practices had stuck. Which only went to show the guy was an idiot for treating her so badly.

Her eyes opened. She flicked a worry-filled glance his way. "Leaving your family in the dark is not the right thing to do."

"What they don't know can't worry them."

"No, Sam. What they don't know leaves the door wide-open for them to worry about more."

He took a bite of the meat loaf and the rich flavor filled his mouth. June was one hell of a cook. He'd rather eat than talk, but he wanted her to understand why his privacy was important.

"I've told you I saw what happened each time my father deployed. My mother put on a brave face for us kids, but she worried constantly. I resolved not to put her through that when I enlisted." He shoved in a forkful of mac and cheese and his taste buds hit the jackpot. He'd never had better, and that was saying something. His mother was a great cook.

"All the more reason to tell her you've left the corps."

"We both know that's a temporary situation if I have my way. You're killing my appetite, Jones. Can we just eat?"

"I'm sorry if I caused a problem. I was trying to help."

Her genuine regret deflated his anger. She hadn't known his whereabouts were secret, because he hadn't told her. There would be hell to pay for her revelations, but he could handle it. Sooner rather than later, if he knew his siblings.

"My family's like a hoard of locusts. If they knew I'd been injured and medically discharged, they'd have descended en masse. Roth refers to their last visit as an invasion."

Her eyebrows slammed down. "They don't even know about your injury?"

"No. And I want to keep it that way."

"But you went through how many surgeries? Without them by your side?"

"Marines don't need their mommies to hold their hands when they get boo-boos."

"A career-ending boo-boo."

He flinched at the blunt and unexpected jab. "Not necessarily."

She opened her mouth, then checked a comment. "Families are supposed to be there for moral support whether you think you need them or not."

"Being a military brat taught me to get through the tough stuff alone. My job reinforced that. In the field I rely on no one but myself and my partner if I have one. There's nothing the Rivers tribe could have done to change my outcome. And I'm not sure my dad won't pull strings to keep me from returning to the corps."

He snapped his lips shut, surprised that he'd admitted something to June that he hadn't even discussed with Roth—the person he trusted more than anyone else.

"If he did, it would be for *your* sake."

"Not his decision."

She searched his face with sad eyes and shook her head. "I understand that moving as much as you did must have made it difficult to maintain friendships. But it should've brought you and your siblings closer."

"Last time I landed in the hospital, they ransacked my apartment and threw out half my stuff and replaced it with crap I never used. They decorated, for God's sake, with pillows and candles and crap."

Her lips twitched, but he could tell reining in her smile hadn't been easy. "Because they love you and were trying to make your home more comfortable, I'm sure."

"You don't know them. My three sisters have seven daughters between them. A Yankees game is quieter than a Rivers family gathering. You have never heard so many shrieks and giggles."

An amused twinkle lit her eyes. "I can imagine. I used to be a camp counselor, remember? But I know that family is the most important thing in the world, and you have no idea what you're missing by putting up walls."

"Says the one whose family bailed on her."

She ducked her head and pushed food around on her plate. Only then did he notice he was packing his away and she was barely touching her food. When she lifted her face again, no trace of humor lingered. He felt like an ass for killing her good mood.

"I left them first. I got tired of being the strong one who held the family together, the shoulder everyone cried on and the one stuck playing mediator. Being that mediator means always upsetting someone. All I wanted was to escape and be responsible for only me. I'd wanted to be a cop since the day I figured out being a veterinarian wasn't for me, and I couldn't do that here with the good-ol'-boy network that existed at the time.

"So I ran off to Raleigh because I thought it would give me enough distance to be my own person and more excitement than Quincey could offer. I ignored my family while I enjoyed the all-about-me time. And then that fell apart. When I came home, my siblings had moved on, and my father had my mother so isolated it would have been easier to get an appointment with the pope than see her. It was only then that I realized what I'd lost. Once those ties are broken, Sam, it's hard to get them back."

"From what Roth and Piper say, your brothers and sisters only show up when they want something. Your brother's a prime example."

"I'm always happy when I can help. They'd do the same for me. Wouldn't you help your sisters if they needed you?"

"I'd die for them," he replied instantly and with certainty.

"Then why cut yourself off? They should be here to help you with this transition."

Tension knotted his shoulder muscles. "I don't need help."

"You've lost a job you loved. And whether you want to admit it or not, your chances of returning are slim. The Marines wouldn't have let an investment like you go if they thought time would bring you around. They'd have given you a temporary administrative position."

Denial screamed through him. But damn it, she made sense. "You've been talking to Lowry."

"Not since our last visit to the range."

And yet she echoed the Army vet's words. Was Sam the only one who believed he could re-up? A cold fist closed off his esophagus. *No.* He would get back into the corps. "My future is my business."

"Talk to my godfather—not about the JROTC job but about the transition and how hard it is. Or talk to Tate. Both have been through what you're dealing with. Better yet, talk to your dad. He's recently had a status change. It'll be fresh for him. Even if his separation was voluntary, it's still a loss and an adjustment."

She reached across the table and covered his fist. "Sam, this doesn't have to be a solo mission. And getting an outside perspective, or three, might be what you need. You can sit back and wait until your year of healing is up to see if you can return to the Marines or you can spend that time exploring other possibilities. That way when the final decision is made, you'll know your options."

He yanked his hand away and shot to his feet. "I came for my phone, not psychoanalysis."

She shrugged. "I care about you, so you get both."

Not what he wanted to hear. "Don't. I told you. We are temporary."

"I know and accept that. But as your partner, I will always have your back, and more important, you need to understand that if I didn't like and respect you and think you were smart and brave, I would never have gone to bed with you. It takes more than a pretty face and a great body to get into my pants, Rivers. Just because I haven't slept around doesn't mean I didn't have the opportunity."

Heartburn hit him hard and fast. He drained his glass of iced tea. And then he realized he wasn't suffering from indigestion. It was the idea of June with someone else bothering him. As much as he wanted to reject it, there was no way he could deny that jealousy was the cause of his discomfort.

He'd get over it. He'd move on. That was the way it had to be. But that meant she would also have other relationships. Other men. After him. She had a lot to offer, and any man would be ecstatic to have her by his side and in his bed.

The itch started between his shoulder blades. "Thanks for dinner."

"You're welcome." She rose, too, gathered their plates, then carried them to the sink. She turned and leaned against the counter, arms braced on the edge, breasts thrust out. The fact that she didn't have a clue how sexy the pose was made it doubly so.

"Do you have to rush off?"

His heart rammed his sternum like an insurgent's truck would bash a barricade. "Why?"

"I don't have to get ready for a few hours. You could stay…awhile…if you wanted."

Desire detonated in his groin. He ought to be satiated after last night's marathon. And he ought to be smart enough to begin his strategic retreat. But she'd made him an offer he didn't have the strength to refuse. Something a woman had never done before.

CHAPTER THIRTEEN

JUNE COULD FEEL Sam withdrawing even before her heart rate returned to normal. His sudden tension and stillness as he lay beside her in bed were unmistakable.

"I gotta go," he said, confirming her observation.

"Do you have time for homemade strawberry ice cream for dessert?" She wanted to lie in his arms a few moments longer. And she hated that because she knew where this was headed.

"Another time." He flung his legs over the side of the mattress and stood. His body was simply... amazing. Taut skin, packed with smooth muscles, corded with thick veins and dusted with burnished whorls. "I have to call my sister. She's threatening to rat me out to my mother."

"You might want to consider calling your mom and telling her yourself. That will pop your sister's power bubble and prevent future threats."

"Good point."

The scar on his stomach caught her attention. She'd felt it but hadn't seen it, since they'd made love only in dim light previously. She rolled to her knees and traced a finger across the barely notice-able white line. His breath whistled inward and his abdomen contracted. "What happened here?" she asked.

"Ruptured appendix."

"You couldn't get to a doctor?"

"I was prepping for an upcoming deployment. I didn't notice a problem."

"Until it was too late?"

He narrowed his eyes. "I had other priorities."

"More important than your life?"

He stuffed his legs into his pants. "Part of my training was to ignore my discomfort to get the job done."

So he had a habit of ignoring the obvious. A festering appendix must have been extremely painful. More so than admitting his military career was over? Probably not.

She sank back onto the mattress. The sheet fell to her waist, leaving her breasts exposed to the cool air. Her nipples puckered. Sam stopped with his uniform shirt on but still unbuttoned and looked at her with so much heat and hunger in his eyes that June felt like the sexiest woman on the planet.

He started to pull his arms free as if he was going to return to her bed. Then he stopped, shook his head and finished dressing.

"Call me if you see anything suspicious tonight. No Jim Bob replays."

"I'll be okay, Sam."

"Damn it, June. Promise me you'll take no risks." He sat, putting them at eye level, and grasped both her shoulders.

His protectiveness made her breath and heart hitch. "I promise."

As soon as she made the vow, he released her and turned to put on his boots. Since he couldn't see behind his back, she didn't have to worry about suppressing the smile on her face or the one in her heart.

No matter what Sam said, he cared about her. The urge to slide up behind him and wrap her arms and legs around him was almost unbearable. Almost. Knowing the clingy gesture wouldn't be welcome was the only thing that stopped her.

If he cared about her, did she have a chance of making their temporary fling something permanent? She didn't want him to leave. Her. Or Quincey.

Then her euphoria evaporated. That road was filled with potholes. Sam needed a fulfilling career. She wasn't going to fool herself into believing that being a small-town deputy would be enough for someone used to as much excitement as he'd had. Regardless, no fraternization was allowed within the department. It had never come up before, but it was in the handbook. One of them would have to quit—if they didn't both get fired.

As much as she hated to admit it, Sam had to leave. And she couldn't earn her father's forgiveness if she left without proving herself.

But who would look out for Sam—a man who cared more about his mission than himself—when he was on his own?

SAM COULDN'T SLEEP. All of his tried-and-true methods for relaxation had failed. He flipped his pillow and rolled over for the umpteenth time, resting his cheek on the cool side. Thunder rumbled in the distance. June was out there alone with an approaching storm.

He checked the weather app on his phone. The front was fifty miles to the east, but it was going to be a real gully washer with lightning and the possibility of flash flooding. Tornado warnings had already been issued along its jagged length.

Thanks to his numerous hikes, he was familiar with the hills and gulches, swamps and forests that compromised Quincey's landscape. How hard would it be to find a missing person in the uneven terrain? After the kind of rain they had coming, tracking dogs would be useless. The river bordering the township only added to the likelihood of someone disappearing without a trace.

What if June ran into someone determined to harm her? Would the thieves even strike on a rainy night? A deluge might actually provide good cover for their ops.

Giving up on getting any rest, he disentangled from the sheets and padded toward the kitchen table. The least he could do was use his insomnia productively to work on the deputy investigation. As soon as he completed his report, he'd have fulfilled his promise to Roth and he'd be free to leave Quincey.

He had to get out of here. He was getting in too deep with June.

The call to his mother had not gone well. As June had predicted, his mom had been relieved to hear he was out of the service. But after she'd scolded him for not calling sooner, she'd grilled the hell out of him about his surgeries and recovery. He'd downplayed the seriousness of the situation as best he could, but talking to her was like taking one of those personality tests. She hit him with a barrage of questions, often the same one multiple times but phrased differently to get you to trip up—a skill she'd acquired working in the ER for decades.

She'd been excessively curious about Quincey and had started listing potential dates for a family trip to town. To avert the Rivers estrogen invasion he'd been forced to admit his position at QPD was simply a favor to Roth and a short-term TDY and that he'd most likely be gone before they could convoy the troops. Somehow his mother had read between his carefully drawn lines—as she always did—and figured out he wanted to return to the corps. Then she'd accused him of being just like his father. Not an insult in Sam's book.

Pushing the conversation to the back burner, he picked up the file on top of the stack. *Justice Jones*, he'd printed on the tab back before he'd gotten to know June. Sam skimmed his early assessment where he'd noted that she was more parent than police officer, that she spent too much time talking on the job instead of doing it and rationalizing crimes rather than dealing with them. He shook his head. He'd been way off. June knew exactly what she was doing. His only complaint with her now was that she was too damned trusting. She expected the best from everyone. And that could get her killed.

He was about to ball up the page and toss it when he remembered he'd written on the back of the sheet. He flipped the page to an extensive list of her good qualities. He couldn't throw out the condemning words before he recopied the credits page. The list was too long for him to remember them all, so he shoved the paper back into the file.

Thunder shook the house, closer this time, bringing him back to the reason he couldn't sleep. June shouldn't be patrolling alone in the middle of the night. And the storm only made it riskier. Aside from the natural dangers it posed, she might not hear the perp approach over the thunder.

He needed to check on her. But he didn't know her cell number. He knew that she was addicted to flowers and a fitness buff, that she sang in the shower, thanks to her always-open bathroom window, and that she was a magician in the kitchen. He knew every inch of her body, what she tasted like and the sounds she made when she had an orgasm.

But he didn't know her damned phone number. How messed up was that?

He rechecked the front page. Her number wasn't in her file. Even if it weren't the middle of the night, he couldn't call and ask Roth for it without raising a flag. Was there a GPS locator on her cruiser? He didn't know and couldn't ask Roth that either. Hell of a mess.

If he wanted to verify her safety, he'd have to do it visually. But how could he do recon without her seeing him? Quincey was a black hole at 0300. If he drove around town, they would eventually cross paths and his headlights would give him away. He didn't have the night-vision goggles for night stalking. And if she saw him, she'd get the wrong idea that he was reframing this thing between them and making it long-term instead of short.

No, damn it, he could do this. His career had depended on him getting in and out of chosen hides unseen. And he was still alive only because he'd been damned good at it. His distance vision might be temporarily out of whack, but nothing had affected his ability to infiltrate. He would find a good hiding place, wait for her to pass, reassure himself she was okay, then get back home for a couple hours' shut-eye before his shift. She'd never know he'd been out there watching.

With his purpose determined, he slipped the file under the place mat and headed for his closet. He dressed automatically in dark clothing—chances were he'd stay in his car, but if he had to get out, he'd be prepared. He had a three-quarter moon to see by at least until the storm clouds blocked it, and he knew June's route. The rest was a matter of timing, position and patience—his specialties.

Five minutes later he was in his Charger, rolling down the street at a slow-enough speed to keep his engine purring instead of growling. Overhead, scattered clouds raced through the sky, intermittently blocking the moonlight. When he reached one of the back roads June patrolled, he stopped at the place he'd decided would offer optimal concealment and reversed into the driveway of an abandoned house. He lowered his windows so he could hear approaching vehicles, then turned off his headlights and killed the engine. Now all he had to do was wait for June to drive past. Then he'd know she was okay and he'd head home.

Warm, humid air so thick he practically needed a snorkel to breathe filled his car. He could feel the drop in barometric pressure. The storm was closing in. After five minutes the night creatures he'd disturbed and silenced with his arrival cranked back up to a dull roar. Thunder rattled the coins in his cup holder. Ten minutes ticked by, second by slow second. Then twenty had passed with no sign of June. He twisted in his seat, looking back down the road, but the curve that hid him so well from westbound vehicles also blocked his view of them.

He checked his G-Shock again—0355. Where

was she? Her entire circuit should take only twenty-five minutes. If she didn't pass soon, he'd have to abandon his hide and go looking for her. He leaned back in his seat, inhaled and exhaled, struggling to suppress the negative vibes and curt patience. Hunger pains gnawed his stomach. Then a knot formed between his shoulder blades, and he was forced to admit it wasn't a food shortage twisting his gut. He was concerned about June in a way he'd never worried about a woman before.

Disturbing stuff. But it didn't mean anything. They had an agreement.

The pounding on his roof scared the crap out of him. He turned and saw June's face in the opening. He hadn't heard her approach.

"What are you doing here, Sam?" The night-vision goggles dangled from her fingertips.

Busted. Lying was out of the question. She was too smart to believe anything he concocted anyway. But he'd give it a shot. "Would you believe I came out to wish you happy birthday?"

"Not a chance. But thanks for trying."

"There's a storm rolling in with tornado and flash-flood warnings. I was concerned about you out here in it."

Her back went ramrod straight. "You think I'm not smart enough to check the weather bulletins? I have news for you, Rivers—I've worked storms before. I know the hazards and can handle them."

He sighed. "That's not what I meant, June. You're

in great shape, but that won't help you if a big guy like Jim Bob comes along. He's twice your size and weight. You'd have to shoot him to stop him and we both know you won't do that."

"Not if I can avoid it."

She didn't get it. That hesitation could be her downfall. "How in the hell did you get the jump on me again?"

"I'm good at my job, and I know this terrain."

"Where'd you come from?"

She pointed toward a blinking light high in the sky. "Quincey's crow's nest."

The only thing over there was— "The water tower? You climbed the tower? With the storm coming?"

"It's the best vantage point in town, and before you ask, I would've come down before the lightning started. I have the weather app on my phone and I've been checking. I saw your headlights the minute you started your vehicle, then tracked your progress down Main Street and saw you backing into the Ackers' driveway."

He felt like an idiot. In combat he'd have been a dead man. He tried to make light of the sobering discovery. "You've been watching my house, Jones?"

She shifted and narrowed her eyes. "I've been watching the countryside. Our homes are part of it."

"You're not afraid of heights?"

She *pfft*ed. "Please. This is a water-tower town. What do you think bored teenagers from the country do when they want to dare someone to the ultimate challenge? Climbing the tower is a rite of passage." Then she grimaced. "And I confess, I used to sneak up there to get away from my siblings when life got too…complicated."

Just when he thought he knew the extent of her bravery, she blew him out of the water. "I'm impressed. You ever make out up there?"

She ducked her head, and he had no doubt if the lighting had been better, he'd have seen her blush. A twenty-eight-year-old who talked tough but still blushed like a schoolgirl was oddly refreshing.

"No. And we're not going to tonight. I'm on duty."

"Another time, then."

She laughed and shook her head, then studied him a full minute. "Admit it. You were concerned about me. Not *me*, a fellow officer, but *me* personally. The woman you're…involved with."

Exactly as he'd feared. She was taking this down the wrong, long-distance path. "I was. But that doesn't change anything. I'm still leaving Quincey. You're not."

"It's okay, Sam. I care about you, too—too much to keep you from following your dream. I appreciate you coming out to check on me, but I can't do my job when I'm chatting with you. Go home."

"I'm not leaving without your phone number. If

I'd had that to begin with, I wouldn't have had to track you down."

Her eyebrows hiked. She recited the digits and he punched them into his phone, then hit a few more keys.

"Now give me yours," she said. "As partners, we should have exchanged numbers sooner." Her phone chirped. She checked the face. "'Be careful, Eagle Eye'?"

She couldn't possibly know what a big compliment that was. "That's my number. Save it."

She shook her head but a tiny smile teased her lips. "See you in the morning, Sam."

For some reason he was reluctant to leave her. The sprinkles dampening his windshield gave him the perfect excuse to extend their visit. "Where are you parked? I'll drive you back to your cruiser."

"Thanks, but no. I'm parked around the bend. I cut through the Ackers' yard and came down the driveway behind you."

All right. He had no reason to stay. And he wasn't disappointed. He *wasn't*.

Hell yes, he was.

"Be careful," he repeated.

"Always am. Go. If you can't sleep, do some work on your Career Day presentation. That's coming up on Monday."

"Did you get roped in, too?"

"I speak to the senior girls every year about nontraditional careers for women. Two have gone on to careers in law enforcement."

She was as devoted to her community as he was to his—the corps. No common ground. And he'd best not forget it.

JUNE'S ENERGY WAS flagging after working the night shift, but as soon as she turned into the driveway and spotted Sam's car parked beside his cottage, a burst of adrenaline rushed through her and she caught her second wind.

He'd cared enough to drag himself out of bed in the middle of the night to check on her. That had to count for something even if she hadn't yet figured out how or if they could take their relationship to the next level.

Her windshield wipers swished, revealing Sam stepping out onto his porch. He looked delicious in his crisply pressed navy blue uniform. Could she steal a kiss before he left for work? Good heavens, the man knew how to kiss. Her body tingled just thinking about it. But she'd be going to bed without a kiss, apparently, since it looked as if he was headed out now.

Then his muscles tensed. It was a subtle change, but June didn't miss it. She parked and alighted from the cruiser. Rain pelted her head and shoulders when she paused to scan the area and see what had wiped the welcome from his handsome face. Madison stood on her screened-in back porch, holding a coffee mug in each hand, one of which she lifted to June in invitation—a common occurrence.

Stifling her disappointment, June waved to her friend, then held up two fingers to indicate she needed a couple of minutes. There would be no kiss, no hug, no discussing the night with an audience. All she could do was hand over the cruiser keys and tell Sam to have a good day.

He waited under cover at the top of the stairs. Smart of him. It put a little distance between them and overhearing ears and would keep them both dry during the exchange. She made her way to his porch.

"I thought you had tonight's shift?" she asked.

The hunger lurking in the depths of his gaze made her breath catch, but he kept his hands by his side. The need to lean into him, to touch him in any way, pulled at her. But she harnessed it.

"I do, but I'm gonna put in a couple of hours at the office this morning. Then Roth wants to have an early lunch. I'll be home afterward."

Anticipation skipped along her nerve endings. "Will I see you then?"

"You should be sleeping."

Did she imagine the spark of anticipation in his eyes that her question provoked?

"I'll sleep. Some." She held out the car keys. His fingertips scraped her palm as he took them and a shiver of desire wound its way to her belly.

"What about our landlord?" he asked.

She definitely did not imagine the deeper timbre of his voice. "She runs a reduced-cost spay/neuter clinic once a month on Saturdays. It's usually packed. She'll be late getting home."

"Then I'll see you this afternoon. Rest up."

Those last two words combined with the hot promise in his gaze sent her pulse rate into the stratosphere. She nodded, then gulped the knot in her throat. "Okay."

Aware of their onlooker, June turned and jogged toward Madison's porch. The raindrops cooled her hot skin. The screen door slapped behind her. She shook off the moisture and hoped Madison attributed her quickened breaths to the sprint across the yard. "What's up?"

"You tell me. Decaffeinated for you." Madison handed over a mug. She was already in her scrubs, which meant she'd be leaving soon but, from the sound of the engine starting behind June, not before Sam drove away. It took everything June had not to watch his departing taillights like a love-struck fool.

She sipped her coffee and sat on the glider. "What do you mean?"

"You and Sam are coming and going at odd hours and working overnights. Piper says Roth's been working every third night. What's going on, June? Do I need to be worried?"

"No." June had to give her something to deflect her attention. "We've had a car theft and another attempted theft. Both incidents have happened at night. We have no suspects. We're trying to catch the perps in the act. Roth assigned the case to Sam and me and swore us to secrecy. The three of us are taking turns covering nights. Please don't mention it to anyone. We don't want to tip off our thief."

"That's it? Work?"

"Yes. What else could it be?" she asked with as much innocence as she could muster.

"I was hoping you and Sam…" Madison shook her head.

"QPD has a no-fraternization rule, remember? Either he or I or both of us could be out of a job if we were…you know, fraternizing."

Which was exactly why she was lying to her best friend again instead of bragging about the amazing sex she'd been having and hoped to have again this afternoon. Guilt settled over her like a cold, wet horsehair blanket. She didn't like her behavior very much at the moment.

"I guess you're right. And if you and Sam did get together and both left QPD at the same time, Roth would be two deputies down. Not good."

June stifled a wince as Madison hammered another nail into the coffin of her dreams. No, not good at all, and something else to worry about. "Any progress with the wedding plans?"

"As a matter of fact, yes. Adam found a place at Wrightsville Beach for the ceremony. It's a pier-slash-restaurant where we can get married out over the water, or if the weather doesn't cooperate, we'll use the banquet room inside overlooking the water and pier. From the pictures he sent me and their webpage, it's beautiful."

"Sounds great. When?"

"The second weekend in October."

"Wow. That's only four weeks away."

"The restaurant had a cancellation because another couple got impatient and eloped, so he snapped it up, then called me. I'm sorry we didn't check first to see if that worked for you and Piper. I hope that's okay."

"I'll make it work, and I'm sure Piper feels the same."

"Four weeks feels like forever *and* tomorrow at the same time. There's so much to do, but luckily, the staff handles most of it."

It was wonderful to witness the happiness and excitement in Madison's eyes after years of seeing her friend's haunting misery, and June would be lying to herself if she didn't admit she was a little jealous. She wanted that kind of love.

"I'm so happy you found Adam."

"You'll find your Mr. Right soon."

June already had, but circumstances would keep them apart. "You'll be moving to Norcross directly after the ceremony?"

Madison's smile faded. "I will, and I'm going to miss you and Piper so much. My in-laws will be moving in while Adam and I are on our honeymoon."

"Do you know where you're going yet?"

"No. Adam still won't tell me. It's a surprise. If you'd told me six months ago that I'd willingly let someone plan not only my wedding but ten days of my life without a clue to my destination, I'd have called you crazy." She smiled into her mug.

"It only works because you trust him completely."

"Yes. I do." Madison paused. "June, are you okay?"

"Sure. Why do you ask?"

"Because we haven't spent much time together lately, and when we do, you seem...I don't know... distracted? On edge?"

That showed what a good friend Madison was. She read June as easily as a billboard sign—and she was being repaid with less than total honesty.

"I guess it's just an accumulation of the thefts, Rhett's baby surprise and my dad."

"You do realize your father may never come around, don't you?"

"I don't want to consider that possibility." But if he found out about her affair with Sam, that outcome was pretty much guaranteed.

What had she been thinking to believe an affair would solve her immediate loneliness? Instead, in just over two weeks she'd very likely created a much bigger problem—a broken heart.

She rose. "I need to get some sleep."

"June...if you need to talk, I'm always available."

She desperately needed advice, but she didn't dare ask for it. "Thanks. Same goes."

She headed back through the rain, walking slowly, but the water wasn't going to wash away her guilt.

CHAPTER FOURTEEN

THE SOUND OF a car engine brought June to her feet. Her heart cartwheeled with excitement. She didn't even bother putting on her shoes before she sprinted to the door. Then her common sense kicked in and she skidded to a halt.

If she ran out there at full speed, she'd look too eager. It didn't matter that she'd thought of nothing but Sam's return since lying down for a fitful nap. Their relationship didn't call for that much... enthusiasm.

Taking a breath, she composed herself, then carefully opened the door and stepped onto her porch. The white sedan stopped her in her tracks. Not Sam. Her excitement did a big fat belly flop. The strange vehicle drove past her cottage and pulled in beside Sam's Charger. The door opened. A tall man, his blond hair threaded with silver, stepped out with his back to her. He faced Sam's place. Despite the casual polo shirt and jeans he wore, everything about him screamed "military," from his haircut to his broad, straight shoulders and posture.

Someone with whom Sam had worked? Or someone to talk to him about rejoining the corps?

Then the man turned and it was as if her boxing bag had swung back and knocked the breath from her. The man looked like Sam—only thirty years older. He had the same bone structure and the same blue eyes. Was this Sam's father? He spotted her and nodded. "Good afternoon," he called out before turning back toward Sam's cottage.

June gathered her scattered wits and forced her gaping mouth to form words. "He's not home."

The man pivoted. Sharply. "Do you know when he's expected?"

"Soon. I'm June Jones. I work with him." She very deliberately didn't include Sam's name—just in case she was wrong about the man's identity.

A crisp nod, then he walked her way with a precise, sure stride. Like Sam's. "You're the one who spoke to my daughter Erin. It's nice to meet you, June. Cliff Rivers. Sam's father."

Shaky knees carried her to the bottom of the stairs. The rain had stopped but the treads were still damp beneath her feet. She extended her hand. "I can see the resemblance. Nice to meet you too, sir."

"No *sir* required. I packed that up with the uniform. Call me Cliff." A tinge of regret lingered in his voice.

She smiled. "Would you like a glass of lemonade while you wait, Cliff?"

"That would hit the spot. It was a long drive and I only stopped once for fuel."

"Where'd you come from?" she asked as she climbed the steps.

"Crossville, Tennessee."

Pretty far. "In that case, I don't mean to be indelicate, but do you need the restroom?"

He grinned and looked even more like his son but without Sam's guarded edge. "If you don't mind, young lady."

She opened the door and motioned for him to enter. "Down the hall on the left."

He went off to do his thing and June wondered if Sam would be upset that she'd invited his father inside. It didn't matter. Southern hospitality demanded she act as Sam's substitute hostess. But she would serve Mr. Rivers outside since the humidity wasn't bad.

She busied herself fixing two glasses of lemonade and a plate of the oatmeal cookies she'd baked earlier. After piling it all on a tray, she carried everything outside to her front porch and propped open the screen door so he'd know where to find her.

Moments later he stepped outside and surveyed the scene the same way she'd seen Sam do dozens of times. "Pull up a chair, Cliff. The weather's too nice to be cooped up inside."

"That it is."

"Help yourself to the cookies."

He wasted no time grabbing two.

"Crossville's not a military town."

"No, ma'am. My daughters—stepdaughters, technically, but daughters to me—all settled near their grandparents, so my wife and I bought a home there when I got out."

"Her parents or yours?"

"Hers. But my in-laws are good people, and it's nice to be near the granddaughters."

"Sam mentioned all the girls. I think he feels outnumbered."

Cliff grimaced but somehow smiled simultaneously. She'd bet he'd been a charmer at Sam's age. "We all do."

"Sam followed you into the Marines?"

"His mother and grandmother couldn't talk him out of it. Trust me, they tried."

"Is it a family thing? Did your father also serve?"

"He did, as a matter of fact. He was a lifer like me."

Sam was following by example. "You know Sam wants back in?"

"That's one of the reasons I'm here. His mother sent me to talk to him and to check on him, of course. She couldn't get off work. It's hard to find a weekend shift replacement at the last minute."

"And are you going to try to dissuade him?"

He shrugged. "Depends. His injury is the determining factor. I don't want him putting himself in harm's way if he has a handicap that could get him killed."

"It's natural for him to be confused and in denial. He's grieving what he lost."

"It's the only life he knows. He was born and raised on or around bases and never lived anywhere else except for the summers he spent with his grandparents in Crossville. Despite trying different summer jobs, he remained focused on a military career. I can see how he might miss it. I certainly do." His gaze sharpened. "How long have you known my son?"

"Only a couple of weeks. Sorry. It's middle-kid syndrome. I tend to analyze and diagnose everybody."

"Understood."

"Sam never mentioned summers with his grandparents."

"Only way to get away from all the females." That Sam-like grin returned. "Love 'em. But they never stop talking and never sit still. No offense intended."

"None taken. I'm one of five. It was the same at our house. Noisy and chaotic. But I wouldn't have wanted it any other way."

The crunch of tires on gravel put a glitch in her pulse. Cliff caught her sudden stillness and set down his glass. "That him?"

The cruiser came into view. She shot to her feet, trying not to look too eager. "Yes."

Sam pulled the patrol car in beside her truck and flung open the door. In two long strides he reached her steps. Then his father rose and he stopped. "Dad. This is a surprise."

He leaped up the stairs and the men embraced. The bear hug of affection looked genuine—nothing like the stiff, dutiful embraces with her father—and it lasted a long time. And then it hit her. Cliff was everything her father wasn't. He was warm and open and hadn't hesitated to admit his feelings for his children.

"I suspect you knew 'the general' would send me," Cliff said.

Sam did the grimace/grin thing his father had done earlier and for the first time she saw him with his guard down. He looked so much younger and more relaxed. "I tried to convince her it wasn't necessary."

"'The general' is your mother?" June asked.

"She issues orders like a five-star," Cliff answered. "You don't disobey." But he said it good-naturedly, not as a complaint.

Then Sam nodded to her with palpable wariness. "June."

"Sam." Trying to mask her disappointment, she returned the stiff greeting. "I'll get you a glass of lemonade. Help yourself to the cookies."

She ducked inside and worked slowly to give them a few minutes alone. She hoped Sam realized how lucky he was. Cliff was the kind of dad she wished she had.

SAM TRACKED JUNE until she was out of sight. His afternoon plans to spend a few hours naked with her were blown, but it was good to see his father. Sam hadn't realized how much he missed him or how badly he needed his guidance until now. His father was a master tactician. He'd help Sam come up with a no-fail strategy to get where he wanted to go.

But that left Sam with a logistical problem.

"I'm pulling an overnight shift tonight, Dad."

"Can I ride along?"

His father's back had to be killing him after the eight-hour drive. Not that a tough sergeant major would ever admit it. Add in an additional eight hours in the cruiser and the same for the return trip to Tennessee and his dad would be in agony for a week.

As much as he hated to, Sam shook his head. "Covert ops."

"No problem. I'll bunk at your place while you work if you have room. If not, point me to a hotel. But if you don't want company, I'll head back to Crossville."

June returned and frowned at Sam as she passed him a glass, making him suspect she'd overheard and disapproved. But she didn't have the facts. "You can't leave without a visit, Cliff."

"I arrived unannounced and uninvited. It was a known risk."

"Don't be silly. There's always room and time for family. I'll take Sam's shift tonight."

"No. You worked last night," Sam objected. He didn't want her out there again, as illogical as that was. And even if it was the best solution.

"Your father drove all day, and you haven't seen him in how long?" June's irritation came through loud and clear.

"Almost a year, but—"

"That brings on another problem, son. If you're working tonight, don't you need to get some shut-eye?" His dad was clearly trying to defuse an estrogen explosion—as he'd done thousands of times over the decades with Sam's sisters.

"I could use a few hours."

"Well, if you won't let me take your shift tonight, then at least go have a nap," June snapped. "I'll show Cliff around Quincey, then take him to the diner for dinner. *He* looks like good company."

The jab didn't go unnoted, but he didn't want to be indebted. "You eat at your parents' every Sunday afternoon."

Although avoiding her toxic father was probably a good idea.

"I can skip it for once, and tomorrow morning while you're sleeping, I'll take Cliff over to Tate's."

She turned to his father. "Tate's an army vet who owns a shooting range and would love to swap war stories with you."

"Sounds good. I haven't fired a weapon since I retired. Don't own one. Allison wouldn't let me bring any into the house."

"No problem. Tate or I will hook you up."

Sam didn't want her cozying up to his family. She was exactly the kind of woman his mother wanted him to bring home, and if Mom heard about June, Sam would never hear the end of it and the whole herd would come stampeding down. They didn't understand that some men, like his mother's first husband, just weren't marriage material.

"Not necessary, Jones."

She folded her arms, stubborn written all over her. "Then let me take your shift, Rivers."

His father's cell phone rang, interrupting the standoff. He checked the screen. "That's your mom. I was supposed to call when I arrived. Excuse me while I check in."

His father descended the porch and strode toward the barn at a good clip, looking eager to escape the escalating tension.

"What is wrong with you?" June snapped as soon as he was out of sight. "I'd give anything for my father to show interest in my work."

He'd bet she would. One more reason to dislike the preacher. "Dad can't ride along because he has a compressed disk in his spine. He's covering well, but he's already hurting. Three long stints in a car will lay him out for a week. He's supposed to take a break every two hours and stretch, but I'd bet my Beretta he didn't stop once on the drive down. He never would have taken voluntary retirement if the pain wasn't getting to him."

A little of the starch leeched from her. "He told me he drove straight through with only one stop, but you can't abandon him. Use your brain, Sam, and let me take your shift. Spend your time with him."

Taking the easy way out put her in jeopardy. He had never intentionally done that to anyone. But she was offering the best solution and he knew it. Damn it.

"Call me if you see anything suspicious. Me. Not Roth. He's taking Piper to dinner and a concert in Raleigh tonight. They're staying there at a hotel."

"I will."

He had the strangest urge to kiss her. Didn't make sense, but he did. Yet he didn't dare. Not with his father's returning footsteps crunching on the driveway. "Thanks, June."

"You're welcome, Sam." She turned to his father. "It was nice meeting you, Cliff. I've talked your son into letting me take his shift tonight. I'm going to get some sleep, but I hope I'll see you again before you leave."

"You will if I have anything to say about it, June."

"This means Sam gets to give you the grand tour,

but I've shown him the best spots. He should do a decent job."

"I'll let you know," Cliff said.

Time to make their exit. "We'll leave you to get some rest." That urge to touch her hit again. Harder. He resisted.

"Take the cookies."

Sam didn't have to be told twice. He grabbed the plate. "I'll text you later. Answer or I'll come looking for you."

Ignoring his dad's curious expression and June's drop-dead glare, Sam headed next door. He paused by the trunk of his father's sedan and passed off the cookies. "Take these. I'll get your bag."

He grabbed the duffel from the trunk and headed into his quarters.

"I like her and your mother will, too," his father said the moment the door closed behind them, confirming what Sam feared. His dad was charmed. But then, who wouldn't be? June was everybody's darling, for good reason. She was just so damned lov—likable.

"Everybody likes June."

"You know what I meant."

"Yes, I do, and we're not going there. Quincey is her home. I'm just passing through."

"No chance you'll stay?"

"No. I'm working on a project for Roth. Once that's done, I'm gone. Small-town police work is not for me."

When he returned from carrying the luggage to the bedroom, he found his father flipping through the stack of tattered targets on the kitchen table. His dad discarded them and parked on the sofa, then pointed to the chair facing him. Sam sat.

"Have you given any thought to what you'll do if you can't go back to the corps?"

The question blindsided Sam. He'd expected his father's support. He'd always had it in the past. "I'll get back in."

"Son, if those targets are yours," he said, pointing at the ragged pages, "you need to start considering other options. Brass has invested too much money in you to release you if they had a shot of still using your skill set."

The same thing June had said. "I have a year to improve."

"So you twiddle your thumbs playing country cop for another six months—then what happens if you haven't regained your skills?"

"Then I'll be an instructor or get a job in the Precision Weapons Section."

"Below your pay grade. Shortage of positions. Surplus of qualified candidates."

Sam's heart jackhammered against his ribs. "You can't know that."

"I made a few calls last night. I haven't been out long enough to lose all my connections. Sam, are you determined to return because you loved your job or because you're afraid you can't do anything else?"

Sam hit a brick wall. Physically, mentally, he stopped in his tracks. Leave it to his dad to smack the nail square on the head with his first swing.

"Both."

"Then it's time for a new battle plan. Assess your skill set."

"I don't have any besides precision shooting."

"You've spent thirteen years in a field where most men don't survive five. You didn't rack up that impressive data book solely by being an accurate marksman. Think. There are other facets to being a scout sniper that kept you on the job."

Sam appreciated the vote of confidence, but making a "new plan" meant accepting failure of the old one. And out in the field failure meant surrender. Death before capture.

He wasn't ready for that.

FROM HER VANTAGE POINT on the water tower's catwalk, June caught the flicker of headlights on the east side of town. In the darkness she didn't have her usual landmarks and without them pinpointing the exact location was difficult.

Her fingers itched to call Sam—this time because she'd promised to, as opposed to every other time tonight when she'd wanted to dial just to hear his voice. But once again she resisted. She wouldn't disturb him and his father for a false alarm. Best to gather facts first.

She tracked the vehicle's progress, mentally mapping the turns until finally placing it on Oak Hill. None of that street's residents worked night shifts. Was Jim Bob out on the prowl again? If so, did Miss Letty know her son was on the loose? June had to check on him and she couldn't call his mother because the Lees didn't have a phone. She started the long trek down, her shoes clanking on the metal treads as she circled the external staircase. Dew had dampened the handrail.

A month ago she never would have believed Jim Bob capable of deliberately hurting anyone, but Sam had planted a seed of doubt. She paused when she reached the tree line for one final study. She needed to determine the direction because descending another round of stairs would put the vehicle out of sight. It looked as if it was heading toward Don Davis's property and his old Suburban.

Could it have been Jim Bob that Don had scared off the last time? Surely not. Miss Letty was a sweet lady. She took good care of her mentally challenged son, and she'd never be involved in theft. And Jim Bob wasn't smart enough to work solo. Even if he had snuck out that one night.

But there had been two sets of prints at the first scene. One big. One small. June didn't like the math on that one. Resuming her descent, she dug into her pocket for her phone and punched Sam. It rang once.

"June?"

His sleep-roughened voice tripped all her triggers. She stumbled and made a frantic grab for the damp rail. Her hand slipped and her heart leaped in panic as she scrambled to find her footing. Then she caught herself and, weak-kneed, sank onto her butt. She pressed the phone against her chest, gulped air and stared at the dark ground hundreds of feet below. Close one.

"June?" she heard Sam repeating with an anxious edge. "Where are you?"

Lifting the phone to her ear with an unsteady hand, she looked up at the half-moon and said a quick silent thank-you prayer. "I'm coming down from the water tower."

She rose. Her legs shook from the near miss, but she didn't have time for weakness now. "I saw headlights on Oak Hill. I think they're heading toward Davis's Suburban."

"I'll meet you there. Don't move in before I'm in position to cover your six, and, June—" silence ticked past "—be careful."

She heard the concern in his voice and emotion swelled in her chest. He cared even if he didn't know it yet. "I will. But you'll probably get there before me. Sam, if it's Jim Bob, please don't hurt him. He's not like the rest of us."

"I'll keep that in mind, but if he's armed or if he resists, I make no promises. The primary goal of every mission is to return alive. Remember that."

"I'll see you soon." She disconnected and, using extra caution, finished her descent. One fright a night was plenty. But she couldn't help thinking that if she'd fallen, she would never have seen Sam again. She wouldn't get to make love with him or lie in his arms. She would never get to tell him how she felt about him. That set off another wave of panic.

Did she have the nerve to tell him? Could she let him go without making a fool of herself? Because unless there was an alternative, a compromise she hadn't yet envisioned, Sam would leave.

She was two steps from the cruiser when her phone chirped an incoming text message.

In position. Blocking rear entrance. Waiting for you. Two people. One small. One large. Looks like Jim Bob and his mother.

Betrayal burned through her. She'd trusted Miss Letty. Had looked out for her. Had taken her food and firewood and treated her like a relative—many of Miss Letty's neighbors had. And Letty Lee was stealing from them? Could Sam be wrong?

June pushed her vehicle to the fastest speed at which she could safely navigate the curvy roads and soon reached Davis's front driveway. She debated going in with lights and siren but was afraid she'd startle the duo into making a bad decision, so she killed her headlights, then texted Sam that she was coming in dark.

Haven't seen the rifle. Be careful, he texted again.

She opened her windows a few inches and heard the sound of the other vehicle's motor running and the rattle of heavy metal chains. The cruiser's engine was quiet. If she kept to the grass instead of the gravel, they might not hear her approach until she was right on them.

She slowly rolled across the field until she spotted a truck, then stopped about fifty yards out. One glance at the dark house confirmed Don had taken his annual fall fishing trip to his son's house in Wilmington. She put on the night-vision goggles, hoping Sam had been wrong about the thieves' identities, but he hadn't. Miss Letty and Jim Bob had already winched the Suburban onto an old farm trailer and were in the process of securing it. Caught in the act.

With sadness, regret and anger in her heart, June depressed the button for the loudspeaker. "Quincey police. Step away from the vehicle with your hands in the air."

She hit the lights and gave the siren a quick blip. Jim Bob's panic-widened eyes swung her way. He covered his ears. Dreading what might happen next, she threw open the door and drew her weapon, but she kept it by her side.

"Put your hands in the air," she repeated, and only Jim Bob, on the right side of the rig, complied.

Miss Letty, on the near side, moved forward, forcing June to take her sight off Jim Bob and raise her weapon. "Miss Letty, stay where you are."

But the small woman kept walking toward the truck's cab. And the rifle? Was the .22 in the cab? "Leave us be, June. We're only taking something nobody wants."

Then Jim Bob copied his mother.

"Jim Bob, remember what your momma told you," June shouted. "You don't want any trouble."

"You're right," Miss Letty hollered back. "We don't want no trouble. Go home, June. Forget about what you seen here tonight."

"The way Butch White did?" June voiced Roth's suspicions.

"Butch knew I needed the money. The new chief shouldn't have fired him."

June's heart sank. Was there no end to the old deputy's dishonesty? "Did Mac and Alan also look the other way?"

"Lord, no. Those two don't know nothing. They'd squeal if they did. You ain't gonna be like 'em, are you?"

Relief flashed through June. Mac and Alan were clear. "I have to take you in, Miss Letty—you and Jim Bob."

"I don't think so, June. I ain't goin' to no jail."

"Remember me, Jim Bob?" Sam said from three yards behind the larger man, yanking mother's and son's attention from June and halting their forward momentum. It gave June an opportunity to get closer, but that meant leaving the cover of the car.

"I'm Deputy Rivers. I work with Miss June. We met the other night. June and I followed you home to make sure you got there safely. Remember, Jim Bob?"

Sam inched closer to him. "That truck belongs to Mr. Davis, Jim Bob. You can't take another man's truck without asking permission first. Come with me. Let's ask Mr. Davis if you can have his old truck."

The child in the big man's body hesitated. Then Sam held out his hand as he would to a youngster and Jim Bob started in Sam's direction. June was surprised and confused. Sam was a man of action, not words. That first week he'd condemned her repeatedly for talking too much and acting too slow. Then Sam met her gaze and nodded toward Miss Letty. He was separating mother and son so June could focus on the woman reaching for the truck's door handle.

"Step away from the vehicle, Miss Letty. You don't want to go for that rifle."

"We're not hurting anybody. Just leave us be. Nobody cares if we take their junk."

"You've been getting away with this for a while, so I know it seems that way, but it's wrong. You have to stop stealing." June circled wide, putting the truck between herself, Jim Bob and Sam and forcing Miss Letty to turn her back on Sam and her son.

"My boy needs medicine the state won't cover."

"What kind of medicine?"

"Something the doctors call experimental. But it's helping him. He's getting smarter. They just refuse to see it. He needs those pills. And I can't afford 'em any other way." Her fingers closed around the metal.

"You just took a truck a couple of weeks ago. Why another one so soon?"

"They raised the price."

Miss Letty would do anything for her son—even break the law, apparently. "If you open that door, I'll have to shoot you. What will happen to Jim Bob then? Who will look after him?"

"You won't shoot me, girl. There's not a mean bone in your body."

June's insides were shaking. Could she shoot this petite woman she'd known all her life if absolutely necessary? Her life and even Sam's might depend on it. What good was she as a deputy if she couldn't protect a fellow officer? "I'd rather not, but I can and I will."

"Momma!" Jim Bob cried out in panic from across the yard, and June took advantage of his mother's distraction to rush forward. She body-slammed Miss Letty up against the cab as the woman's thumb depressed the door handle, then caught her wrist, yanked it free and pulled it behind Letty's back, immobilizing her but being careful not to injure the older woman. Through the windows June spotted the rifle propped against the front seat…and Sam leading a handcuffed Jim Bob to the cruiser. The big man was confused, but she could see Sam talking into his ear to calm him.

Miss Letty struggled, but her frail frame was no match for June's strength. June cuffed her and forced her to march back to the patrol car. Without another cruiser, mother and son would have to ride together. Not a desirable outcome. But calling Alan or Mac was out of the question until both captives had been thoroughly interrogated and the other deputies' involvement could be totally ruled out.

After both Lees had been confined, June looked at Sam over the roof of the car. Their gazes held. She ached so badly to tell him she loved him that she had to bite her tongue. Now wasn't the appropriate time. Would there ever be one?

He opened the front passenger door. "I'm riding with you. My father will follow in my truck."

"You brought him with you?"

"He wouldn't have missed it for anything. He has my Beretta, and he insisted on providing backup just in case."

June smiled. Sam had been blessed with a father who'd work *with* him instead of questioning every move he made. He had the kind of family that she'd always wanted. But he avoided them. Someone needed to make him see how lucky he was before it was too late. And she was the one for that job.

JUNE SAT BESIDE Sam in front of Roth's desk Monday morning with lingering traces of last night's adrenaline still pumping through her exhausted body. "I drove the Lees to the county jail, where they have facilities and round-the-clock supervision for a detainee like Jim Bob."

"And you're certain neither Morris nor Aycock are involved?"

"I interrogated each of the Lees separately. I'm satisfied that Alan and Mac are clean. I also discovered Mrs. Lee was stealing to pay large sums of money to some charlatan doctor for a miracle drug he claimed would cure Jim Bob's retardation. The doc just upped the price on them. That's why she tried to take another vehicle. A warrant for the doctor will be issued today. He's not in our jurisdiction. Not our problem."

"Good work, Jones."

"Sam helped. I'd also like it to go on the record that he did a great job with Jim Bob last night."

Sam swung a surprised glance her way. "I did nothing."

She looked at him, then turned toward their boss. "He's wrong, chief. Sam distracted Jim Bob while I dealt with his mother. If I'd tackled Miss Letty in front of her son, I'd have been in a world of hurt this morning. Or worse. I've logged their .22 as evidence and put it in lockup. Miss Letty's cousin is an assistant manager at the closest scrap yard. He's been buying the vehicles from her. He'll need to be charged, too. I can do that—"

"Go home, Jones. I'll take it from here."

"But, sir—"

"You've covered two night shifts in a row and have caught our perps. Get some sleep."

"We secured the Lees' truck last night, but I need to go back over to Davis's for photographs this morning."

"Go home," the chief repeated. "I'll get the pictures. And, Jones…"

"Yes, sir?"

"Good job."

"Thank you, sir. It was a team effort. But I won't lie. It's hard to arrest someone I've known all my life, and I'm worried about what's going to happen to Jim Bob."

"We'll keep an eye on the case and I'll try to locate a reliable relative to take custody of him if he isn't sentenced."

She nodded her gratitude. "And no disrespect, Chief, but I can't go home yet. It's Career Day. I promised to speak at the high school."

"I should've guessed. I got roped in last semester."

"It's not an imposition. I love talking to the senior girls. In fact, when—" she glanced at Sam "—*if* you have an opening, one of our Quincey High graduates would like to apply for a position. She graduated the police academy last year. Top female recruit. She'd like to be near her family."

"I'll keep it in mind."

Finally June rose. She had no reason to stall any longer.

"Jones, is that blood on the back of your pants?"

June froze at the sound of Sam's voice and glanced down. A dark stain marred the hem of her left pant leg. She lifted the fabric a few inches and saw a raw scrape about two by four inches long over her Achilles tendon. "I guess that's where I slipped when I was coming down from the water tower. Funny, I didn't notice it until you mentioned it."

"Adrenaline often overrides pain," Roth said. "Get it checked out."

"Yes, sir." Then her gaze met Sam's and the sheer lack of emotion on his face confirmed a sinking feeling that her time with him was evaporating like the early-morning mists on the fields.

CHAPTER FIFTEEN

IT WAS TIME to clear his debt to June and start cutting their ties, Sam decided after saying good-bye to his father. He owed her a steak dinner.

He showered and shaved, not because he was dressing up but because he and his father had gone fishing this morning and he stunk of bass and catfish. Then he hiked the short distance to June's cottage and knocked.

Her door opened almost instantly. She smiled, then looked beyond him. "Where's your dad?"

"He left." Sam took in her fitted white blouse and the ripped jeans with slivers of pale thigh peeking through and his purpose for coming over vaporized.

"Already?"

"Yes." He'd never been a fan of the ragged-pants trend, but they looked good on her. He'd bet his bank balance she didn't wear them to follow the current fashion style but rather because she preferred old, comfortable clothes. That was June. Easygoing, practical and unpretentious.

"I didn't get to tell him good-bye."

"You were sleeping. He didn't want to wake you."

She opened her door and a mouthwatering aroma drifted out. "Come in."

"What is that smell?"

"Fudge pie. I was hoping to offer your dad a piece with some homemade vanilla-bean ice cream." She checked her watch. "It's kind of late. He won't be home until well after midnight."

"I made a reservation for him at a pricey hotel halfway there and told him I'd forfeit the cost if he was a no-show. He'll take the offer and rest because he can't stand to waste money."

Her slow grin made his toes curl. "Devious."

"Strategic." The urge to stroke the gaps between denim threads hit him hard. He shoved his hands into his pockets to keep them out of trouble.

Debt. You're here to pay your debt. "I owe you a steak dinner. How about tonight?"

She blinked, then nodded. "Give me five minutes to change. We can have the pie for dessert later."

The look she shot him, accompanied by a suggestive wiggle of her eyebrows, hit him with a howitzer blast of desire. "Okay."

She waved at the sofa. "Have a seat. I know how much you like chocolate, but stay away from the pie."

And then she disappeared into her bedroom. He'd never known a woman who could get dressed in under an hour, so he picked up a gun magazine, settled in for the long wait and tried not to think about having "dessert" later. He hadn't even finished the first article when she returned wearing a yellow sundress that skimmed her curves and sandals that showed off her sexy legs.

She looked as edible as a lemon-drop candy—his favorite. Hunger—for her—kicked him in the teeth. He staggered to his feet, his plan to pay his debt and begin easing out of the relationship going off the rails. "How about dessert first?"

She frowned. "The pie's not cool enough to cut."

"I meant you."

Her breath hitched and her cheeks flushed. She ducked her head and twisted her torso, the picture of a shy young girl. Then her eyes met his again and the all-woman heat in them roasted him. He closed the gap between them in two strides and reached for her.

But June, being June, met him halfway. Their bodies collided, winding him so much he kissed her soft lips, gasped, kissed and gasped again. His heart beat double time and his lungs labored to ward off dizziness. He skated his palms over her waist, her hips, her bottom, kneading. Then, needing her skin against his, he went for her zipper. The dress hit the floor, leaving behind yellow panties and a bra that were like bows and ribbons on a package. He scooped her up and carried her to her bedroom. Seconds later scraps of yellow were on the floor and magnolia-soft breasts filled his hands.

He thumbed her nipples and her back arched. Eager for the taste of her, he dipped his head and sipped his way from her neck to the puckered tips. She smelled of her usual flowers but also a hint of the chocolate pie she'd baked. Her short nails raked his back. Then she cupped his face and held him while he laved and suckled her. That lasted until his teeth gently grazed her; then she whimpered and plucked at his belt.

He was too triggered for a slow unveiling. He stripped bare in record time and tumbled her back onto the covers, landing between her legs and holding her captive when she tried to wiggle away. He kissed a path down her belly, registering the way she tensed when he approached her center, then jumped when he hit the sensitive flesh, and the way she moaned to confirm he'd found the right trailhead and set the right pace.

He pleasured her relentlessly, pushing her hard and fast to her first orgasm, her second. He would have gone for three if she hadn't grabbed him by the ears and pulled him up for a kiss so hot he almost misfired. Then he slid home for a race to the finish. Pressure and heat, already simmering below the surface, rose with each of her gasps, her cries. Then she lifted her hips and grasped his and he was done. The explosions seemed to go on forever. Blast after blast until he was empty. Like a spent casing, he fell beside her and sucked wind.

She curled into his side, resting her cheek over his hammering heart. Giving her up was going to be a bitch. But it would be for her own good.

A GENTLE JOSTLE woke Sam. Without opening his eyes, he took a mental inventory—a habit that had saved his bacon during more than one deployment.

A soft surface beneath him. A gentle breeze carrying the scent of flowers and birdsong. His muscles more rested and relaxed than he could remember them ever being. A warm body spooned against him. The jostler.

June.

His tension returned as fast as the crack of a rifle, followed by smoldering arousal, and his eyes snapped open, slowly adjusting to the near darkness. Curtains danced by the open window and moonlight seeped in. He eased up on his elbow. June slept with her folded hands tucked beneath her chin. The soft breaths escaping her pink parted lips fluttered a golden lock of hair draped across her nose.

The digital clock on her nightstand read 0500. He'd spent the entire night in her bed. Not part of his plan. He'd meant to ease out of their relationship, not build expectations he couldn't meet. Staying all night delivered the wrong message.

He had to get out of here before she woke. But he didn't want to move. Didn't want to slide away from her bottom tucked into his lap or wake her. Didn't want to deal with a morning after emotional fallout. Not just hers—his, too. Because he didn't know what to make of the past thirty-six hours.

He hadn't wanted her to cover his shift, and he'd barely slept until she'd called for assistance. Then when she'd boldly confronted the Lees, he'd been terrified that Jim Bob or his mother would hurt her and he'd be helpless to prevent it. When he'd seen her blood during the debriefing with Roth and learned that she'd slipped while descending the water tower, he'd been slammed with fear so fierce it immobilized him.

He'd faced death too many times to count and not once had he been paralyzed by fear. Until yesterday. And then not for himself—for June.

She'd snaked under his skin and made him want more—more than he was capable of giving. He had nothing to offer. And June deserved better. If he got out of the way, maybe she'd find it.

The thought made him about as uncomfortable as lying still in his hide while a venomous snake slithered over him.

Paying his steak-dinner debt last night had felt more like a date. A damned good one. Where had his plan to disconnect derailed? Before dinner when he'd had dessert first? Or after their steak dinner when they'd returned here and she'd served him fudge pie with homemade ice cream before he'd lost himself in her body again?

Now here he was. Rested and reluctant to leave but determined to think with his big head instead of the little drooler in his drawers. If he wanted to be out of here before she woke, he had to haul ass.

He eased away, leaving her warmth behind, and gathered the clothes he'd worn last night. He found his shirt, pants and shoes but only one sock. No time to search for the other one. He dressed in her den before slipping out her front door, shoes in hand.

On her porch he carefully closed and locked her door before turning and spotting Roth in the glow of his front porch light looking straight at him. There was no hiding where he'd been or what he'd been doing.

Roth's spine and jaw went rigid, but he said nothing as Sam covered the distance between them. "What in the hell, Rivers? You don't shit where you sleep," Roth snarled when Sam reached his side. "How in the hell are you going to give an unbiased report when you're sleeping with a suspect?"

Sam's molars snapped together. "June's not a suspect. She's the best damned deputy you have on your force."

"I'm supposed to trust your opinion now?"

"Inside." Sam shoved the key into the lock and turned it with so much force the old metal broke off in the keyhole. Damn it, he should have called a locksmith back when the lock started sticking, but he'd figured he wouldn't be around long enough for it to matter. At least the door opened. He wouldn't have to kick it down.

Roth followed him into the cottage. Sam shut the door. "June's not guilty of anything except caring too much for her neighbors. That'll be in my report, along with info clearing Alan and Mac. I'll write it up tonight. Then at the end of the month I'm out of here."

Roth's expression turned serious. "You're giving me two weeks' notice?"

"You knew this was only a TDY for me. I was here to investigate your team and I've completed my assignment. Nothing left but the paper shuffle."

"I wish you'd reconsider, Sam. You have a permanent position with QPD if you want it."

"Thanks, but police work is not for me. June loves her job and one of us would have to go. No fraternizing. It's in the handbook you sent me."

"Yeah, but as chief, I can rewrite—"

"There is no *but*. I'm leaving."

"Piper's going to have your hide if you hurt June. Hell, she'll have mine, too. I brought you here."

"June and I both knew that this was a temporary affair." Sam paused before going on. "Was there a reason you came by this morning?"

"I wanted to see if you were interested in breakfast and one of these before your shift." He pulled out a fat cigar.

"A smoke before breakfast?"

"Piper's pregnant. I'm going to be a daddy. Again. And this time I'm not gonna miss one second of the process."

Taken aback at seeing his usually cool and composed friend wearing a shit-eating grin and oozing jubilation, Sam took the cigar. "Congratulations. Quincey seems like a nice place to raise a kid."

The moment he said the words, Sam rejected them. Settling down and populating a neighborhood was for people who had jobs, not for a man who had no idea what his next step was.

Roth's breakfast invitation would have been welcome any other day, and yet today it had underlined another reason Sam needed to get out of Quincey. He would never fit in here.

But he wouldn't refuse Roth's request, because it meant Sam could delay being alone with June to discuss last night or the future they couldn't have.

He was being a coward and he knew it. But avoiding that conversation was better for both of them. Besides, he couldn't explain what he didn't understand.

JUNE AWOKE WITH a smile on her face and satisfaction in every atom of her being. She scooted backward but didn't encounter Sam's hot, firm body.

Disappointed, she rolled over and slid a hand across the empty side of the mattress. The sheets were cold. Sam must have left her bed a while ago. Was he still here? Getting a glass of water, maybe? She checked the clock. Six! She'd overslept.

She headed for the kitchen and found it empty, then looked out the window. His Charger was there. He must have gone home to shower. She yearned to join him under the hot spray, but due to the time shortage, she raced through her morning routine solo. As she made the bed, a sock fell out when she untangled the sheets. Sam's sock. The perfect excuse to say good-morning.

Madison's truck was not in its usual spot when June headed next door, meaning no witnesses. She couldn't remember the last time she'd been this excited. Last night had been...amazing. Not just the lovemaking but everything—from the way Sam's appreciative gaze had coasted from her face to her toes, then rebounded with desire burning in its depths, to dinner, during which she'd felt his hunger with each glance he stole. His response had given her hope for the future. Hope but not certainty.

Her feelings were bottled up and it wouldn't take much for the cork to pop and emotional words to froth forth—words Sam wasn't ready to hear. She loved him, was in love with him. It had been all she could do not to bubble over last night during their candlelit dinner. She'd promised herself after her slip on the water tower that she would tell him, but...something had held her back.

She jogged up his steps and knocked. The door swung open. "Sam?"

No answer. No Sam. He always locked his door. He had even locked hers when he left this morning. Was he in the shower? Had he left the door unlocked for her? She stepped inside but didn't hear water running. "Sam?"

Had he fallen back asleep? They hadn't rested much last night. That made her grin. She pushed the door closed. It bounced back open. She tried

again with the same result, then jiggled the knob.
The latch assembly wasn't working. Had his cottage
been broken into? She checked the jamb. No signs of
forced entry. But the lock was definitely damaged.

"Sam?" she repeated, louder this time. The total
silence of the house made the hairs on the back of
her neck rise. With her hand on her service weapon,
she cautiously moved down the hall. His bed was
empty and made. Then she spotted the chinos and
black polo shirt he'd worn last night draped over a
chair along with a solo sock. He'd been here. And
he'd left. But not in his car and without securing
his door. Both were out of character. She dialed his
phone. It rang nearby. She located it in his pants
pocket. He'd left his phone behind.

Retracing her steps, she scanned his living space
for clues. There were none. No dishes in the sink or
on the counter. No keys. No signs of a struggle. He
must have gone for an early run even though he was
cutting it late. She checked his closet. His running
shoes were there. But his uniform was not.

Disappointed that she wouldn't see him until
she reached the station, she headed out. A stack of
file folders on the kitchen table caught her eye as
she passed. He must have brought work home. But
what? She'd finished the paperwork on the Lees.
The sight of her name on the top file stopped her
in her tracks. Then she noticed two more tabs beneath hers. Mac Morrison and Alan Aycock were

written on them. Why would Sam have files on each deputy?

She picked up the one bearing her name and read the top page. The typed data listed her hire dates, training and credentials, and other information that could have come only from an official personnel file to which the chief had sole access. Then she read the first line written in Sam's bold script.

"More parent than police officer."

The shot came out of nowhere and it hurt. She sucked a bracing breath and read the next line. "Spends too much time talking on the job instead of doing it." The hole in her heart opened wider.

"Rationalizes crimes rather than dealing with them. Nosy."

Her knees started to shake and her chest to ache. All the while Sam had been making love to her, he'd been condemning her. She continued reading. The words whirled in her head like debris in a tornado's funnel cloud. By the time she reached the bottom of the page, her hands were shaking so badly she could barely focus.

"No sign she's involved in or had knowledge of the moonshine production/sales."

Sam had been investigating her to see if she was part of Quincey's illegal activities, and only one person could have ordered that investigation—Chief Roth Sterling. Her best friend's husband. Her boss. A man she'd thought liked and respected her. The betrayal burned like alcohol poured into an open cut. Had Piper known?

Her gaze traveled to the other folders. She recalled a dozen conversations when Sam had asked her about Mac or Alan. She'd believed him interested in his coworkers and hadn't held back. Had he slept with her to get information? Had she given incriminating evidence against them? They were both nice guys, not crooks. Could something she'd said cost them their jobs? How could she live with herself if that happened?

Feeling as if she was violating Mac's privacy but needing to know if she'd inadvertently betrayed him, she opened his file and read. Snippets of conversations she'd shared with Sam were there on the page and her words, taken out of context, had been used to discredit her fellow officer. She checked Alan's file and found more of the same.

The pain cut deep and guilt weighed heavily on her heart. She prided herself on being an expert at reading body language, at understanding people and their motives. But this was the second time a man had duped her into handing over her heart and her trust only to violate both in the end. How could she have missed the signs? Not once but twice.

Was she that stupid?

Sam's duplicitous actions not only threatened her, they threatened her self-made family. Hurt morphed into fury. June rarely got angry. But when she did, everyone in the Jones clan knew to run for the hills.

And the longer she stewed, the bigger the boilover.
Sam didn't know that.

Too bad for him.

THE STATION WAS dark except for the light in Roth's
office when June arrived fifteen minutes before her
shift. Was Sam in there with him? Heaven help him
if he was. She strode across the tiles and entered
without knocking. The chief was alone.

Roth looked up abruptly. "You need something,
Jones?"

"You ordered an investigation. On all of us."

Roth rocked back in his chair, eyes filled with
caution. "Yes."

She gave him credit for not lying or denying it.
"And you brought your buddy in to act as hench-
man and hang us all out to dry."

"Only if you were guilty."

"Do you trust none of us?"

"Butch White's corruption went on for a long
time, and you all worked with him and supposedly
saw nothing."

"You interrogated each of us after Butch's arrest.
That didn't satisfy you?" She held up a hand when
he opened his mouth to respond. "Rhetorical question. Obviously, it didn't. Then you set me up by
putting Sam next door and getting him to…make
nice." She wasn't going to admit to the affair. That
had been her stupidity.

"There were no vacancies in Quincey's only

apartment complex, and the relationship between you was ill-advised. You work together."

So he knew. Had Sam reported that, too? And in how much detail? Humiliation stung her cheeks. "Where is the traitor?"

"Sam's not a traitor. He did what I hired him to do."

"Where is he?" she repeated. "I'm not going to shoot him." Still Roth hesitated. "You don't trust me with that information either, Chief? Then maybe I shouldn't be working for you."

"Don't be rash. You're the best officer on my team. And before you condemn Sam, you should know he told me that."

"And you trust *him*?"

"With my life."

"Where is he?" she asked once again.

"He's at the shooting range," Roth admitted with obvious reluctance. "Jones—June, don't do anything stupid."

"You don't know me very well if you think I'd break the law because some bastard screwed me over. I was taught to turn the other cheek rather than seek vengeance. But Sam messed with people I care about and he used me to do it, and that makes his deception unforgivable."

She turned to leave, but then indignation got the better of her. Sam was guilty of betraying her and all of Quincey, but Roth had betrayed him, too. What kind of friend did that? She rounded on her chief.

"You claim to be Sam's friend. You should be helping and guiding him to a new career, not encouraging him to chase a dream that isn't going to come true and isn't in his best interest."

"I'm giving him time to figure that out."

"Well, he's not figuring it out. He's determined to go back. What if by some stroke of bad luck he gets reinstated and he's killed in action because you didn't discourage him from returning to a job he's no longer physically able to perform? Will you be able to live with yourself?"

She bit her tongue. Why was she fighting Sam's battles? He'd betrayed her. But fighting for the ones she loved was second nature, even though Sam didn't want her concern. Or *her*.

She pivoted and headed out the door. Five minutes later she parked beside the patrol car outside the hunt-and-bait shop. The front door of the building was unlocked. She didn't bother calling out to Tate and instead steamed straight to the red door and yanked it open.

Sam stood in the center lane, ear and eye protection in place. Her heart contracted as if someone had reached into her chest and crushed the organ in a giant fist. Pain, betrayal, loss and disappointment rained down on her like a hail of gunfire. And fear. Fear that he might succeed on his suicide mission of resuming his sniper career. The target, covered in a tighter pattern than before, exacerbated her concern. His marksmanship was improving. Would it be good enough at the end of the year to resume his old job?

Sam must have felt the change in air pressure caused by the opening door, because his gaze swung her way. He laid his weapon on the rubber-matted shelf, removed his eye and ear protection and stepped out of the booth. The hunger and welcome in his eyes ramped up her anger because it was a lie. But it looked real and that only hurt more.

"Did you sleep with me to get information?"

He snapped into alert mode, going still, watchful, and rolling to the balls of his feet. Then resignation settled on his face. He'd obviously known this moment would come. She could see all of that so clearly now. How could she have missed his deception?

"No."

"I trusted you, Sam." She hated the crack in her voice. "I trusted you with things I'd never told anyone. And you betrayed me."

"I was up-front from day one about my intentions. You came on to *me*. Remember?"

Shame parked its big butt on her shoulders. "This isn't about us, you conceited ass. This is about you putting personal information that you pried out of me in Alan's and Mac's files and using it to discredit them."

His jaw tensed, his expression turning stoic. "How did you find out?"

"I went to your place this morning to return the

sock you left in my bed. The lock was broken. Stu-pid me, I rushed in worried about you. I saw the files."

"I had a job to do. Getting involved with you was never part of the plan. But nothing you've told me discredits Morris, Aycock or you. It does the oppo-site. It clears you all of collusion with the crooked deputy."

"'More parent than cop. Talks too much. Nosy.' Those weren't your words?"

"Those were my initial observations, not my final analysis. Did you read the back of that page?"

No, she hadn't, because she hadn't been able to take any more condemnation. She reined in her hurt. *This isn't about you, remember?*

"You called Mac a 'momma's boy' and Alan an 'overworked, overstressed single father always short of cash.'"

"All true. But my final report will say that none of those affects their job performance." He stepped toward her. She backed abruptly and he halted.

"What did you tell Roth about us?"

"Nothing. He was waiting on my front porch when I left your place this morning. I was carry-ing my shoes and one sock. There was no way to cover what we'd been doing. I shouldn't have stayed the night. I'm sorry, June, if I misled you into ex-pecting something I can't give you."

His pity nauseated her.

"This is not about me, Sam. I've been stupid

enough to fall in love with the wrong man before."
He flinched at her unintentional confession. She
ignored it and plowed on despite the humiliation
burning through her.

"I survived his betrayal and I'll survive yours,
too. But before you load your car and move on with
your life, you need to figure out what it is you're
really afraid of. If it's failure, then you're too late.
You've already failed at everything that matters.
Your parents and sisters love you and would do anything to hear from you, but you ignore them. The
love and respect of family and friends are all that
counts in this world. Anything else is fleeting and
worthless."

Her throat and eyes burned. "So go ahead and
run. Run from the fact that your military career is
over. Run from your fear of attachment. But I can
tell you from experience, your fears will always
find you."

She turned and fled with all the dignity she could
muster, because if she stayed a second longer she
would lose the slippery grip on her control. She'd
already given Sam too much—she refused to surrender her pride by bawling in front of him. She
wouldn't let him know how badly he'd hurt her.

CHAPTER SIXTEEN

SHE LOVED HIM. June's confession left Sam reeling, his chest tight and his thoughts spinning out of control. He ached to run after her, but he let her go. A clean cut was the best kind. He could never be the man she needed. Not without a job or a plan. But she was wrong—he wasn't running, damn it. He was looking out for her.

He turned his face to the camera. Was Lowry watching?

Time to pack up. He'd burned a lot of bridges during his short stay in Quincey. He reeled in his target and went through the motions of packing his gear by rote. But even routine couldn't erase the knot in his gut, and not even the fact that every shot had hit the target made him feel better.

He should have known a woman like June couldn't have an affair without giving more than her body. He wanted to make it right. But he couldn't. Not for him and June.

He'd screwed up. Big-time. The thought plagued him on the drive to the cottage and as he loaded his meager belongings. It stayed with him while he turned in his report along with his gun and badge to Roth and said good-bye to his friend. And it was still with him as he headed out of town.

Then it hit him. He could make things better for June—she'd told him how. He did a U-turn and hit the gas. He drove straight through town to the church. Her father was walking from his house to the rectory. Sam flagged him down. "Sir, I need to make a confession."

"I'm a pastor, son, not a Catholic priest."

"I need forgiveness."

The preacher studied him. "Come in."

Sam followed him to an office and parked in a chair. He didn't know where to start. But he knew he was already pissed off. The man had dropped everything for a stranger, but he wouldn't give his daughter five minutes.

"What's troubling you, Deputy?" The preacher's tone was patient and kind, neither of which Sam had heard when the man spoke to June.

"I've killed a lot of men, some women and even a few children." June's father looked taken aback. Funny how the same green eyes that sparkled with warmth in June could be so devoid of emotion in her father. "I was a sniper in the Marine Corps. Do you think God can forgive me for taking those lives?"

"Of course. You were defending our country."

"But I broke a commandment. Multiple times."

"It was your job. And our Maker forgives the sins of anyone who truly repents."

"You're a hypocrite, Pastor. You know that?"

June's father stiffened with indignation. "I beg your pardon?"

"Our Maker can forgive anything, but you can't forgive your own daughter for making a mistake when she was young, naive and too trusting. She's not the one you should be condemning. That slimy piece of shit who took advantage of her is."

"It takes two to commit adultery."

"June didn't know he was married. He was the liar and adulterer. She was his victim. She came running home to you for your support and forgiveness and you withheld both." Sam rose and slapped his tattered pocket-size Bible on the desk. His mother had given it to him before he left for boot camp. He'd never deployed without it.

"There's an old saying, 'There are no atheists in a firefight.' And it's true. Out there where there's nothing but you, the enemy trying to kill you and Him, you get real familiar with the Word. I'm beginning to think I know this book better than you. It says you're not fit to judge June or anyone else. And yet you do."

"My relationship with my daughter is not your concern."

"I'm making it my concern because I care about her—probably more than you do. I watched you at June's birthday party. You turn on the charm for your parishioners like a snake-oil salesman. But your own children are denied your attention.

Preacher, you've run off your sons and daughters. Even your grandchildren barely speak to you. Have you ever asked yourself why they all avoid you?

"How June grew up to become such a caring, forgiving, understanding person with a two-faced asshole like you for a father is the real miracle. If any of us burns in hell, sir, it will be you."

The preacher stood. "It's time for you to leave."

"A very wise woman—your daughter—told me love of family and friends is all that matters. Pray on that one, before you die alone." He snatched up his Bible. "And maybe you'd better go back and read this again. You sure as hell aren't living what it teaches. But June is."

JUNE'S CHEEKS HURT from the effort of keeping a smile stapled to her face while she'd numbly trudged through her day ever vigilant for Sam. She hadn't seen him, but looking for him and trying to keep everyone else from guessing her heart had been crushed had exhausted her. But the day was finally over. All she wanted was a long hot bath and solitude to lick her wounds.

As she drove up to their cottages after the longest-feeling shift of her career, she noticed Sam's parking space was empty. Hollowness welled in her stomach. She killed the engine, gripped her steering wheel and stared at his cottage.

How could she have fallen so hard and so fast?

How could she have been so blind and stupid?

How could she have made the mistake of falling for an emotionally unavailable man twice? And then a possibility hit her and she frowned. Her father was emotionally unavailable. Was she choosing men like him? That idea made her a little queasy.

Her father was a judgmental, hypercritical control freak who never saw her successes. He only saw her shortcomings. She'd never please him, she realized. She had to stop begging for his approval and work for her own satisfaction. That meant no more crawling over to their house on Sunday for dunch. The sad casualty of that would be losing time with her mother, but her mother needed to meet her halfway. June had been carrying the entire weight of their relationship for too long.

Sam's door opened and June's hopes sailed like a kite catching the wind... Then Madison stepped onto his porch carrying a mop and bucket, and June's hopes crash-landed. Was she crazy? Even if it had been Sam, she could never love a man she couldn't trust.

Good riddance. Right?

But that didn't make her hurt any less, worry any less or feel any less disappointed in herself... and him.

Madison waved and smiled and June suddenly wanted to back her truck out of the driveway and disappear for a few days. She couldn't fake a cheerful attitude anymore. But she wouldn't run. Running solved nothing.

And she couldn't tell Madison the truth right now. June refused to spoil Madison's happiness due to her upcoming wedding by crying all over her. And she couldn't confide in Piper either. Doing so would cause dissension between Piper and Roth.

Usually June was the one everybody ran to with their problems, yet she had no one to go to. So she'd suck it up and deal with her heartache solo. Forcing a smile, she climbed from the cab. "Cleaning?"

Madison joined her in the driveway. "Yes. Sam moved out."

The news shouldn't have pierced like a nail through her heart. But it did.

"He taped his broken key to my door and left a note saying he'd forfeit his deposit in lieu of giving notice. Did something happen at the station?"

June wrestled with all she knew and all she couldn't say and shrugged. "You'll have to ask Roth."

"I will. Feel like a celebratory dinner?"

"Celebrating what?"

Madison's eyes sparkled and her face glowed with happiness. She pressed a hand to her tummy. "I'm pregnant. I guess that makes two of us."

June tried to make sense of the information. "Two?"

Madison's eyes widened. She slapped her hand over her mouth. "Piper hasn't told you she and Roth are expecting?"

All the more reason to keep the Sam situation

to herself. "No. I haven't seen her, and Roth didn't mention it. Congratulations!" June hugged her friend. She was truly happy for her even if it left June feeling even more isolated and empty.

"Piper and Roth were trying. Adam and I weren't. But it's a wonderful surprise. You're going to be an auntie times two sometime in May."

Their successful relationships only underlined June's lack of one. But she would never let that show. "I'll arrange a baby shower for each of you."

"Are you okay?"

No. "Sure. Long day."

Tires crunched in the driveway. June's heart jumped in anticipation again—foolish of her. Then she recognized Rhett's car and her hopes sank. She mentally kicked herself for forgetting him and his baby. Still, she didn't know if she had the reserves to handle whatever his crisis was this time or the strength to turn him away. But she was thankful for the excuse to escape Madison. And that made her sadder. She'd told Sam that friends and family were everything, and yet she was fast distancing herself from both.

"I guess I'll have to take a rain check on that dinner."

"I'll hold you to it." Madison waved to Rhett, then disappeared into her house.

June faced her brother, bracing herself. He approached, carrying a pizza box and a six-pack of sodas. "Got a few minutes? I brought food."

Her brother never brought anything. "Come in."

"Can we invite Sam to join us?"

Another arrow hit home. "No. He's left Quincey. Why?"

He set his offerings on the table. "I wanted to thank him for his advice."

That stopped her. "What advice?"

"He's a tough talker. Really ticked me off. But once I calmed down and I thought about what he said at your birthday party, it made me think." Rhett popped the top on a can and opened the pizza box. Typical of a college kid, he didn't wait for a plate before digging into the pie.

"What exactly did he say, Rhett?" she asked again, and slid a dish in front of him. She had no appetite, but she went through the motions of serving herself while she waited for Rhett to finish his story.

"A lot, but the upshot is that we've put the baby up for adoption."

A pang of loss and regret stole her breath. It was the best decision for all concerned. But Rhett's child was family. Her nephew. For one fleeting moment she considered adopting him, moving away and starting life over where no one knew her and without a man to complicate things. But no, that would be selfish and unfair to the baby.

"What made you decide to do that?"

"Sam said it was time for me to start solving my own problems instead of always running to you.

Until he said that, I hadn't realized that's what I do. Jolene and I talked, probably our longest conversation to date. She has no interest in being a mom—ever. I want to be a dad. One day. But not now. I can't afford to keep up myself, let alone a baby. He's so…tiny and helpless. And perfect. And—" He put down his pizza and sadness filled his face. Tears pooled in his eyes but he blinked them back. "I hate it, June. I want to be the daddy he deserves. But I can't. And giving him to someone who can… It's the right thing to do."

The splash of water on her hand surprised June. Only then did she realize tears were streaming down her cheeks. She wasn't sure who she was crying for. Rhett. His baby. Or herself. She suppressed the twister of emotions and wiped her face, then grasped her brother's hand.

"I know it wasn't an easy decision, but I'm proud of you for putting the child's welfare first."

"Sam was a good guy. I'm sorry you and he didn't work out."

"Sam and I weren't—"

"Give me credit. I may be young and dumb about a lot of things, but I saw the way you two looked at each other, and I liked the way he stuck up for you. If you need an ear, I'm here."

That was a first. Rhett never put himself out for others. Her baby brother was finally growing up. "Thanks. I'll be okay. I always am."

"Yeah. You've set a good example. Better than

Mom or Dad. But the offer stands. And nothing you say will go any farther than my ears…unless you need me to kick Sam's butt."

That surprised a laugh out of her. "Think you could take him?"

"Hell, no. But for you I'd try to get as many licks in as I could before he cleaned my clock."

That was the reward she'd been waiting a lifetime for—for someone in her family to stand up for her. And Sam had given her that gift.

FOR THE SECOND TIME in recent weeks Sam had no plan. The highway junction came into view. His family was to the west, but he wasn't ready to face them. So he turned east toward unfamiliar territory, with his stereo blasting to drown out his thoughts. He kept his wheels turning until he ran out of road in Hatteras, North Carolina.

He had two choices: turn back or wait for the ferry to Ocracoke, the next island in the Outer Banks chain.

He wasn't running, damn it. He was just enjoying his freedom—the first he'd had since enlisting.

He drove onto the ferry. As soon as the boat left the dock, people climbed from their cars and mingled by the rails. Kids fed the seagulls squawking and diving for snacks. Sam didn't feel like socializing. He stayed in his car with only the black gaping hole of his future to keep him company.

June was wrong. He wasn't afraid of attachment.

If he'd spent his life forming temporary relationships, first on bases as a kid, then in the service himself, it was because it was the military way of life. So yeah, transient interactions were all he knew except for Roth and a couple of other friends he seldom saw. But that wasn't a flaw. Was it?

He'd never wanted what Roth had, never even considered leaving a wife and kids at home worrying about him while he fought for freedom. He didn't need letters during a deployment to remind him that others were losing sleep over him.

So why was he a little envious of his friend?

What if June was right? What if he was incapable of sustaining anything more than a superficial connection? Had he screwed up the most basic relationship of all—the one with his family? He'd chewed out the preacher for shortchanging his kids. But had Sam done any differently with his parents and sisters? The answer jarred him. No. He hadn't.

The boat docked. Rattled by his discovery, he fell in with the line of cars heading down a narrow road flanked by the Atlantic Ocean and the Pamlico Sound. When he reached the next ferry terminal, the gates were closed. He'd missed the last ride off the island. He was stuck. Couldn't go forward or backward. He had to find a place to take cover. Good thing he had his camping gear in the trunk.

He found an isolated spot along the shore, ate an MRE and lay there half the night listening to the wind rustling through the sea oats, on guard for the nocturnal animal sounds. But nothing was stalking him except his own dark thoughts.

He missed June. Leaving her behind had been harder than he'd expected. He should have been able to make a clean break and move on. He was no good for her. Not now. Maybe never.

Both his dad and June had claimed Sam was fixated on the corps because he was afraid he couldn't do anything else. But what else *could* he do?

Holding out for the corps meant living in limbo for the next six months. Should he move on? If so, to what? What were the other strengths his father was so certain he possessed?

He stared at the stars. Tooting his own horn was an unfamiliar task and it took a while for the rusty mechanism to engage. He was disciplined. Dedicated. Intelligent. A good team player. Self-motivated and reliable. What job could he do with those skills and his military training? Would he have to go back to school? The thought of joining a bunch of kids like Rhett on campus was about as appealing as bedding down in a viper pit.

He shifted on his sandy bed. His wallet caused an uncomfortable lump. He pulled it out of his pocket and caught a glimpse of the white corner of a business card. June's godfather's card. John Page's open invitation to visit pricked Sam's interest.

John seemed like a smart guy, one who wanted to talk about all things military—things Sam knew and loved. John had found a career he enjoyed after being medically discharged—what Sam had to do. Sam could use a little unbiased wisdom right now. His father's advice, while appreciated, was that of a parent to a child. John's would be soldier to marine—he had nothing vested in Sam's outcome.

Sam had a plan, albeit a short-range one. That was a start. In the morning he'd call June's godfather and see if his invitation was still open.

His last thought before sleep ambushed him was of June. Her ready smile. Her green eyes. Her fit body. Her big heart. Her quick mind. Her brownies. Did she like camping? Would she have been excited about bunking down beside him in the sand? Would she have made love to him in the moonlight under the stars?

She was the first woman who'd ever made him think about a life outside the corps. And he'd let her down. Because he was afraid, he admitted. Afraid of failing himself, but mostly he was afraid of failing her, he realized.

Before she'd found the files, she'd looked at him as if he were a hero. But he was just an out-of-work bum. She deserved a man who could protect her and spoil her the way she did everyone she loved. And that wasn't him.

JUNE'S EYES WERE crossing from fatigue. Converting the old files to digital was going to be slow, tedious work—just what she needed to keep her mind off Sam.

The station door opened and she glanced up from the computer screen, then did a double take. Her father entered the main room, looked around, spotted her and headed her way.

She sprang to her feet. "What's wrong? Is it Mom?"

"Nothing's wrong. Your mother's fine. Can't I stop by to visit my daughter?"

Not the response she'd expected. "You never have before."

"Well, I've never had someone call me an asshole and tell me I was going to hell before."

Dumbfounded over hearing her father swear, June gaped. "Who?"

"That new deputy."

Sam. Her breath caught. "When did you see him?"

"A few days ago. It took a while for his words to become palatable. Then when I told your mother what he had the audacity to say and she had the nerve to agree with him…" He looked away, shifting uncomfortably—totally unlike him.

"What else did he say?"

Her father glanced at Mac sitting at the desk a few yards away trying very hard to hide that he was eavesdropping. "Can I buy you lunch?"

Another first. "Sure. It's time for me to take my break. You got this, Mac?"

"You bet. Take your time."

"So this is where you work," her father said as they headed for the door.

"I have for almost five years, Dad." His face flushed and she wished the words back. "I'm sorry. That was rude. I've just never known you to show any interest in my job."

"My mistake. I hear you're very good at it."

The surge of happiness and pride stopped her in her tracks in the parking lot. Hadn't she decided his opinion didn't matter anymore? Then worry set in. "What's this really about? Are you sick?"

He shook his head. "I can see why you'd believe I'd only repent if I were on my deathbed, but I owe you an apology Justi—June. As your deputy pointed out, I've been preaching the Word…but I haven't been living it."

"What exactly did Sam say to you?"

"He hit me with a few home truths that forced me to reexamine the past. I have alienated you and your brothers and sisters. I've been rigid and judgmental. I held my children to a higher standard, an unattainable one, because I believed we needed to set an example. I expected perfection, and only our Father is without flaws. I am very sorry, June. I want to try to mend our family. But I'm not sure how to go about it."

He looked sincere. But did she dare trust or believe in the unbelievable? A lump rose in her throat, corking the hope swelling in her chest.

"Thank you for admitting your mistakes, Dad. I

know it wasn't easy. And I'm sure all of us would love to heal our family."

One thing was certain. Sam might have exited her life, but he'd left behind a huge impression on two of her family members. For that she would be eternally grateful.

And she would miss him even more.

SAM STOOD IN the high school gym, listening to the shouts of young voices calling cadence, the stomp of marching feet and the slap of hands on mock M1 Garand rifles echoing off the walls as John's JROTC students carried out the drill almost flawlessly. It reminded him of boot camp.

Then John blew his whistle. "At ease," he called out, and the young men and women snapped into position, straight lines, eyes forward, perfect posture. "Good job. Dismissed."

As though a light switch had been flipped, the students suddenly morphed into regular sixteen- to eighteen-year-olds, talking and jostling each other as they filed out of the building.

"Told you my crack squad was good, didn't I?"

"Yes, sir."

"Takes dedication, discipline and teamwork, but they have it. Every last one of them. If they don't have it when they get here, I make sure they learn it before they graduate." The pride in his voice was unmistakable.

John had listed all the qualities Sam missed from the corps. "You've done a great job."

"Our teams have placed in both armed and unarmed drill competitions. I'm going to miss them and *all* this."

"I can see why you would."

"I get these young men and women for four years, and I get to see them mature from adolescent to adult, something the rest of my fellow teachers are denied. I teach them citizenship, leadership, geography, history and first aid in the program. Some of my students will head straight to boot camp after graduation. Others will go into college ROTC, but even the ones who don't pursue the military will carry the discipline they've learned in my JROTC for the rest of their lives."

When Sam had spoken to John's students in the classroom prior to the drill, they'd shown the same excitement and commitment he'd had at their age. Being in front of them and also the Quincey students and sharing some of his experiences and fielding their questions had been energizing.

Sam's mental wheels started turning. His life was a train wreck. If he wanted it to be any different, he was the only one with the power to put the cars back on the track. Was this an option for him?

"June suggested I consider JROTC."

"She's a pretty astute judge of character."

"How did you end up as an instructor?"

"Applied. Talked to everyone who'd listen. Pulled strings. Need me to pull a few for you?"

Taken aback, he looked at June's godfather. "Would you?"

"My girl's taken a shine to you. Of course I would."

That took the wind out of his sails. The man deserved honesty. "I left the Quincey PD. June and I aren't together anymore. I couldn't saddle her with a man who has no job."

"But would you be interested in her if you had one?"

"Yes, sir." The answer sprang out before Sam had a chance to think about it. But once he did, he knew it was the right answer. The only answer. June was more than his equal. She was the strongest woman he knew. She didn't hesitate to lay her heart on the line for others.

John clapped him on the back. "Thought so. You were mighty protective of her at her party—a man's not that territorial without a reason. I'll make some calls tonight. I won't lie—these are difficult positions to land. Not many to go around. But with your recent medical discharge, you stand a good shot because right now they're actively recruiting wounded warriors. Where can I reach you?"

June had been right about a lot of things—one of which was his need to visit his family. In trying to protect them, he'd inadvertently hurt them. He owed them, particularly his mother, an apology.

"I'm heading to my parents' in Tennessee, but I'll give you my cell number."

"I'll see what I can find and get back to you, but, son, let me give you a piece of advice. Life and marriage don't come without obstacles. If something means a lot to you, you'll find a way to make it happen. If you find yourself making excuses, then maybe you're headed in the wrong direction. If you're not absolutely certain you'd give your last breath trying to make my Junebug happy, then leave her be."

The wisdom he'd been seeking. Sam nodded. He needed to find a way to be with June. If this job didn't work out, he'd find another one. Then he'd go after her. If she'd still have him.

CHAPTER SEVENTEEN

JUNE STOOD AT the end of the pier watching the sun set over the Atlantic Ocean and tried to find the inner peace that she'd been lacking of late.

Her heart was broken. Shattered. Destroyed. When she'd promised Madison she'd be at this wedding no matter what, she hadn't realized how hard it would be to hide her pain while she watched two people pledge forever to each other.

But now that the ecstatically happy bride and groom had left on their honeymoon and their guests had dispersed, June could drop the pretense. Behind her the restaurant staff worked quietly to dismantle the flowered arch and put away the folding chairs and reception tables. In front of her a pod of a dozen porpoises surfaced and dove as if performing a water ballet.

Wind teased her hair from its pins, tugged at the hem of her dress and ruffled the sheer silk shawl wrapped around her bare shoulders, but she didn't care. She had the solitude she craved for the first time this wedding week. Not that she wasn't happy that her friends had found their soul mates—she was. But she had decided she was never going to find hers. She'd thought Sa—

No. No more thoughts of *him*. He was gone. She'd erased his name from her vocabulary, and soon—if she was very persistent and lucky—it would be gone from her heart. She'd been marking time, renting her cottage and waiting for Mr. Right. No more of that. When she returned to Quincey, she would buy a home and put down the roots she yearned for— solo. Thanks to her inheritance from her grandfather, she had enough money to do that.

The raised voices of the staff behind her caught her attention. She turned and saw them pointing at the beach beside the pier. A man was bent over, his back to her, writing in the sand. She shielded her eyes against the glare. It was a marine in dress blues with his white hat and the red stripe down the side of the pants. His black shoes were so well polished she could see the glare of sunlight on patent leather from here.

Her heart ached. Would Sam get back into the service? Would she turn on the news one evening and see his face accompanied by the story of a casualty? Her eyes stung. She blinked, grabbed the flower bouquets and crossed to the opposite railing.

She should have guessed that she'd see marines at Wrightsville Beach. Camp Lejeune, the home of more than one hundred thousand of them, was only a short drive from here.

But curiosity nagged her. Why would anyone

come to the beach in dress blues? The man hadn't been a wedding guest. From her vantage point beside the bride, she'd have seen him. And there wasn't another ceremony scheduled for this evening. She returned to her previous position and read the words he'd scratched into the wet sand.

I'm sorry.
I love you.
Please give me—

She shook her head. Some guys were such romantics. Wouldn't it be nice to find one of them? A man who actually told you what he was thinking instead of just staring at you with inscrutable eyes and making you guess—incorrectly—what was going on in his handsome head?

She glanced at the bouquets. It figured she'd finally catch the bridal flowers once she'd given up on finding Mr. Right.

The marine finished his message, then stepped aside and turned to face her. He laid one white-gloved hand over his heart and removed his hat with the other. Sam.

The bottom fell out of her stomach. Dizziness swamped her. She clutched the rail for balance.

He snapped his hand from his chest to point at the words.

"—a second chance," he'd finished.

Her heart soared like a seagull; then it dive-bombed like a pelican. No. *No!* She backed away from the railing. Sam had used and abandoned her. He'd lied to her and betrayed her friends. Why would she want him back?

Time to go. This was an encounter she didn't want to have. She bolted for the parking lot, but she couldn't find the valet to get her keys. Sam rounded the building at a dead run, then stopped abruptly when he saw her.

He was so handsome in uniform it hurt to look at him. She searched for the missing valet and spotted him on the far side of the lot, then tugged on the key cabinet handle. It was locked.

"June. Wait," Sam called out in the deep voice that haunted her dreams.

She debated hiding out in the ladies' room, but a large party leaving the restaurant blocked her retreat. And Sam was persistent. He'd very likely be waiting whenever she returned anyway. Best to get the confrontation over with. "I have nothing to say to you, Sam."

He searched her face. "No response to what I wrote out there?"

"No. My answer is no, not that I have no response."

She could have sworn pain and defeat flashed through his eyes before he stiffened with determination. But she'd misread him before. She didn't believe what she thought she saw now. "Give me five minutes, June."

The valet had lit a cigarette and was leaning against the low wall on the other side of the parking lot. Since she couldn't get her car, what choice did she have? "Clock's ticking."

A family of five headed up the walkway toward the restaurant. Sam motioned her around the side of the building. Reluctantly, she followed, then paused on the edge of the sidewalk beside the sand. Her heels would sink if she went any farther. Before she could remove her shoes, Sam swept her into his arms and covered the distance to a nearby picnic table in three long strides.

Her body betrayed her with a racing pulse and a flush of heat. It felt so good to be held against his muscled chest and in his strong arms that she had to fight the urge to lay her head on his shoulder. "Put me down."

He gently set her on top of the table. "I screwed up. I know. And I hurt you. I'm sorry. I'm a no-excuses kind of guy, but you need to understand what was going through my head."

She folded her arms. "Give it your best shot. But there's no excuse for lying to me and using my words to hurt my friends."

"Didn't Roth show you my final report? It cleared all of you of wrongdoing."

Roth had. And as Sam had said, there'd been nothing condemning in it. If anything, he'd explained why she, Alan and Mac were ideally suited to police work in Quincey. "He did, but that doesn't change the fact that you deceived me."

Sam removed his hat and ran a palm over his closely cropped hair. Nervous. Sam was nervous. She'd seen him in a lot of ways, but not that one. Or was she misreading him again?

"I was on a mission. Roth saved my butt too many times to count and I owed him. When he asked, I couldn't refuse. My goal was to get in. Get it done. Get out. I had tunnel vision. I never expected...you.

"I've told you before that my mother was married to a deadbeat before she met my dad. The day my mother landed her first job after nursing school, that jerk quit his. He sat on his butt while Mom worked two and sometimes three jobs and struggled to raise my sisters. He was a useless piece of shit who made her life miserable. But she loved him, so she stuck it out. She's a lot like you that way—too generous with the ones she loves. He took off when Erin, my youngest sister, was three months old. I heard those stories all my life, and I swore I'd never be a man who leeched off his woman."

She dammed the flood of sympathy.

"Mom struggled for six years before she met and married my dad—a career marine and the love of her life. He was a stable provider and a good husband when he was home. But when he was deployed, she worried and walked the floor. Some of my earliest memories are of her crying at night and no matter what I did or said, I couldn't make her better. I always knew I would follow in Dad's foot-steps, but I swore I'd never put a woman in the po-sition to cry over me. And I figured what my mom didn't know, she wouldn't worry about."

Typical male logic. Not that she was making ex-cuses for him. "It doesn't work that way, Sam."

He grimaced. "I know that now. I spent a week with my parents after I left Quincey. I learned that my 'the less she knew, the less she'd worry' theory was completely backward.

"June, I've lost a lot of friends over the years, and I've attended too many of their funerals and posthu-mous medal ceremonies to count. I decided a long time ago to keep my distance because it's easier and less painful that way. Seeing a wife or kid receive a folded flag graveside…" He paused, swallowed and looked off into the distance as if he was battling memories. "I didn't want to inflict that on anyone. So you were right. I avoided attachment.

"Then I met you. And even though I knew Quincey was a TDY—temporary duty station—you got under my skin. I have never desired a woman the way I did you, and I didn't know how to handle it. You wrecked my plan to get in and get out and leave no trace."

She wanted to run. And contrarily, she wanted to stay and hear everything he had to say even though she knew it would likely hurt and make forgetting him doubly difficult. But this was the first time she'd seen beyond the facade Sam showed the rest of the world. It was the first time he'd said he wanted her.

"Oh, you left more than a trace, Sam. You told my father he was going to hell. I don't know that anyone's ever been that bold before."

"Somebody needed to. His judgmental attitude was hurting you. Did it do any good?"

She couldn't help smiling. "It did. We're not out of the woods by any means, but he's trying hard enough that my brothers and sisters are bringing their families for dunch every Sunday."

"Dunch?"

"Dinner-slash-lunch. Like brunch, only later." She paused before going on. "You also talked some sense into Rhett. He's actually acting like a responsible adult. He found a part-time job, and he and Jolene gave the baby up for adoption."

"I couldn't let you become a struggling single mom, not after hearing the hell mine went through. And I know how much you would have invested in the baby, only to give him up when your brother wanted him back. It would have crushed you. That little boy deserves two loving parents in it for the long haul."

"I agree."

He looked down the beach and again he swiped his head. Then his eyes met hers and the turbulent emotions in them squeezed her throat.

"You were beyond my scope, June. Strong, both physically and mentally. My equal. No doubt about it. Tough as nails on the outside but soft as a marsh-mallow in the middle. Caring, loving and under-standing of everyone. Even me.

"And you were right. I was scared. Of you. Five and a half feet of in-my-face attitude. You gave one hundred percent of yourself and expected nothing in return. You're the generous kind of woman that a selfish bastard could end up draining dry.

"What you made me feel flat-out paralyzed me, June. And in Roth's office when I saw your blood and found out you'd slipped on the water tower and thought about what could have happened—" he shuddered "—I was sick to my stomach. Me. The tough guy who's belly-crawled past dead bod-ies without flinching. And I started wanting to pro-tect you from your too-trusting nature, but mostly from me. Then when you told me you loved me..." He shook his head.

"I freaked out. I had nothing to offer. With my discharge I had become exactly like my mother's first husband. No job. No prospects. Not even a clue of where I was headed next. If I'd taken you up on your offer—"

"I never offered more than sex."

"Wrong. You offered everything. It was there in your eyes every time you looked at me. And if I'd accepted your gifts, I'd have been no better than the parasite who fathered my sisters. And I couldn't be him, June. I couldn't drag you into the pig pond of my life. So I shipped out believing it was for your own good and that like everyone else in my past, you'd soon be a vague memory."

That hurt. It shouldn't have, since she'd been hoping the same about him, but hurt it did.

"But that didn't happen. After I retreated, I realized that I didn't want to go back to the corps. Not because I don't love that life. I do. But because if I did, no matter how many of the bad guys I took out, I couldn't bring back the good guys we've lost. They're gone and me joining their number wouldn't solve anything. And the hole in my heart... Well, the corps wasn't going to fill that.

"It hit me that if I wanted to do something positive with the rest of my life and stop hurting the people I cared about, if I ever wanted to have a chance with a woman like you, then I had to make changes, beginning with finding a job. Only then could I meet you on a level playing field."

"I don't understand. Are you back in the Marines?"

"Yes and no."

She shouldn't care and shouldn't ask. "Sam, I won't stand here all day and play games. What are you trying to say?"

"My first stop was your godfather's. I spent some time with John and his students. You were right. His program has all the positives of the corps but none of the negatives. No danger. No deployments or frequent moves. John was able to put down roots and have a normal postmilitary life. But the best part is he spends his days building kids up, not taking them down. He teaches them survival and real-world skills that will stay with them forever. That positive outcome appeals to me.

"The corps is actively recruiting medically discharged marines who were injured in combat. That made me eligible to be a Marine Corps JROTC instructor even though I'm short a few years of service. With John's and my dad's help I've landed a position. It means going back to school. I'll have to get my bachelor's degree, but I'll start teaching a Marine Corps JROTC in January, and I'll be earning a paycheck while I learn. It's won't be easy. I'm not going to have a lot of free time. But at least now I can ask you to be a part of that. Because I have something to offer."

Her heart soared. Then she remembered all the reasons why she shouldn't get her hopes up. What he'd told her explained a lot of it, but still…

He must have read her refusal on her face, because he laid a finger over her lips. "What I'm asking, June, is a chance to start over and give us a shot."

She pulled her head away from the warmth of his touch. "Start over? What does that mean?"

"It means I want to date you, Miss Jones. I want to get to know you, hold hands, learn your favorite foods, colors and flowers and all that stuff we skipped. And I want you to know me—the man, *not* the marine on a mission. Then if you can find it in your heart to forgive me for my part in investigating you and your team, and if you love me as much as I love you, I'll ask your daddy for your hand and marry you."

He loved her. A well of emotions overwhelmed her. Sam was offering everything she wanted, and everything she was terrified to accept. How could she survive losing him again?

"Sam—"

"Slow and easy. You set the pace," he insisted with a touch of desperation. "My position will be in Greenville, North Carolina. Close enough for us to stretch out this courtship until you have no doubts. And close enough that we can buy a house in the middle and you can commute to Quincey and keep the job that you love. You're Roth's best deputy. You see the big picture, not just the laws in black and white. And one day, when you're ready, I'd like to make beautiful green-eyed babies with you and raise them in a quiet town like Quincey."

He cupped her face, his eyes earnest and sincere. "I love you, June. Just say yes, say I've still got a chance, and I'll make it happen."

She wanted to say yes so badly her chest hurt. "How can I be sure you won't run scared again? I need someone brave enough to fight for me, Sam. For us."

He dropped to one knee beside the table and took her hand in his. "You've got it, June. I gave my *Semper Fidelis* oath to the corps. Now I'm pledging it to you. I will always be faithful and always loyal to you. You have my heart and I swear I won't let you down. And I will prove that every day for the rest of our lives if you give me the chance."

"Yes," she choked out over a heart so full it blocked her throat.

His golden brows dipped. "Does that mean yes, you'll give me a chance, or—?"

She slid off the table and tugged him to his feet. "Yes, I'll give you—give us—a chance. Yes, because I love you, Sam Rivers. Yes, I'll marry you if it all works out. And I know it will. Because you're *my* equal. Because you stood up for me and tried to heal my family because they were important to me. Because you stole my heart when you waded into that swamp and spent hours holding a stranger's head above water with no thought to your own safety.

"You may think you're always looking out for number one, Sam, but in everything you've done, you've put others first. How could I not love you?"

* * * * *

LARGER-PRINT
BOOKS!

HARLEQUIN *Presents*

PASSION
GUARANTEED
SEDUCTION

GET 2 FREE LARGER-PRINT
NOVELS PLUS 2 FREE GIFTS!

YES! Please send me 2 FREE LARGER-PRINT Harlequin Presents® novels and my 2 FREE gifts (gifts are worth about $10). After receiving them, if I don't wish to receive any more books, I can return the shipping statement marked "cancel." If I don't cancel, I will receive 6 brand-new novels every month and be billed just $5.05 per book in the U.S. or $5.49 per book in Canada. That's a saving of at least 16% off the cover price! It's quite a bargain! Shipping and handling is just 50¢ per book in the U.S. and 75¢ per book in Canada.* I understand that accepting the 2 free books and gifts places me under no obligation to buy anything. I can always return a shipment and cancel at any time. Even if I never buy another book, the two free books and gifts are mine to keep forever.

176/376 HDN F43N

Name	(PLEASE PRINT)	
Address		Apt. #
City	State/Prov.	Zip/Postal Code

Signature (if under 18, a parent or guardian must sign)

Mail to the **Harlequin® Reader Service:**
IN U.S.A.: P.O. Box 1867, Buffalo, NY 14240-1867
IN CANADA: P.O. Box 609, Fort Erie, Ontario L2A 5X3

**Are you a subscriber to Harlequin Presents books
and want to receive the larger-print edition?
Call 1-800-873-8635 today or visit us at www.ReaderService.com.**

* Terms and prices subject to change without notice. Prices do not include applicable taxes. Sales tax applicable in N.Y. Canadian residents will be charged applicable taxes. Offer not valid in Quebec. This offer is limited to one order per household. Not valid for current subscribers to Harlequin Presents Larger-Print books. All orders subject to credit approval. Credit or debit balances in a customer's account(s) may be offset by any other outstanding balance owed by or to the customer. Please allow 4 to 6 weeks for delivery. Offer available while quantities last.

Your Privacy—The Harlequin® Reader Service is committed to protecting your privacy. Our Privacy Policy is available online at www.ReaderService.com or upon request from the Harlequin Reader Service.

We make a portion of our mailing list available to reputable third parties that offer products we believe may interest you. If you prefer that we not exchange your name with third parties, or if you wish to clarify or modify your communication preferences, please visit us at www.ReaderService.com/consumerschoice or write to us at Harlequin Reader Service Preference Service, P.O. Box 9062, Buffalo, NY 14269. Include your complete name and address.

HPLP13R

LARGER-PRINT BOOKS!

GET 2 FREE LARGER-PRINT NOVELS PLUS

2 FREE GIFTS!

✦ HARLEQUIN®

Romance

From the Heart, For the Heart

YES! Please send me 2 FREE LARGER-PRINT Harlequin® Romance novels and my 2 FREE gifts (gifts are worth about $10). After receiving them, if I don't wish to receive any more books, I can return the shipping statement marked "cancel." If I don't cancel, I will receive 4 brand-new novels every month and be billed just $4.84 per book in the U.S. or $5.24 per book in Canada. That's a savings of at least 19% off the cover price! It's quite a bargain! Shipping and handling is just 50¢ per book in the U.S. and 75¢ per book in Canada.* I understand that accepting the 2 free books and gifts places me under no obligation to buy anything. I can always return a shipment and cancel at any time. Even if I never buy another book, the two free books and gifts are mine to keep forever.

119/319 HDN F43Y

Name _____ (PLEASE PRINT) _____

Address _____ Apt. # _____

City _____ State/Prov. _____ Zip/Postal Code _____

Signature (if under 18, a parent or guardian must sign) _____

Mail to the **Harlequin® Reader Service:**
IN U.S.A.: P.O. Box 1867, Buffalo, NY 14240-1867
IN CANADA: P.O. Box 609, Fort Erie, Ontario L2A 5X3

Want to try two free books from another line?
Call 1-800-873-8635 or visit www.ReaderService.com.

* Terms and prices subject to change without notice. Prices do not include applicable taxes. Sales tax applicable in N.Y. Canadian residents will be charged applicable taxes. Offer not valid in Quebec. This offer is limited to one order per household. Not valid for current subscribers to Harlequin Romance Larger-Print books. All orders subject to credit approval. Credit or debit balances in a customer's account(s) may be offset by any other outstanding balance owed by or to the customer. Please allow 4 to 6 weeks for delivery. Offer available while quantities last.

Your Privacy—The Harlequin® Reader Service is committed to protecting your privacy. Our Privacy Policy is available online at www.ReaderService.com or upon request from the Harlequin Reader Service.

We make a portion of our mailing list available to reputable third parties that offer products we believe may interest you. If you prefer that we not exchange your name with third parties, or if you wish to clarify or modify your communication preferences, please visit us at www.ReaderService.com/consumerchoice or write to us at Harlequin Reader Service Preference Service, P.O. Box 9062, Buffalo, NY 14269. Include your complete name and address.

HRLP13R

ReaderService.com

Manage your account online!

- Review your order history
- Manage your payments
- Update your address

> *We've designed*
> *the Harlequin® Reader Service*
> *website just for you.*

Enjoy all the features!

- Reader excerpts from any series
- Respond to mailings and
  special monthly offers
- Discover new series available to you
- Browse the Bonus Bucks catalog
- Share your feedback

Visit us at:
ReaderService.com